The Mysterious Abandoned Cars

Edward Joseph Germick Sr.

Disclaimer: All names, places, and situations are purely fictional. Any resemblance to real life is a coincidence and has no relation.

DEDICATION

This composition is dedicated with love to my wonderful wife of 50 years, Margaret. Her confidence in me is what always kept this old, worn, and rusty engine block of life firing on all eight cylinders. Her praise, encouragement, and never-ending faith in me always inspired me to do my best when I needed it most. Thank you for being you!

CONTENTS

1

The Early Abductions

Tuesday, July 23, 1991

An unstable twenty-year-old, seemingly perverted laborer named Arthur Owind was spending the last day of his vacation several hundred miles away from where he lived in Porktown. While he was relaxing on a peaceful beach, his thoughts veered drastically from being such. Owind was planning an evil act that would make even our prisons' hardest lifers cringe. The beach was alive with the sounds of gayety, music, laughter, children amusement, and splashing from a nearby water park.

The sun had just set and fireworks on the beach were getting underway. Arthur already had his victim picked out and was lingering, waiting for the opportunity to act. When all eyes turned to the magnificence in the sky, and the loud noises would deafen the screams for help, Arthur Owind seized the opportunity he had eagerly awaited. Little 5-year-old Tammy Chilk's parents, Tom and Bonnie, who didn't realize that they should always clutch a child's hand in a crowd and who were entranced by the spectacular fireworks event themselves, lost the child for just the briefest moment. Meager little Tammy was just another screaming and crying child to the rest of the crowd. No one even noticed that she was being taken against her will. When Tammy's parents turned to check on their child, she was gone. A search was initiated immediately by her parents, security, and boardwalk police. Surprisingly, the emotionally damaged little angel was found otherwise unharmed.

Arthur, a dirty, unshaven, full-body tattooed, hippie-like scumbag, had it all planned. Take the girl and get out of town before anyone might involve him. As fate would have it though, just a few miles from

1

the beach, he was involved in an accident. A rather massive off-duty sanitation truck parked along the road was in the way when an oncoming vehicle forced Arthur out of his lane.

Unfortunately, Mr. Owind was not killed in that brush with death. It would have been the justice he deserved, along with saving everyone a lot of time and trouble. He was relatively unharmed, except for a broken ankle when a steel portion of the truck pierced through the front door on his side of the car. Unlikely as it may sound, the putrid sexual predator was taken to the same hospital to have treatment for his injuries that little Tammy Chilk was taken. Tammy was examined by doctors and had D.N.A. evidence gathered for the start of an investigation. Unbeknown to everyone involved, this investigation was about to wrap up rather quickly. When Tammy and Owind locked eyes in admittance, she screamed and identified her attacker. There must have been some feeling of satisfaction for the Chilks to see the attacker grimace in pain as he tried to run away on his ankle. Owind was informed of his rights and promptly arrested. He received treatment for his ankle that included surgery and steel pins to strengthen the joint, and eventually stood trial for his crime. The sex offender was found guilty at trial and sentenced to ten years in prison. Though he was persistent about his innocence, he was frequently sodomized by his fellow prisoners.

About fifty miles away in the small town of Orville, at about the same time as little Tammy Chilks attack. In the dark, just outside a dance hall, two unidentified eyes are watching an unsavory looking motorcyclist, Mr. Charles Stint, also known as "Cycle Chuck." The somewhat notorious motorcycle gang member drove into the halls' parking lot and walked into the establishment. The eyes approached and peered in through a window ostensibly interested in the cyclist's activities. Shortly, he returned to the shadows of the parking lot and gazed at two scantily clad young ladies, Mary Hardau and Betty Bell, that had just arrived and were walking into the hall. Like before, the cold-eyed man watched the pair through the window with apparent interest.

As the unidentified man observed the cyclist and the two young ladies mingling with the crowd, he went over to the ladies vehicle. With a jimmy of the lock and disabling of the cars dome lights, he felt ready and went back to the window to peer inside the hall. He continued to watch until he saw the two young ladies saying goodbye to some of the people they had met. As they started outside, he snuck in the rear floor area of their vehicle and waited for them. When the car drove off and reached a desolate area, the perpetrator came up from the floor area and surprised the young ladies. Mary Hardau, Betty Bell, and their vehicle were never seen again.

The twisted assailant proceeded to return to the hall that same night and went over to the motorcycle. He fiddled with the gas line and returned to his vehicle where he waited for "Cycle Chuck." With no problems, he started his motorcycle and drove off down the highway. The cold-eyed man also left the parking lot and followed at a distance. Within minutes, the cycle sputtered and the engine shutdown. "Cycle Chuck" coasted the bike off of the roadway and attempted, unsuccessfully, to restart the engine. The follower slowly pulled in behind the motorcycle and offered his assistance, which was graciously accepted. He nor his bike were ever seen again.

2

Cutting the Pipeline

Saturday, April 23rd, 2005

Two young men from the small town of Benton, named Isaiah
Watkins and Dennis Honner were up well before the crack of dawn.
The two were anxious to get to work fulfilling a new large contract they
signed with a natural gas company to clear felled trees from the land the
company had leased. The company had designs on putting in a new
grid of pipelines to reach thousands of potential new customers.

The pipeline would cross approximately twenty miles of flatlands
and mountains consisting of straight runs and some turns along the way.
The gas company leased one hundred and fifty feet to ensure their
operation didn't infringe on properties not under a lease. Only sixty feet
on each side of the centerline was to be cleared. It was a given, under
contract, that no remaining debris from the removal would be visible
when they were done. Burning brush and branches was not an option.
A crew of earth moving operators and equipment would precede them
to uproot the enormous and mighty trees that lined most of the way.
They would return after Isaiah and Dennis were finished with their
cleanup to retrieve the large roots and haul them away before the
pipeline crew came in. If Isaiah and Dennis completed the job ahead of
schedule, they would likely be at the top of the list to do future jobs and
be awarded a two-thousand-dollar bonus each.

The best part of the contract was that it allowed them to dispose of
the timber, branches, and brush, anyway they presumed fit, other than
burning. They could also keep all profits they made, if any, from the
sale of the removed cuttings. They were somewhat restrained due to
stipulations that they do not backtrack heavy equipment or loads of
material over any pipe less than a week old. This stipulation meant each

time they began a new stretch of pipeline clearing from a highway, they needed to stay far enough ahead of the pipe-laying crew that they could remove their cuttings.

Dennis and Isaiah were lifelong friends coming from families that were not very well to do. Subsequently, before getting old enough to know any better, both had been engaged in somewhat undesirable behaviors with unsavory groups of people. Not being of a class able to even consider going to college after high school and jobs in the area remaining scarce, options were limited. They were thinking of joining the military when Dennis came up to Isaiah and told him of the excellent job opportunity he heard about shortly before that.

There was a job ad that ran in one of the local newspapers up in the vast Northwest Territory where a friend of his was visiting. When his friend returned, she showed him the ad because she knew Dennis needed a job and didn't want to see him join the service. The girl's name was Tammy Wright, and she was just a friend, nothing more, nothing less, though she would have liked it to be more.

Isaiah was even more excited about the job prospects and the high pay that went with it. They would have to sign for a full two-year hitch to be considered employable. If they for some reason, were not able to honor any portion of the two-year obligation, they would forfeit all of the completion bonus, a bonus which was worth almost three times the high wages they would have already been paid.

Being very young, energetic, and naïve, they both signed, became highly skilled lumberjacks and worked very hard, counting the days, weeks, and months till they would get their bonuses. Their bonuses would allow them to start any business they wanted, or they could sign back up again for another two years with a bonus. Everything went well for them until the last four months when they both found tremendous effort being placed against them to quit. They were being treated like dogs and given things to do that were beneath them. They were forced to do dangerous jobs that required skills they had never been trained for. They talked with each other about how they were feeling, and both confided in one another that they were feeling scared for their lives.

Isaiah and Dennis watched out for each other very closely during those last months and thankfully saved each other from disaster several times. They were down to just two days more to go till bonus time when a massive tree was unexpectedly felled on the mountainside they were working on, causing a considerable mudslide that surely would kill them

5

both. As the raging pile of tree, rock and mud were about to sweep them away, Isaiah saw a ledge overhang that formed a small but open-fronted cave. He grabbed Dennis and without uttering a word, pulled him to safety under the ledge with him.

When the foreman and the lumberjack that fell the tree came down to investigate, both Dennis and Isaiah grabbed them and gave them the beating of their lives. When they got back to camp, they were told they were fired and that their bonus offer was now invalid.

After coming back home to Benton, Isaiah's father directed them to a friend of his that was an attorney. It took about eight months, but the court found in their favor, and they received a massive pile of money. Of course, it wasn't as huge as it would have been if they didn't have to give 35% to the attorney.

Now, getting back to the boy's new pipeline contract. They were able to swing the deal because of the tremendous experience they had gained as lumberjacks. As they were waiting to see how the verdict for their lawsuit would turn out, they had become interested in finding ways to use their newly acquired skills and were already taking orders for firewood. Of course, they didn't have a vast resource for free trees to cut and sell, so it wasn't anything more than a way to make some spending money until they found jobs or received a settlement.

While cutting and selling firewood, they discovered a pretty good market for not only lumber, which was getting mighty scarce, but also wood chips for mulching. There were new ways of wrapping fireplace logs and selling them in small bundles. There was a relatively inexpensive process for drying and treating wood chips and bagging them for selling as landscaping mulch too, all at incredible prices!

When the young men received their money from the settlement, they immediately opened outlets to sell their commodities. They hired a couple of people to run the outlets while Dennis and Isaiah did the log cutting for firewood and ran the chipper to make the landscaping mulch chips.

A crew would come in at noon each day to load the timber, logs, and chips, take them to their respective outlets, process them for sale.

There were some others in the town that were passed over for the contract because Isaiah and Dennis outbid them. This success inadvertently led to their equipment being sabotaged as a form of retribution. Dennis and Isaiah had to take their expensive chipper home with them every day when they were finished working to protect it from damage at the worksite.

On that unusually warm Saturday morning in April of 2005, Tammy Wright who didn't have to work on Saturdays, and was now officially engaged to become Mrs. Dennis Honner, joined the two young men to assist them and make a noon picnic.

It was still dark when they towed their chipper behind their truck and stopped at a local truck stop to get gas. There in the shadows, was a figure with two very familiar eyes, not seen since Tuesday, July 23rd, 1991. It was an unusually warm day for April, and the group was dressed as if they were going to go for a walk on the beach more so than going logging. The mysterious eyes were very interested in the young bunch.

No one noticed the man in the shadows, but Tammy told them as they pulled out and drove away about a weird, strange feeling that came over her while they were getting gas. This was a sense of imminent danger that she was having a peculiar time shaking. Woman's intuition, I guess.

Shortly after the three left the truck stop, the mysterious eyed figure got into his car and drove in the direction the trio went.

Arriving at their work location, the two young men started their chainsaws and prepared to start cutting the fallen trees that were directly in front of the truck pulling the chipper. The combination of vehicle and chipper totaled approximately fifty feet in length. It was the young men's standard procedure to clear a path about twenty feet wide and around 200 feet long so they could drive the machine into position for chipping as needed. As they started cutting the fallen trees before them, they would select those for timber, trim the branches off of them and throw the branches to the side out of the way. They would do the same thing for the trees they selected to be fireplace logs, trimming, and throwing the branches just to the side of the pathway. The men didn't have the time to stack fireplace logs for pick-up by the other crew so they would just let them lay where they were cut. Typically, when the pathway had been cut, and the chipper was in place, they would trim the branches and throw those that were too small for firewood right into the running chipper.

The men knew they had to keep a clear area for them to do their tasks safely. Safety was tantamount, and if either were to get hurt or ill, it would jeopardize their future. However, the duo seemed to have little respect for good safety practices when it came to dressing appropriately.

They were wearing shorts, and instead of good steel-toed shoes like Isaiah had on, Dennis wore sneakers. Other than wearing proper quality ear protection and eye protection with side shields, they dropped the ball big time.

Tammy was a good worker, and she pitched right in helping the guys. It was about 8:45 a.m., and the crew had opened up approximately 200 foot of pathway when Tammy started to get hungry for both food and conversation. One can't communicate very well over the sounds of the machinery, especially when wearing ear protection.

Over the loud sound of the saws and the chipper, Tammy finally got the attention of Dennis. He pulled his earmuffs to the side enough so he could hear her, and she told him she was going to pull the truck up as far as they have cleared. She planned to make a campfire off in the shade of the trees, brew up some fresh coffee, and cook some hotdogs for their break.

Tammy brought the machine up, the duo started the chipper, and they began cutting and throwing branches into it. They would have already had their pathway for the entire day cut, several cords of firewood cut, and a large pile of landscaping chips chipped by the time the snack was ready. Tammy left the area to find a sweet spot for the picnic she had planned for the boys. She only walked slightly out of the view of the boys when the mysterious eyed stranger came up behind her and rendered her unconscious.

After what seemed like a very long time, Dennis became aware that it had been a while since Tammy told him she was going to prepare for their break and yet she hadn't called them. He got concerned, put his saw down, and went to check on her. She was nowhere to be seen. He looked all around, and still, he did not see her anywhere. He thought maybe she was using natures ladies' room and called to her. Tammy, who was just out of sight behind some fallen trees and into the woods, had come to by then and was being held forcefully by her captor. Her captor told her to call out to Dennis. Gripped by fear, she did as she was told, and the mysterious assailant put an abrupt end to her short life. An end made simple by a crushing blow to her skull with a metal bar he held in his hand. The psychopath then went behind a large uprooted tree root in the direction Dennis was heading and repeated the same gruesome murderous method.

Just a few minutes after Dennis was killed, his friend and partner Isaiah began to feel something was not as it should be. He had looked several times and did not see either of the other two. Feeling tired, hungry, and a little lonely himself, he shut his saw off and looked around the immediate area. Seeing no one, he took off his ear protection and called out. No one answered. Knowing how young lovers are today, he assumed they wanted to be alone for a while. When he looked and smelled for the intended campfire site hoping to get a cup of coffee while he waited for them to return, he was concerned that he couldn't find any trace of a campfire nearby. Isaiah called out louder and louder, each time facing in a different direction and moving from here to there. He was hoping to hear or see something that would explain the ordeal.

Isaiah approached the spot where both Tammy and Dennis met their fate. From behind the same fallen tree root, the assailant unexpectedly approached and instilled the same future upon Isaiah as he did the others.

Putting on his own feet the same sneakers that Dennis had been wearing before his demise, the campfire killer removed articles of clothing from the young woman and Isaiah. He left them near a blanket from the truck. The killer proceeded to deposit each of the bodies into the chipper one at a time with Dennis' body being the last to go through. Reaching into his pocket, he pulled out a pair of hospital type disposable slippers. He removed Dennis' sneakers and put the disposable slippers on in their place. He then threw Dennis' sneakers into the chipper also. Afterward, he went back to the blanket area, gathered any potential evidence, and left town stopping only once far away from the site to remove the disposable slippers and put his shoes back on. He carried the disposable slippers with him as he walked away.

When the pick-up crew arrived at noon to load the harvested material and take them to their processing and sales outlets, they found the remains and called the authorities.

A thorough investigation into the untimely deaths took place and revealed no evidence as to the cause, reason for, or any motivation for the happening. No one was identified to have even the slightest thing to gain from any of the trios' deaths, other than possibly the awarding of the pipeline contract the duo would no longer be able to fulfill.

Since the clothing belonging to Isaiah was found next to the blanket with Tammy's' clothing, authorities suspected it could have been the gory results of a love triangle gone awry, resulting in a double homicide and suicide. Dennis' remains as the surface covering of the shredded human remain pile supported that theory.

3
The Empty Car

Tuesday, July 17ᵗʰ, 2007, 12:15 am.

It's the middle of the night; a car is seen stopped alongside the highway in a small rock and knolly area just off the road within Oreville's city limits. This is a town that is located on the part of Interstate highway 50 where there are few homes or other buildings. It is not uncommon to drive for twenty or thirty minutes in one direction and not see another car traveling in either direction.

The vehicle is seen parked just off the newly improved portion of the highway. At the rear of the parked vehicle is the owner of the car, later to be identified as Mr. Cal Sutter. Mr. Sutter, a businessman from Rawlins, Wyoming and traveling in casual attire, is being held at gunpoint by an unidentified man.

Mr. Sutter is vehemently questioning the event.

"What is the meaning of this? Who are you? Did I do something to you? You must have me mixed up with someone else!" Says Mr. Sutter.

He worriedly receives no reply.

The silent unidentified person, while holding Mr. Sutter's car key, depresses the remote trunk button to open it up.

"Get in!" The person commands.

Mr. Sutter objects and becomes belligerent.

"I will not! What... what do you want from me? What are you going to do to me? Please, please, don't do it!" Pleads Mr. Sutter frightfully.

The would-be assailant hands him a blanket and says reassuringly in an attempt to calm Mr. Sutter, "Just put this down you can lie on it and pull it over you. It might get pretty cold in there tonight if they don't find you soon."

"Now either get in or die!" the unidentified person again says forcefully.

Mr. Sutter reluctantly complies. "Don't hurt me, please! I'll... I'll do anything you say. I can give you money. I have connections. I know people!"

As the unidentified man assists him, Mr. Sutter was feeling some relief and less threatened. The man helps him place the blanket around his entire body and while doing so, brings the end of the blanket up over Mr. Sutter's head.

Unseen and unknown to Mr. Sutter at this point, the perpetrator points and places his gun at Mr. Sutter's head. A single gunshot rings out. The assailant shoots him through the blanket and immediately kills him. The murder weapon was loaded with evidence elusive bullets, a type of birdshot to make the gun harder to trace. It eliminates the potential for a slug to go through the head and lodge into or go through the car. The blanket was used to eradicate gunshot residue, and blood spatter from being found in the trunk.

Tuesday, July 17th, 2007, approx. 7:10 a.m.

Somewhere on that very same stretch of I-50, a lone police officer, Randy Dobbs, is driving west on his way back to his town from a news conference in Justice the evening before. He is a sheriff of a small town called Roxi, located just 35 miles west of another small towns center called Apollotown.

While barely still in the town limits of Apollotown, and about two miles before he would reach the Roxi town limits, he observes a car stopped up ahead. The vehicle is blocking the westbound right lane and appears to be abandoned.

The Sheriff turns on his patrol car lights, pulls up, and stops immediately behind the abandoned vehicle. He radios a report asking for any wants or warrants for the car or its owner. A Mr. Cal Sutter reportedly owns the car from Rawlins, Wyoming. No wants or warrants exist. Sheriff Randy gets out of his patrol car and investigates the scene. He notices that the vehicle is not running, appears not to be broken down, and that the car's transmission lever is in the drive position. All its doors are locked, and its keys are still in the ignition.

He was thinking someone might have suddenly had a nature call and left the vehicle in a hurry, intending to return and found they locked themselves out. The officer walked away from the car into the terrain and climbed up on a high knoll to look in all directions. He saw no one and called out, but there are no replies.

Officer Randy radios dispatch and says, "Reported (I-50) vehicle has been abandoned, visual surveillance of the area turned up empty. The car fits the criteria for other abandoned and missing person vehicles found near the area in the past." Randy requests it be roped off, investigated as a possible crime scene and taken in for forensic analysis.

The Sheriff's requests were confirmed. He put out flares and cones to prevent any potential rear-end collisions.

4

The Empty Car "Follow-up"

Thursday, July 19th, 2007, 10:30 am

Thursday morning finds Sheriff Dobbs busy on the phone talking to authorities from various police and investigation commissions. The vehicle Sheriff Dobbs reported found, was still being examined by a forensic specialist. The owner could not be located, and his wife said that he was late, and she had not heard from him in more than 30 hours. She was worried about him as he always calls to notify her of his location and when he expected to be home. His cell phone was going right to voicemail when she called.

The circumstances around the discovery of the vehicle were remarkably similar to several other reported missing persons and their cars. None of the prior vehicles turned up any clues as to what transpired or hints as to what may have led to the disappearance of the cars' owners. No signs of any foul play were substantiated. No one even knew if any criminal acts occurred and if they did occur, where or when they happened. One thing they did know for sure was that none of the missing persons were ever heard from again. Would it be the same this time? Nobody knew. At the same time, police also had a concern due to what seemed to be an unusually high number of missing persons reported with-in the same area of interest — the same area where many of the vehicles were abandoned. There appeared to be no similarities or connection between the two types of events.

Further investigation turned up that the abandoned car, as was similar to the prior abandoned vehicles, had an empty gas tank and had run out of gas. More shocking, though, was that recent disappearances might be related to disappearances that were reported across county lines as long as fifteen years ago.

Due to public outrage over the disappearances, State Police were pursuing help from federal agencies that had better investigative equipment, trained persons, and methods. A conference was being set up for next week to bring together all persons, private, or public that might have information pertinent to the case. It was to be conducted by some of the best know criminal and investigative minds alive today. Though this had been attempted to some degree in the not too distant past, this meeting would be inclusive of all instances dating back many years. Sheriffs, Deputies, Constables, Rangers, and the State Police were working hand in hand. This effort spread across towns, counties, interstates and rural roadways to hopefully find a lead; any lead that may help them begin to finally see a focal point to start a fruitful investigation.

5
Sheriff Dobbs Gets Involved
Thursday, July 19th, 2007, Background

No one seemed to be more interested in getting a start than Roxi's own Sheriff Dobbs. He is a soft spoken, six foot handsome man, with sandy hair and blue eyes who was a lifelong resident of Roxi, and his family was one of the oldest and most established in the community. Randy's Great Grandfather Hiram had started a mining supply and support business early in the 20th century. A company that provided jobs, commerce, and helped the small town prosper. They were considered pillars of the community and did substantially well for themselves living what many thought the great American dream.

Unfortunately, it all began quite depressingly while still living in the Scranton-Wilkes-Barre coal mining area of Northeastern Pennsylvania, where Randy's Great Grandfather worked laboriously in a coal mine. Randy's Great Grandmother died from pneumonia treatment complications while in the state correctional institution for the criminal and mentally challenged. She was incarcerated for feeding an early day version of rat poison to the guests and patients of a nursing home where she was employed as a caregiver. Two elderly patrons died and several more patrons were hospitalized as a result. She was determined to have had an uncontrollable vindictive persecution complex for which there was little if any treatment.

After Randy's' Great Grandmother died, his Great Grandfather left the mine. He and his 12-year-old son, (Randy's very young future grandfather) moved to Roxi. He felt it would be better for the child because in coal towns, gossip travels fast, and such events are never forgotten. It was back in the days when coal ruled the roost. They wanted to get away and leave the troubled past behind them.

Randy's Great Grandfather, with what little earnings he had saved working the coal mines in Pennsylvania, bought a few acres of land and began raising mules to work in the mines. Randy's young grandfather was a good helper and learned fast. He was a big help to his father as they worked side by side, building their empire.

Available water limited the number of mules they could raise, but the venture was so successful he was able to buy a rather large tract of farmland, dug a considerable water well and began receiving more and more mining contracts. Great Grandfather was becoming rather wealthy and genuinely the pillar of society he was reputed to be. He paid off his land purchase, built an extravagant home; one many referred to as a mansion by its sheer size alone. Additionally, he built a large barn and many smaller buildings necessary to his occupation. He invested heavily in mules, harnesses, wagons, blacksmithing, and fabricating equipment. He had envisioned making the coal cars, tracks, and everything that the mines needed.

While all this was happening, Randy's Grandfather met, fell in love with, and married his Grandmother. Randy's father came along about one year later. Things were going very well.

But unfortunately just as quick as their good fortune came, their plans now began to unravel. New and better mining techniques were being discovered; steam, gas, and diesel. Large factories were built all around the country to make mining equipment faster and cheaper than they could compete with. All this after they had poured so much money into the purchase of what was now becoming obsolete equipment and supplies. The Dobbs probably would have weathered the storm by their hard work and determination alone, but then one day, as the nearby mining company was preparing to blast a new tunnel, an accidental explosion killed dozens of miners as it ripped open the natural crevices below the standard water levels underground. It collapsed, flooded, and permanently closed the mines. As the mines flooded, it drained Great Grandfathers huge well and permanently rerouted the once vast underground caverns of water elsewhere. The well became forever useless. The abundance of water on their property was reduced significantly. The shock of his latest dream shattering event was too much for Great Grandfathers heart, and he died on July 7th, 1944 at age 74.

Realizing that his father's entrepreneurial dream was now firmly quashed, Randy's Grandfather with the help of Randy's father and mother took to farming to make a living. Farming was hard and not very lucrative. It would ultimately take Randy's adored Grandfather's life in May of 1987. He died from working in those fields.

Young Randy, who was born Tuesday, May 6th, 1975, worshipped his grandfather. He swore this would never happen to him. He did not want to be a farmer for the rest of his life. Randy remembered and lingered upon a phrase his Grandfather once told him, "The man who knows how to do a job will always have a job, but a man who knows why you do a job will always be your boss!" Randy felt the profoundness of those words of wisdom.

The farming business is seasonal, so profits vary year to year. This uncertainty forced Randy's Father and Mother to find other ways to make ends meet. His Father had a standing agreement with the local funeral parlor to handle the removal and transfer of human remains from the site of death to the funeral home morgue and help with the preparation of the bodies for viewing. He usually only did the undressing and redressing of corpses, for which he received an equal share of the billing. Randy's Mother worked part-time preparing funeral bouquets and meals for the loved one's family. However, clients were few and far between at times in that rural community.

6
Roxi Townfolk

Friday, July 20th, 2007, 7:30 am

Sheriff Dobbs frequents the town's only diner by day, bar by night establishment.

"Good morning Randy," Marge Betley said with a soft and loving voice as she bent over the bar to kiss him. The Sheriff sat down at the counter for his usual mid-morning coffee and sandwich. Marge, who has grown very close to the Sheriff, some even say they are a couple, owns and runs the Diner during the daytime hours. Evenings, she relinquishes the establishment and its customers to Troy Conway, a former friend of her late husband Frank that used to run the bar and grill evening business before his untimely death about two years ago. Marge's husband, Frank Betley, was a successful farmer and bartender. Frank was killed in a terrible barn fire one sweltering summer afternoon in 2005.

He and a few hired hands had relentlessly fought against time to harvest and bring in the second cutting of hay before the impending thunderstorm was to arrive. With only half of the last wagon of hay to put into the loft of the barn, Frank dismissed his crew saying he would finish and tidy things up before he went home. Some think maybe Frank, being so overtired, fell asleep in the hay. Others say it might have been a bolt of lightning or perhaps spontaneous combustion trapping him in.

Anyway, Frank's barn caught fire, and he never got out alive. Dental records were needed to confirm it was indeed Frank's remains they found afterward. Sheriff Dobbs took his death almost as severely as did his wife, Marge. Frank and Randy were very close growing up. He was going to be Sheriff Randy's best man at his wedding to Kathy Johns, Randy's childhood sweetheart, a marriage that never happened.

The wedding was planned, and reservations were made when a motorcycle-riding hippy type rebel named "Spokes" came riding into town. He and Sheriff Randy's fiancé, Kathy Johns, hit it off immediately. Kathy seemed fascinated with his devil may care persona, wild lifestyle, and flashy expensive motorcycle. Things were never the same between her and Sheriff Randy after that. Two days before the wedding, Kathy Johns visited Randy and told him it was over. She was leaving town that very day with Spokes to travel and see all the states. Nothing Sheriff Randy or Kathy's parents could say or do would change her mind. She left with Spokes and has never contacted any of them since.

As Sheriff Randy and Marge are about to engage in some serious conversation, in walks the towns grumpy old Mayor, Ralph Samms. "Glad you're here Sheriff," the Mayor exclaimed. "I need to talk to you right now," he growled.

"What's the trouble, Mayor?" Randy Inquired.

"That car you found yesterday! That's what's the trouble! So far, we've been pretty lucky that Roxi hasn't been riddled with the missing persons and cars scandal that has hit most neighbors to our east," replies the Mayor.

"Scandal!?" Replies the puzzled Sheriff.

"Yes, a scandal!" Growled the Mayor. "You know how important it is to the welfare of our small community that travelers stop and stay in our rooming houses and establishments. Not to mention, fill up their tanks at our service stations, buy produce from our farms, knick-knack sales, tourism! Something like this can ruin it for all of us. We can't go scaring these visitors, our guests, away!" the Mayor snarled.

"What did you expect me to do Mayor? Just pretend like I never saw the car blocking my side of the roadway. Suppose someone ran into it in the dark, would you be happy then?" the Sherriff snarled back.

"You know very well what I'm talking about Sheriff. We don't need any more bad publicity. We all need to help make this all go away, not escalate it." Scolds the Mayor as he turns and storms out the door.

"What was all that about?" Asked Fred Baynes, Randy's lifelong friend, and a twenty-year Army veteran that is Sheriff Dobbs only and reliable part-time deputy.

"The Mayor is just his same old usual, ornery self." Replies the Sheriff.

"Don't let him get to you, Randy. You do a great job as Sheriff! He doesn't appreciate you. Maybe you should tell him to shove it. You got too much on your plate for just one man anyhow, you know?" Says Fred. Sheriff Randy thanks him for his kind remarks.

"Don't you wish things could be like they were when we were boys Randy? Before the all too complicated, the hustle and bustle, the unpeaceful modern world came to our town?" Questions Fred. Fred goes on to say, "Remember how nice, quiet and peaceful things were back then? Remember those early days on your dads' farm? We never had to worry about anything. The whole world seemed as if it were in our grasp." Fred says goodbye and leaves Sheriff Randy in deep thought about times and days gone by.

7
Reminiscing

Friday, July 20th, 2007, 8:00 am

Randy recalls when he was very young. He never got to know his grandmother because she died when Randy was very young. Randy's grandfather, who helped his father build their business, was still alive when Randy was born. Randy and his grandfather had been the best of friends, did many things together and had a great love for each other.

Randy and his father both shared, [the more things you do, the more things you learn] philosophy; a belief taught to them by his grandfather. Randy would, upon occasions, and as his busy schedule permitted, join his father at the Munson's Funeral Home. He would pitch right in and help his father prepare the deceased members of their society for a funeral. He would learn new things, and they would get done sooner so he and his dad could spend more time together doing things they liked.

Randy remembered on one particular occasion when the body of a man was being prepared; the man had a real attention-getting tattoo on his upper left arm. Randy was taken with the tattoo.

"Father, this is an elegant tattoo this man has on his arm." Said young Randy.

His father grunted... he didn't care.

"Do you think I could get a tattoo like this one?" Randy inquired. "Perhaps someday," father replied. "I have my reasons for not appreciating tattoos. First, I believe what the bible says; that a persons' body is the Lord's Temple, and one must not alter, demean or destroy that temple or they face being punished by the Lord. Secondly, I for one, do not want to parade in front of St. Peter and the Lord someday wearing those drawings. The Lord might say something to me like, 'Didn't you like the body I gave you, boy?' Uh uh... no... not me, I'm not going to tempt the Lord. And lastly, they cost a lot of hard-earned money, even more, if you ever want to have them removed and that would be very painful, I hear." Randy had the utmost respect for his father's words of wisdom and the subject of getting a tattoo ended.

Randy worked hard on the family farm, helping his father to the best of his ability, but he had other interests.

Randy's father always would tell Randy, the more things you get involved with, the more things you will learn, and Randy was involved. His father once told him what his father and his father before him always said, "If a man is comfortable in what he is doing, he is not learning and growing."

One day while Randy was hard at work in their large farm building, his delighted father saw him fabricating some unusual but very helpful farm implements. Randy had designed and made them all by himself with the new welding equipment they bought for repairs.

"Randy, you are one very talented young man. Your great grandfather and grandfather would be so proud of you, as I am! You'll be able to make a good living someday with the skills you have developed. Perhaps some big farm equipment company will hire you to make their products." Father said.

Randy insisted that he would indeed find a way to use his more than adequate skills, perhaps in his own business right at the farm. He knew both his beloved deceased grandfather and his father, would not want to see the family farm they all worked so hard to own and run sold to some outsider.

8

The Hungry Hogs

Friday, July 20th, 2007, 8:05 am

Sheriff Randy's dream bubble burst as he was awakened to current reality by his police radio. It was the County Coroner Bill Masten.

"Sheriff, a 911 came into my office. There's been a farm accident over at Ted Smifht's hog farm. You'd better come with me." said Masten.

"Ok," replied Randy as he prepared to respond.

Sheriff Randy Dobbs got into his police car and followed the coroner to the site of the farm accident. When they arrived at the hog farm, a farmhand named Dick Bowden met them and guided them to the scene of the accident. He was rightfully shaken up and extremely concerned about giving the bad news to Mr. Smifht's wife, who was away at her job in town.

"This is the way I found him, Sheriff," said Bowden. "My tractor broke down while working out in the field, and I came back for some help and tools. I searched for Ted and couldn't find him anywhere. I called out but no reply. I heard the fuss the hog's outback were making and figured I'd better see what was disturbing them. I saw they were all in a tight bunch routing something in the mud. I couldn't see what it was at first. Then I saw what looked like a, a body. It scared the be-Jesus out of me! I couldn't get them off of him. It was a real feeding frenzy. I got scared! So, I ran into the barn and grabbed the fox gun. I fired several shots, and that finally broke them up. I forced them all into the barn and closed all the gates. Then I went to get a closer look. I saw it was Mr. Smifht or at least what was left of him. I didn't touch anything else, I ran inside and called 911. I hope I did the right thing Sheriff, maybe... maybe I should have called his wife... maybe I should have called the Chaplin… but I… but I… I couldn't do it. I didn't want her to see him this way. I didn't want anyone to see him this way. I mean look Sheriff… look at him all torn to pieces and he… he isn't wearing anything but his trousers, and they are down at his ankles. I… I don't know what to think! I don't know how this could have happened?"

The Coroner and the Sheriff could see how badly the event had shaken poor old Mr. Bowden.

"Why don't you just sit down over here in the shade" Sheriff Randy directed the excited farmhand. "Try to relax. It's ok now; we've got it. We'll take care of everything, relax."

Sheriff Randy and the Coroner, although both visibly affected themselves by the sheer horror of the event, professionally performed their duties. Randy waited to make further notifications until he had a better picture of what likely happened there. He watched intently as the coroner examined the remains to make a preliminary diagnosis.

"I'm afraid I'm not sure just what did happen here, Sheriff," said Coroner Masten, "But I believe he was already dead at the time the hogs were consuming him. Though there is a tremendous amount of blood from the predatory behavior of the pigs where they feasted, I think the blood pattern would be different and spread out more."

"Are you suggesting he may have possibly met with foul play Bill?" Question Randy. "I don't know Randy. I don't know for sure." Masten replied. "Possibly, if the pigs didn't kill him, something or somebody did. Let's both take a closer look and see if we can figure this out," suggested the coroner.

Though pretty thoroughly riddled with hoof prints, there was one seemingly tell-tale trail of blood and drag like marks leading to where the body was found devoured. It came from the cement feed trough the pigs ate out of approximately eight feet away. Only one footprint other than that of the hired hands footprints were found close enough to the body to be that of a potential assailant. It was a partially un-trampled footprint that matched that of the victim. Some visible blood and hair that matched the victim's hair color were found splattered on the sharp corner edge of the trough nearest the hog frenzy area.

"I can't say for sure sheriff, but it appears that Ted may have walked into the pen for some unknown reason, tripped, lost his balance and hit his head on the edge corner of this trough, killing himself instantly. That would account for the lack of blood being pumped out of his body while being drug and consumed by the hogs." Masten concluded. "Yeah…

yeah, it fits. It sure does look that way" the Sherriff agreed.

"Dick Bowden naturally has to be considered a person of interest if an investigation is started." Said, Sheriff Dobbs.

"Do you want me to arrange for a formal investigation?" asked Sheriff Randy.

"Ted and Dick have been the best of friends forever, I can't believe he would have any reason to hurt Ted, but I'll leave that up to you Sheriff," said Masten. "By the way," Masten inquired, "What do you make of the way Smifhts was dressed?" "You don't think…?"

Sheriff Dobbs stopped the Coroner before he said anything that he might regret or have to release if an investigation did in-fact ensue. Randy called Mr. Bowen and Mr. Masten together and said,"Look, I don't see any good that would come out of any of us speculating about why Mr. Smifhts' pants were where they were when he was found, and it would only subject Mrs. Smifhts to ridicule. Let's just let Ted and his good name rest in peace, shall we?" suggested Sheriff Randy. They all agreed never to let the subject resurface, and that was the last time the issue came up.

9
The Hungry Wolves
Tuesday, August 30th, 1994

The event reminded Sheriff Randy of two somewhat similar incidents that happened a few years earlier in the nearby town of Justice. The first incident occurred when Sheriff Randy was entirely new to the job, and he didn't take it nearly as well as he did this event. Lou Crocket, the Sheriff of Justice, was in Massachusetts visiting relatives on a two-week vacation and had asked Randy to fill in if there was a need. Lou had not returned yet when Randy received a call from the Justice Coroner that some Elk hunters had found the remains of a person presumed to have been a hiker. He did not want to remove the body until police had been notified to investigate the occurrence. The Coroner did not tell Randy what had been found and he just expected to see a dead body, something he was quite used to seeing at the town funeral parlor. Randy almost heaved his guts when he saw what presumably a pack of wolves did to that unfortunate hiker, later identified as Sam Koolidge.

Sheriff Randy did a preliminary, then called the State Police and County Coroner to do a full investigation. The investigation could not conclusively identify the manner of death due to the condition of the body. No motive for murder was found, and no one was arrested. The cause of death ultimately was listed as unknown with a probability of natural causes.

About three weeks later, Sheriff Lou Crocket from the small town of Justice again called Randy and asked him to assist with another remains situation that occurred a short distance from the hiker event. The area had been plagued by several cattle being killed by wolves over the past few months. A hunt to kill the rogue wolves culminated with the killing of three wolves and everyone figured the threat was gone. While all this was going on, Brent Wahle, who owned the cattle farm where the cattle were attacked, strengthened all the fence that surrounded his grazing pastures. He put in all-new stronger and higher fence posts, stronger and more heavily barbed wire, and strung rows of the barbed wire closer together to prevent wolves from being able to enter, hopefully.

During grazing hours, he electrified the fencing. This change, though perhaps suitable for Farmer Wahle, angered many local fishermen that formerly would park on the dirt roadway that ran along the north boundary of the fence. Now it meant an additional 10 to 15-minute walk (depending upon a person's age and gait) to go around the fence.

As Randy approached the scene, he saw Sheriff Crockett waving to him as he stood by his patrol car and a small trail bike. A bike that Randy recognized immediately as belonging to young Timmy Travis, the son of a small newspaper publisher in Justice. Since he got his driver's license, young Timmy delivered papers to Roxi for his dad. He always brought one, free of charge of course, to the Sheriff's office so Sheriff Dobbs could stay abreast of events in Justice. Sheriff Randy was not surprised to see Timmy's bike there, as he did naturally expect that young Timmy was there covering the story for the newspaper.

"What's up, Sheriff?" Asked Randy.

"Bad news Sheriff... Real bad news," replied the Sheriff.

"Brent Wahle called me this morning. When Brent turned on the power to his electric fencing at around 7:00 am as he was putting his cows out to pasture, he heard some loud humming coming from his fence's transformer. He had heard that kind of noise in the past, and he thought maybe a tree fell across the fence somewhere, so he took his quad-runner and drove the perimeter looking for a cause. Just above the fishing hole, he found the body of young Tim Travis caught in the barbed wire; his fishing pole was nearby. It appears he tried to short cut across the pasture to go fishing, climbed over the fence and somehow managed to get himself firmly tangled and impaled in the heavily barbed wire. I guess nobody could hear him screaming for help way out here."

"Electrocuted?" asked Sheriff Randy.

"No... much worse than that," answered Sheriff Crocket.

"Wolves got him, must have heard him screaming... maybe they smelled his blood from the barbed wire punctures and took advantage of the situation. Maybe he bled to death before the wolves found him. I hope that was the case anyway! Terrible way to go. I don't know how on Gods beautiful earth I'm ever going to be able to tell his family! Not much left of him. It's going to be so hard for everybody!" said Sheriff Crocket as he held his head in his hands, with tears in his eyes.

After Sheriff Crocket composed himself, he told Randy that he called him over to help comfort Farmer Wahle who was still kneeling over the boy sobbing. Randy needed to help the Coroner examine the remains, do an investigation, and remove the body. Sheriff Dobbs obliged, and he called for the National Guard to help hunt the remaining rogue wolves.

10
Randy's Development
1989-1996

It had been a long grueling day for Sheriff Randy as he lied in bed trying hard to fall asleep. His thoughts returned to the question his deputy asked him. "Don't you wish things could be like they were when we were boys Randy? Before the all too complicated hustle and bustle?" Randy slipped into deep thought.

Randy remembered when he was young, how he wanted to be involved hands-on with things, not behind a desk. He knew he would need to have additional skills someday, so he took an upholstery course at the local tech school. At the same time, he went to work part-time after school at the Buttons Tool and Die Machine Shop right in Roxi and only a few miles from his farm. He started as a cleanup person, but it wasn't long before the boss recognized the un-haltered skills and ambition young Randy possessed and used him in a much higher capacity. The owner was able to create a position for Randy in the state-sponsored youth apprenticeship program for which they both received money from the state and federal government. Randy learned many new skills and was a cinch to get a permanent job close to the farm when he finished high school.

A young man's fancies, interests, and needs do change rather quickly and unexpectedly as he speeds through those early years of his life. Then one day while hunting Whitetail on the family farm, Randy was fortunate enough to harvest a magnificently antlered huge buck. It had 12 almost perfectly symmetrical very long and sharp tines on its very thick of girth antlers. It weighed 212 pounds dressed out. The long sought after buck had been seen and heard grunting by other not so fortunate hunters for the past several years and was the talk of the town pretty regularly. It had been given the handle "Old grunt" by those who were at least fortunate enough to see and hear it. People came from miles around to see Randy's prize trophy, and many encouraged Randy to have it mounted because it was so magnificent and extraordinary. Randy was so proud of his trophy buck. He beamed ear to ear. He wanted to be able to relive and enjoy the experience and excitement of the hunt for years to come and to be able to continue to show his catch to others.

Randy visited and talked to the only taxidermist for miles around, Mr. Russel. He was an old, very mannerly gentleman, his eyesight was failing, and he was recovering from a broken wrist he sustained from a bad fall he took a few months earlier. His incapacitation had hampered his progress and put him many weeks behind in his work. He had many dissatisfied customers because he had not gotten their mounts back to them as promised. When he told Randy that it would cost $300.00 to mount his trophy Whitetail, he was extremely depressed. He knew there was no way he could afford that much. The kindly old gent, seeing the extreme disappointment in young Randy's eyes offered to let Randy work off the charge helping him in his shop where he needed the help of two strong arms. It was an offer and an opportunity Randy couldn't resist, and he burst with joy. He was thrilled because now not only would he be able to get his trophy mounted for all the world to see, he would also learn more new skills. Randy grew to respect and love Mr. Russel as if he were a member of his own family and kind of thought of him as another grandfather.

Though Randy continued to build upon his plans to start a potential part-time upholstery business of his own, over the next few years, Randy had little interest in anything other than taxidermy, that was where his real love was. This interest became evident when Randy had mounted his magnificent kill. It made a tremendous promotional figure to advertise the quality and professionalism of their work.

In the back of Randy's mind, he had entertained the notion that after he finished high school or perhaps college, he would have full-time employment at the tool and die shop and run his upholstery and taxidermy businesses part-time on the farm. Randy realized and accepted the fact that at least for the time being, except for the machine shop job that his life would depend upon, the other jobs would be on more of a need and can-do basis.

Randy's notion got much stronger one day when Mr. Russel, the taxidermist encouraged Randy to take over the business he had started a lifetime ago.

"Randy," he said, "You have more motivation and drive than anyone else I have ever seen. You seem to love this work. You can do great things with my business!"

"I do... I do!" exclaimed Randy, "It's what I think I want to do for the rest of my life."

Thus, Randy accepted the offer and moved the business into his shop on the farm.

He was using a new name: The Dobbs-Russel taxidermy shop. Both were very happy. Mr. Russel stopped by occasionally and helped Randy as much as he was able to when Randy was overloaded with customers. This usually happened for a short period each year, immediately following the state deer season.

Randy finished school and forgot all about college ambitions. He knew what he wanted to do. He had a plan that could not fail. Things went pretty well for several years. Advancement at the machine shop improved revenue as did both of his home businesses. Engaged to the girl of his dreams, his childhood sweetheart, everything was fulfilling the great American dream.

11
Randy Gets Elected

Thursday, January 4th, 1996

Good things and good times don't last forever. Unfortunately, Randy's mother died unexpectedly, and as fate would have it, the country fell into a deep recession. One of the top three automakers was on the brink of bankruptcy. You guessed it; it was the same automaker that the machine shop Randy worked at, designed, and made engine parts. The machine shop that had survived the Great Depression and two world wars making tank parts failed and closed their doors forever. This was a massive blow for Randy. At the same time, his now older and ailing father needed further care that Randy was ill-equipped to provide and despite Randy's monumental efforts, he had to place his father in a nursing home, where he ultimately died in 1994 at age 62. Randy knew his father and his mothers' deaths were premature because of the hard lives they had both lived.

Like during all recessions, money was tight. People stopped spending on things that weren't necessary at the time. Much fewer people were patronizing Randy's home businesses. Randy had to pick up his father's former duties at the Munson's Funeral Parlor as they became available, but it still was not enough to pay the bills. There were no jobs. Randy's plans were all falling apart, and he felt like the whole world was against him.

Fortunately and timely for Randy, he had made many friends at the different jobs he had, one day in August 1995, he received a call from Bob Knole who was the machine shop nightshift foreman where he formerly worked and who had fortunately retired before all his retirement assets would have been lost in the shops closing.

"Randy," Bob said boldly "I want you to run for Sheriff of Roxi!" Bob went on to tell Randy about the current Sheriff. Bob Raynes decided to not run for Sheriff again, and his deputy was not interested in the job and not well-liked enough to get the job anyway.

"We need a good man like you to be our Sheriff Randy!" said Bob.

"But there must be others that would jump over a full moon to get that job, recession, and everything!" Randy replied.

"There are, but none are as qualified or as well-liked as you are. It would be a sure win if you did run!" Bob proclaimed.

"But what about my home businesses? I've worked hard to build them up, and that's what I want to do. What would I have left if I closed them and if I didn't get re-elected to future terms? Besides, the job doesn't pay that well." Randy questioned.

"Randy we're a small town here, you know that Sheriff Rayne owns and operates his lawnmower repair shop and two bus shuttle services while still doing his Sheriffin'. You can do yours too. Just need to be there when and if any Sherffin' needs to be done, and you get to pick a deputy of your choice to be there when you don't want to be or can't be. Plus, you get a full pension after eight years and lifetime healthcare. Can't get a better deal than that no how, and I think you'll learn to love the job, knowing you like I think I do!" Argued Bob.

Naturally Randy couldn't turn down an opportunity like that at a time like this, a Godsend he thought, and of course, he wouldn't want to miss out on learning new things.

The election was held, and on Thursday, January 4th, 1996 Randy was sworn in as the sitting Sheriff of the small town of Roxi. He had won the election by a landslide. Randy may have been considered the sitting Sheriff because he filled that position, but there was not then or ever had been a sitting Randy Dobbs! Randy immediately screened potential deputies. One candidate which he tested had also run against him for Sheriff. His name was Tom Adams. Tom Adams was well known around Roxi and not very well-liked.

He had been in trouble in just every year of his teens and just about every town in the entire county at one time or another. He wasn't involved in anything severe, or at least as much as anyone could prove, and he did not have a record, but many believe that was only because the police could not find incriminating evidence to prosecute him.

Randy felt a particular uneasiness about Tom Adams as he sensed Tom firmly held it against him for beating him in the election. Randy was partial to a young however inexperienced young crop farmers son named William Fedox. Randy knew if you came from a farm, you were a prompt, reliable, honest, and a hard-working person. The people generally liked Will and respected him and his family very highly. Will was eager to show the Sheriff and the town what he had to offer. Randy thought to himself, "What a great opportunity for young Will to learn new things," so he gave him the job on a probationary period. Tom Adams was rumored to be even more angry with the new Sheriff now. Randy's thoughts of days gone by began to fade, and he fell into a deep sleep.

12
The Missing Persons' Investigator
Saturday, July 21st, 2007, 7:45 am

The next day Randy returns to his office and gets word that the detective the State Police had assigned to investigate the latest missing person and abandoned car found was Officer Matthew Ezekiel Sharkey. That was the same officer that had been the investigating officer in the other more recent missing person & abandoned car cases.

Abandoned car and missing person occurrences have reportedly been an issue of importance since the problem began more than twelve years earlier. Officer Matthew Ezekiel Sharkey was a dedicated investigator who once received an award as a rookie cop for suggesting a new way to help get drivers to wholly and accurately stop at lights and signs. Sharkey was no longer that young rookie but now one of the oldest officers in his division. Unlike the champion of change he once was, he soon was more of a misoneist, a non-believer of the value of change, especially when the change wasn't right for him.

Sharkey also used to be a person who had always believed the adage about attracting more bees with honey. He once suggested the Governor give several certificates worth $25.00 each to random State Troopers throughout the state and while they were watching for people who run or jump stop signs or lights. If they saw someone who completely stopped with-in the proper boundaries, carefully looked both ways before pulling out, and pulled out without jackrabbiting, the officer was to pull the driver over and give the driver the $25.00 gift certificate and a Governors citation. Their insurance company would recognize that citation as a person potentially qualified to receive safe driver discounts. The Governor heavily publicized the promotion which turned out to be a great success and helped get the Governor to get re-elected.

Officer Sharkey, a tall statured, gruff 49-year-old balding and slight overweight man who was a constant source of negativity; yet still a dedicated police officer. Those that know him say the only time Officer Sharkey is ever happy or at least pleasant is when he is assigned to investigations. He has done nothing but complain that he has to go back and do what he did as a rooky after each investigation detail is over with. This complaining started when the State Police initiated a policy where all officers, investigators, and patrolmen rotate through all assignments to give learning opportunities to the newer officers and to maintain all the skills the various duties require. Thus, Officer Matt Sharkey is happiest when he is investigating these strange person disappearances. Some of his peers say he could be doing more, but they think he doesn't want to work his way out of the job he loves the most.

Another reason Officer Sharkey does not like duties other than investigations is that he does not have the freedom to take on or perform tasks at his own pace as he would if he could prioritize them. Some days he would have to sit behind a desk for hours.

The dedicated officer's negativity and grumpiness do not come from a relationship with coffee. That relationship between the two ended many years ago when Sharkey was rushed to the emergency room for what he and the Paramedics thought was a heart attack. Thankfully it was not a heart attack but was diagnosed to be a problem with the cardiac or purse-string valve between his stomach and his esophagus; a valve that is supposed to shut off the back-drifting of stomach acids into the throat.

Sharkey had been suffering from severe acid reflux disease for years and had to be very careful about what he ate. Particular food and drinks, as well as anything putting even the slightest bit of weighted pressure on his chest area or abdomen, would severely inflame his esophagus and cause him tormenting chest pains similar to those experienced when someone has a heart attack. Sometimes the effects would last days or even weeks once an attack was initiated simply from overdoing any of the mentioned potential causes. Sharkey eventually had to stop wearing a belt around his waist because of the tremendous tightening effect it had on his abdominal area. He habitually loosened his pants at the snap or button when he sat down to reduce the pressure or tightness he felt there.

Sharkey seldom carried his handcuffs on his person and complained about his shoulder holster, causing him severe discomfort at times, especially when he was in a sitting position. Thus, he seldom wore it when he was doing office work at his desk, attending meetings and while driving his car.

Officer Sharkey is well known by most persons that reside in the area where he typically investigates crimes and is not well-loved. His only daughter, Sara, is no Cinderella and hangs out with a crowd that makes most peoples' skin crawl. They're unclean, spaced-out looking youngsters that look like a cross between hippies, yuppies, and some dark, death-loving cult. The men, if you want to call them that, make Harry from Henderson's look healthy and clean-shaven and the women resemble recently rescued war refugee, flower child, intoxicated, high, spaced-out bag ladies.

In spite of everything else and knowing his daughter and her lifestyle are the number one reason he has the health problems he has, Officer Sharkey loves his daughter very much and wants what's best for her. However, he has not been able to reach her and save her from herself and the riff-raff that is corrupting her.

Those around Officer Sharkey believe his lack of involvement in his daughter's life, and her lifestyle is why he is so miserable to everyone he meets. Once when a peer tried to befriend him, he told the peer, "If you need a friend, get a dog!"

Bill Fedox was no longer Randy's deputy at this point as he had taken a law correspondence course, done very well for himself and became a law clerk at the courthouse. That's how Fred Baynes got the job. This development further angered Tom Adams, "The Sheriff wanna-be."

That same evening while the Sheriff's girlfriend, Marge Betley was driving into town on her way back from her mother's house, a large tractor trailer came up immediately behind her. Though she was doing a little more than the speed limit to begin with, the tractor trailer was unsafely right on her bumper. She felt threatened for her life. She sped up, and the truck sped up. She slowed down, and the truck slowed down. As she approached a gas station up ahead, she quickly sped up and turned abruptly into the gas station before the truck could react. She sat there, shaking like a leaf, frightened right out of her mind! Marge called the Sheriff on her cell phone, and Randy came to her aid immediately and comforted her.

When Marge calmed down, Randy questioned her to see if she might have done anything to provoke the truck driver. Marge couldn't come up with anything. Randy asked her if she recognized the driver. She said she could not see the driver, but she did notice a sort of license plate on the front of the truck that had the Dixie flag on it and that the vehicles' exhaust emitted a high level of dark smoke from its stacks. Marge stated that as the truck continued by her when she pulled off into the gas station, she noticed occasional sparks coming from under the truck as if something was hanging down and hitting the road.

Randy saw Marge safely to her home and started back to his office. He radioed ahead to the Sheriff's offices east of Roxi with the data that Marge had given. Later that evening Randy remembered that someone told him that Tom Adams hadn't been able to find work in law enforcement and was now driving a tractor-trailer. Randy became concerned that Tom might have harassed and endangered Marge to get back at him for not picking him as his deputy. As soon as Sheriff Randy could locate Tom Adams, he examined his rig. It met the description Marge had given. Randy confronted Tom and warned him to leave Marge and him alone, or he would arrest him.

Additionally, Randy told him to clean himself up, as he had degraded in appearance substantially since Randy last seen him. Tom denied that he had harassed Marge, but Randy didn't believe him. Since Toms failed attempt to become Sheriff and to become deputy, he started hanging around some unsavory motorcycle gang thugs, and now he resembled them. Many people were pointing the finger at Tom for just about anything that happened in town.

13

The Meeting Invitation

Sunday, July 22nd, 2007, 10:00 am

Officer Matt Sharkey was scheduled to meet with Sheriff Dobbs 10 o'clock the next morning. He had already asked Sheriff Dobbs to clear his schedule for the planned information-gathering meeting being held in Oreville next Friday at 8:00 am sharp.

Monday morning, July 23rd, 2007

Officer Matt arrived and being his usual delightful self, said "You look like shit, Sheriff, you need to get some rest!"

Sheriff Randy quickly thought to himself, O.K. you want to play rough, we'll play rough and retaliated by saying, "Watch this shit don't step in you!"

The two immediately felt a bond indicative of trust and respect. They developed an open and honest rapport with each other.

After those niceties were out of the way, Officer Sharkey informed Sheriff Dobbs that Sheriff Mason from Championsburg, the easternmost small town currently known to be associated with missing drivers of found vehicles, would not be able to attend the meeting because of a new development he was faced with.

Officer Matt, as he typically did when he was making new acquaintances, took the time up-front to get to know the person and tell the person about himself. Randy went first and filled in Matt about who he was, what he did as Sheriff, what he liked to do for fun. When it was Officer Matt's turn, he showed Sheriff Randy a photograph of his daughter Sara and talked little about himself and more about his daughter Sara, what she was doing to herself, how spooky she looked, the people she hung out with, and how disappointed he was in her. It was apparent his daughter's behavior was eating him up inside, and he just needed somebody, anybody to talk to about it.

After the introduction and all the niceties were now out of the way, Officer Matt took off the gloves and got down to serious business. He started by filling Sheriff Dobbs in on the current events that brought him there.

"Just yesterday," said Sharkey, "As daylight began to appear, a truck driver returning to his rig at a Championsburg truck stop startlingly discovered the remains of what later was identified as the body of a young woman that had been chained by her legs to the underside of the tractor that was pulling the trailer."

"The woman had been placed between the tires where she would not have been easily seen by passing or trailing vehicles, especially in the dark. Little was left of the body when it was found. Steps were now being taken to identify the body. Because the truck had traveled to and made stops in towns both east and west of Championsburg during the hours of darkness, it was near impossible to know when or where the body had been attached, how long it was attached, or how far it had been drug."

"Damn these obstructions!" hollered Officer Sharkey. "Things like this seem to keep happening. No one has the time to focus on the big problem because of all these other little problems that keep popping up. Takes up too damn many man-hours. Feds spread out all over because many are interstate problems. Can't these other cases wait?" Officer Sharkey complained.

"Are there really that many murder cases around here?" asked Sheriff Randy. "Well, enough anyway," responded Officer Sharkey. "The Feds had a double, gangland-style homicide over in Bedloe a good month ago and they assigned a couple of dozen agents to it. They've been there since. It seems someone found two severely mutilated corpses just off the interstate, park. They think the incident might be related to the drug war and drug gang problems down in Ciudad Juarez, Mexico. Both of the deceased individuals, a man, and a woman were found bullet-ridden, with their heads severed. They had been heavily doused with sulfuric acid. The acid destroyed all possible identifiable scars, marks, identifiers, and fingerprints. The incidents so closely resemble a similar case in New Mexico a few months ago, when two unidentifiable women were found in a vacant parking lot. Because both instances so closely resemble tactics used by Mexican warlord rivals to intimidate each other in their bloody drug war, the Feds are afraid the violence may be spreading over into our country and have given the situation their highest priority." Finished Officer Sharkey. The Sheriffs' Office door opened and in walked Sheriff Randy's girlfriend, Marge Betley.

"Good morning!" Marge said with enthusiasm as she interrupted their meeting.

"Thought you both might like a nice steaming fresh pot of coffee and some of my fresh out of the oven cinnamon buns." she said.

Officer Matt Sharkey instead of being annoyed as one might think he would be, gleamed with approval. It just so happened that Officer Matts' favorite baked goods were just that, cinnamon buns. Matt had to wonder how she knew. Of course, she didn't, it just worked out that way.

"Wow!" said Officer Matt enthusiastically, "Cinnamon buns are my favorite! Thank you very much!"

"Marge Betley, meet Officer Matt Sharkey with the State Police, Matt Sharkey meet Marge Betley, she's a very close friend of mine, and she runs the best diner in this part of the country!" said Randy.

Officer Sharkey had just taken a bite and savored it during the introductions and said, "How very pleasant to meet you and by how wonderful this cinnamon bun tastes, I'm sure Sheriff Dobbs' words ring true!" said he.

"When Sheriff Randy told me about your coming today, I just had to meet you." Said Marge, "Randy has been very concerned ever since he found that abandoned car on the highway the other day. You've got an excellent resource in Sheriff Randy. He's very dedicated."

"I'm sure he is, and I have big plans for him and the other Sheriff's around the vicinity." Said Officer Matt.

A little small talk and pleasantries took place, then Marge Betley, feeling she was in the way, apologized for intruding upon and interrupting their conversation. She told Randy she would come by later, then told Officer Matt that she was delighted to have made his acquaintance and left.

Officer Matt was taken by Marge Betley and her cinnamon buns and said so to Randy.

"That's one hell of a swell girl you've got there Sheriff, treat her right. Girls like her are hard to come by." Said he.

Randy took a few minutes to tell Sharkey about Marge and her deceased husband, Frank. Officer Matt felt terrible for her.

"Sometimes, things are just destined to happen." Said Sharkey, "I'm glad she found you. She seems to be recovering from his loss and has hope. I wish my daughter Sara would find a nice guy to take her away from that wasted life she's living!"

"I'm sure she will," said Randy.

"Well anyway, getting back on track, that's why I came to invite you in person Sheriff," Stated Sharkey. "I want you to come prepared for this meeting as if you were studying for a final exam! Think about anything you might have seen, heard, smelled, even thought about when you found that car. Things that might have slipped your mind or perhaps you didn't know might be necessary when you filled out your report. Anything ever so small could be the lead we need to solve this case!"

"You can count on me, Officer Sharkey!" Sheriff Randy replied. "I'll give it my highest priority!"

Sheriff Randy Dobbs has no love for anyone that abuses their authority, bullies, threatens, swindles, or cheats people, (especially the ill or elderly). Sheriff Randy being a quite large fellow, six foot three, a good 245 lbs. and strong as an ox, always stuck up for people that were picked on, threatened or taken advantage of. Matt Sharkey was glad to have a person like Randy on his side.

14

The Dangerous Chainsaw

Monday, July 23rd, *2007, 11:45 am*

After Officer Sharkey left, Randy was deep in serious thought. Then his phone rang. It was Walt Devons, the rural delivery mailman in Apollotown but also known well to the people in Roxi and the Sheriff. He was calling the Sheriff on his cell phone and was extremely excited. "Sheriff, he said, I called Sheriff Tom Keets office and got a message that he and his deputy were testifying at a trial in Justice today and that I should call you in an emergency. You'd better get out to Ed Shontis's farm right away. I just found young Ed lying on the ground. I... think he's dead!" Walt said.

"I'll have an ambulance sent out immediately Walt, then I'll round up Bill Masten the County Coroner if I can, and I'll be right out." Replied Sheriff Randy.

The mailman, Walt Devons waited with dead Ed. When Sheriff Dobbs arrived with the Coroner Bill Masten, the ambulance was there, and the crew had already examined young Ed. They had pronounced him dead at the scene. "Hello, Sheriff," Walt said, "Poor Ed, no one around to help him, he bled to death." Commented the attending E.M.T. Len Hontz.

"What the hell happened?" asked Randy.

"Don't know for sure." Said Len, "All I know for sure is that he has sustained significant, potentially fatal chain saw blade induced injuries to his hand, arm, leg, neck, face, and chest. I think the wounds to his upper torso by themselves were enough to cause his death."

"I guess we'll have to leave the cause of death up to you Bill," Randy told the coroner.

Following up on the 911 call the Sheriff made, several state police units arrived. Accompanied now by the Officers, Sheriff Randy began an investigation to try to piece together what might have happened. Len and Walt stayed around to help.

"It appears Ed was cutting small fireplace sized logs from this big pile of long stacked up logs over here," said Randy.

"Not a smart thing to do!" said Walt. "When logs are stacked upon each other like that, the chainsaw can unexpectedly grip one of them under logs and rap you in the shins. Happened to me a time or two before I learned better. Hurts like hell!"

"Maybe that's what happened to cause all of this? Looks like he was standing on some pretty slippery, uneven ground by the looks of his footprints." one of the State Police officers noticed.

"I think maybe it did" commented Len. Look at that partially cut through log over there, it has blood on it. Could be that he got unexpectedly clobbered in the shins by that log when the saw started into it, that could explain why it's not cut clear through. It may have knocked him off balance, and the saw blade fell into his leg."

"But... how did he get all the other wounds he has?" asked Sheriff Randy.

"Hell, I don't know for sure, but he sure wasn't dressed properly for this kind of work. No shirt, wearing shorts, worn-out sneakers, no socks, no gloves. These young kids today, I don't know where they get their brains!" commented Len.

Bill Masten, the coroner, came over to share his preliminary findings as the conversation was unfolding and added his two cents. "If Ed was right-handed as I suspect he was,"

"He was." interrupted Walt.

"Then..." Continued Bill, "The inflictions Ed had on his chin and neck potentially were the result of the simple involuntary reflex action when the saw chain struck his upper right thigh the one that is badly ripped and scraped raw. He probably and understandably jerked the saw upward away from his leg so fast and hard it came up so high it struck him about the chin and neck. Then the same simple involuntary reflex probably caused him to reach up with his free left hand, the hand, and arm that have extensive injuries. At that point, he fell to the ground with the saw, inflicting the other injuries he sustained."

"Makes sense Bill," Sheriff Randy stated. "However, what about the degree of damage we see? Wouldn't the saw chain have stopped turning by now? I mean... look at the way it has ground up to his chest and upper left arm!"

45

"That part puzzles me too" Bill answered, "The only explanation I can see is that he was so frightened he squeezed the trigger so hard his grip didn't release immediately when he collapsed."

Len interrupted and said, "I know of two reasons that the chain would keep moving when the throttle trigger was released. First, the throttle screw may have been out of adjustment. Many times, when operators have problems with the saw stalling because of R.P.M.'s get too low, they adjust the throttle screw, so the R.P.M.'s don't get low enough for the engine to stall. This is serious business because the saw's chain will continue to run around the chain bar when you let go of the trigger. Another reason the saw engine runs at high enough speed disallowing the chain to stop traveling is because of a too rich of gas to oil ratio. The less oil mixed with the gas, the faster the saw's engine will run without depressing the throttle trigger. Chainsaws usually speed up when you are almost out of fuel as the mixture tends to favor all gas and little if any, oil."

A State Police Officer asked, "Is there some way we can test any of these theories to narrow down the most probable cause?"

Len exclaimed, "Sure, can! Are you done gathering forensic data you need from the saw now, Bill?" Len asked.

"I'd like to remove the chain and gather data from the bar's pathway groove yet. However, as long as your testing doesn't compromise that data, go ahead." Bill replied.

Len shook the saw vigorously to thoroughly integrate the gas with the oil, gave two powerful pulls on the recoil start cord and the engine came to life. Giving it a few seconds to warm up, Len released the throttle trigger. The saws engine was reluctant to slow even close to a speed that the saws chain would not keep turning.

"Well, Said Len, we now know the chain didn't stop as it should have. If you want to know for sure why, we will have to find out what the correct gas and oil mix ratio is for this particular saw, make a mix and try it. If it still runs extreme, then it would be a throttle screw adjustment cause. Do you want to go any farther with this?" Len asked.

Bill the coroner commented. "I guess we found out what we wanted to know. If we need to, we can find out later. Anyone disagree with that?" asked Bill. All agreed.

All present paused for a moment of silence as young Ed's body was placed into Coroner Bills vehicle, reflecting and lamenting about how Ed returned home from San-Francisco only a few months ago, to die like this. He returned when his only living parent, his father, died and left him the farm. Ed was a wayward youth, and he and his dad never got along well. That's why he went, to begin with.

Just as the State Police prepared to depart, they all heard over the police radio about remains found when employees reported working that morning in a vat of acid at a business in Bigelow about 80 miles away.

"Sure glad this one's out of our district. One like this is enough for one day!" commented one State Police Officer.

"I couldn't agree with you more!" replied Sheriff Randy.

15
The Missing Persons Meeting Begins
Friday, July 27th, 2007, 8:00 am

The meeting began with Officer Matt Reviewing the agenda and giving a brief synopsis of the problems he had been facing; trying to sort through the myriad of strange occurrences, events, and happenings. Many of these problems have muddled and clouded the facts and detailed information he so badly needed to solve the strange disappearances that have plagued the large area in question.

Officer Matthew Sharkey shared the data about the strange human remains cases that may be related to Mexican drug lord violence. He explained that the Federal Authorities were heavily involved with these few cases and how it has made it difficult for him to get the workforce he requested.

Officer Sharkey made it very clear about what he wanted from each participant and reminded them that he had personally, face to face, met with every participant before the meeting. The purpose of these meetings was asking them to give special consideration to any possible but maybe not so apparent details regarding their individual experiences and encounters with potential evidence.

Officer Sharkey said he would one by one, allow each participant as much time as they needed to present their experience(s) with the group in any way they best feel fit to do so. He asked that as each shared their data, that no-one distract them with questions until after they had completed their presentation so as not to disrupt their train of thought. He stressed how valuable and necessary data goes unrepresented many times because of interruptions and distractions.

Officer Sharkey promised and ensured all participants that there would be ample time for questioning each presenter immediately after each finished. Then, after all data is shared there, would be an open question and answer forum and time to hypothesize about the how, why, and motives.

He cautioned everyone to pay particular attention to similarities and questionable dissimilarities.

"Write things down as you hear anything questionable, so you don't forget." Instructed Sharkey.

Officer Sharkey specifically wanted to take advantage of the testimonies of the presenters, witnesses, or others in any way involved with some of the earliest disappearances recorded. This would prevent them from mixing up their data with any more recent occurrences.

Officer Sharkey said. "Let's begin. Our first presenter will be Mr. Tim Keaston. As far as our records show, Tim was the first person to be involved with one of these cars found and person disappearances. Tim, the floor is yours." Gestured Sharkey.

"Thank you, Officer Sharkey, I hope I can help," responded Keaston. "Good morning, everyone. It was about 7:15 am, it had just broken daylight on a pleasant Sunday morning, February 9th, 1992. I was driving through Benton, going west on I-50. I saw a car (later identified as belonging to a Mr. William Rapsey, from Russell, Kansas.) up ahead.

As I gained on it rather quickly, I began to realize the car was not moving and had no lights on. I began to slow down, not knowing what the story was ahead. When I realized the car was stopped, blocking the right lane, the one I was traveling in, I slowed way down. I got pissed that the driver didn't pull off of the road and was causing a dangerous situation for others approaching in the same lane.

I thought to myself well, maybe the car broke down in a way that didn't allow the driver the opportunity to curb the vehicle. However, I felt that in almost every case, surely the driver could have coasted off of the pavement. I put my passenger side window down to offer help and was preparing to hurl a few words at the inconsiderate driver if appropriate. However, to my surprise, I saw no one. I suppose I could just as well have only driven on and minded my own business, as I think most people would do. However, I guess my curiosity got the best of me. So, I put my car in reverse and carefully went back

I wanted to see if everything was all right. I parked my car well off of the pavement, got out, and walked up to the car and looked inside. There was no one inside. The doors were all locked. I saw what looked like a belt buckle, some change, and a pair of glasses lying on the front seat. Then I noticed that the keys were still in the ignition. I remember thinking to myself; something about this feels wrong. I walked around the car to see if it showed any signs of a breakdown, flat tires, or some foul play. Nothing stood out to me. I saw a tractor-trailer approaching from way off in the opposite lane and across the medium. I hurried across the swell and flagged the driver down. I specifically asked him if he saw anyone walking the roadway. He said he didn't notice anybody but he wasn't inclined to look way over on that side. I told him what I found and asked him to call the Sheriffs' office. There weren't too many cell phones back in those days, and I sure didn't have one.

I tied my hankie on the wrecked cars door handle and went on my way. As I drove into Benton, I passed what looked like the Sheriffs' car that was coming fast in the opposite direction on the eastbound highway and across the median. It approached much too soon for me to get his attention. I had assumed that he was responding to the call from the trucker. When I arrived in Benton, I left word with the Deputy. I was contacted about it back then, and I told the Sheriff what I just told all of you today, and that was the last of it... That is until I heard from Officer Sharkey last week."

"Does anyone have any questions for Mr. Keaston?" asked Sharkey. There were no questions.

"Great job, Tim!" said Sharkey. "Now we will hear from the Sheriff that responded and investigated that incident. Former, Benton Sheriff, Mr. Bill Blasty."

"Well, I guess I could just as well have stayed home today. You did an excellent job of presenting the facts, Mr. Keaston," Said the former Sheriff. "I have only a few things to offer that Mr. Keaston was not aware of. First, when I arrived, I looked the area over carefully for any clues to what might have happened and who might have done it. There were no fluids under the vehicle or anywhere on the highway leading up to where it was stopped that might have indicated it had a mechanical failure. I found no footprints. However, the ground was quite firm. There was no apparent reason for the car to be disabled. There was no one to be seen in any direction. I called out. No one answered. I reported the incident to the State Police, and they had the car towed into Benton where it had been examined by the State Police Crime Lab and Hank Roweland, the best mechanic in Benton. In a short while, I received a report on what the inspection revealed.

They found out that the doors were all indeed locked. The cars gas tank was empty, bone dry. It had been run out of gas, as there was none in the fuel pump or carburetor. The shifting apparatus, which was between the two front seats on that model, had been left in the drive position. The ignition key was found in the on position, and the light switch was in the on position. The car took on the appearance of having been driven, possibly during night-time hours, until it finally ran out of gas and rolled to a stop where it was found. No disabling mechanical or electrical failures were discovered. Other than the findings Mr. Keaston already shared, only a wedding ring and wristwatch belonging to the owner of the vehicle was found on the front drivers' side floor mat. Forensics found no helpful clues. There were only the fingerprints of the owner found inside the car. There were absolutely no visible signs of foul play. To the best of anyone's knowledge and because of lack of data supporting otherwise, (except the fact that the driver was never seen or heard from again), there was no scientific reason or evidence found to suspect that any foul play had even occurred." Summed up the former Sheriff.

"Does anyone have any questions for Mr. Blasty?" asked Sharkey.

A voice called out from the audience asking Mr. Blasty if he felt the automobiles radiator area or hood to feel if there was any heat coming from them, which might be an indication of how long it had been since the automobile's engine had run.

"No," bashfully replied the former sheriff, "I never thought to do so." There were no other questions.

"Thank you, Bill, that was very helpful." Said Sharkey.

"Next up to bat, we have Officer Anthony O'Brien, with the State Police. He was working the Championsburg district during the Thursday, April 30th, 1992 disappearance of Madge Crackest from Championsburg. Welcome, Officer O'Brien!" said Sharkey.

"Morning, folks," started Officer O'Brien. "I'm afraid you'll be looking in the mirror here folks. Other than the date and possibly the time it happened; the location, persons involved, and type of car, my incidents facts and data are extremely similar to what you've heard from both Mr. Keaston and Mr. Blasty."

Officer O'Brien went on to relay his experience. The only thing added was the fact that Officer O'Brien did indeed check the precise temperature points on the vehicle. He explained that the car did not feel even warm to him, but it was 9:05 am when he arrived, and the car had already been discovered and reported some 35 or 40 minutes earlier.

"The caller left no name or number to reply to. Probably just doing his patriotic duty and didn't think it peculiar," he said.

When the next presenter, Sheriff Lonnie Potts from Bigelow representing the disappearance of Mr. Ted Basinn of Alamosa, began, he stopped abruptly and said, "I sound like a summer rerun!" and questioned the time being spent by running the meeting in the fashion it was being done. Most of the other attendees also pitched in and suggested that an open discussion be held asking for anyone with any new, different or potentially helpful data speak up rather than wasting precious time repeating the same theme. A show of hands decided the change to the agenda.

"All right, all right! However, before I ask you, is there anyone here with any new, other, or different data than what we already know and discussed?" Stated Sharkey. "I must insist that we do take the time to hear from Sheriff Randy Dobbs from Roxi, our most recent member of 'Found the Car but not the Driver Club.' It might help and sure can't hurt!"

Randy told the story as we already know it to be. Indeed, there was nothing new. We knew that. However, Randy did caution that the potential for any car to be displayed on the roadway and not be reported by a motorist encountering it, was far less likely now because of the heavy use of cell phones today as opposed to 15 years ago.

"Now, let me ask you again," restated Sharkey. "Is there anyone here with any new or different data than what we already know and discussed?"

16
The Not So Missing, Missing Person
Friday, July 27th, 2007, 10:00 am

Before anybody could reply to Officer Sharkey's question, the door flew open unexpectedly, and in barged Sharkey's chief assistant. He whispered something into Sharkey's ear as he handed him a paper. Sharkey looked stunned, took a moment to study the letter that was given to him, and began.

"Damn it! Another sprag in our spokes gentleman!" Exclaimed Sharkey. "Our most recent missing person, Mrs. Silvermann from Beaumonte, her car was found in Championsburg last week."

"Yes, I worked that case," interrupted John Trotter, the Sheriff of Championburg.

"Well, thankfully, she was just reported found alive and well." reestablished Officer Sharkey. "Seems she and her husband had a falling out and she went on the cruise she couldn't get him to go on, and never told him or anyone else for that matter. Now do you see why the priority to work these disappearances are so low? No one is even sure these people are missing, have met with foul play, or aren't just someplace where they don't want to be found."

One attendee spoke up. "Wait, wait just a minute," commanded Officer Sharkey.

"This report doesn't address the fact that Mrs. Silvermanns' car was found exactly as the other missing person vehicles were."

"That's right!" shouted several of the other attendees.

"Let's get someone in here right now to fill us in on the connection!" requested Officer Randy Dobbs.

"Take five fellas," said Officer Sharkey. "I'll be right back."

Officer Sharkey, not at all happy about being left in the dark about the found missing person vehicle link, stormed out of the room looking for answers. Officer Sharkey returned about 15 minutes later, more unhappy than he was when he left.

"I hate my job!" Sharkey decried. "Can you all believe that I talked to officials at the Beaumonte Sheriffs office, the State Police, and the F.B.I., nobody, I mean absolutely nobody has any clue or even any idea how Mrs. Silvermann's car wound up like all the rest. Mr. Silvermann didn't even know Mrs. Silvermann's car was missing until the police notified him that they found it nine or ten days ago, that's when he filed the missing person report about his wife. Anyway, Matt Helmsler with the State Police crime lab will be here in a few minutes to fill us in."

The group tried to hypothesize a scenario that would explain the unusual circumstance but came up with too many question marks to make any significant progress, so they decided to wait for Matt Helmsler. Hopefully, he would have the answers that would make things piece together. Matt Helmsler arrived just before 11:00. Everyone was getting pretty hungry by then. Matt had a critical 12:15 appointment in Porktown, so lunch would have to wait.

"Good morning everyone, I'm Matt Helmsler with the State Police crime lab. I've been as close as anyone has been to this particular disappearance because Mr. and Mrs. Silvermann and the Captain are friends and he had me work full time on investigating her mysterious disappearance. I can sum up the distinction between this found car and all the others rather quickly. No personal wear items were found on the drivers side floor mat or the seat. That's it, nothing else, everything else is the same as the others!" stated Helmsler.

"Well I'm glad to hear that spoke one jokester, I was starting to think Martians had vaporized all these drivers!"

Everyone laughed as they could relate to that thought.

"Any questions before I depart?" asked Helmsler.

"I've got one," Sheriff Lou Crocket from Justice spoke up. "Did anybody feel the Radiator, engine, or hood when the car was found?"

"The engine was cold," Helmsler replied.

"Was the battery dead, possibly drawn down by the lights being left on?" Asked yet another.

"Yes," replied Helmsler, "Same as all the others from the reports I've read."

"Do you know if any investigators, in any of the cases, tried to find out if anyone driving by or camping out, saw or reported any cars parked on the portion of the highway with their lights left on at night?"

Asked Tom Keets, Sheriff of Apollotown.

"No, not to the best of my knowledge," replied Helmsler.

There were no more questions. Helmsler left, and the group broke for lunch.

After lunch, everyone felt more refreshed, and all were very interested in continuing to hypothesize a possible reason or motive and setting direction for the future.

"Let's pick up where we left off," said Officer Sharkey choking down a sandwich as he spoke.

The poor, busy officer had canceled his 12:15 in-person appointment in Porktown and done it by teleconferencing instead. He got no break or lunch.

"Let's try to reason this thing out." He said, "To me, I can only see one of two possible theories for the car not having the personal property found in it like the others and showing up for a person that wasn't missing. Either the perpetrator of the other disappearances knew Mrs. Silvermann and knew she left town, or, someone formerly uninvolved played a very clever game of copy-cat,"

"But why?" several attendees harmoniously responded.

"We need to revisit and delve into this case again and penetrate every bit of data and evidence we possibly can. I'll bet there are more differences to be found." Said Lou Crocket.

"Perhaps someone thought she was really missing or dead and not coming back." Said Mr. Keaston.

"Did she keep valuables in her car?" asked another.

"How about her kids, she must have told one of them." Questioned Sheriff Tom Bones from Bedloe.

"No children." spoke up Sharkey.

"That's it. That's it!" encouraged Officer Sharkey. "Keep the questions coming in; that's what will keep this investigation alive. Someone, please, get up to the flip chart and start writing all these questions and what ifs down," said Sharkey, "We need to get all the ideas out on the table. Then I'll compile all the data, publish it in full detail and disseminate to all of you so we can compare. Please, everybody, jump in. Add your own two cents." Sharkey pleaded.

"Let's work the found car scenario." Suggested Dick Logan, Sheriff of Oreville. "How do you suppose the perpetrator got all those cars out on the highway like that without anyone seeing him? I think there had to be more than one person involved to pull it off."

"I do too!" suggested Sharkey. "The way they were scattered almost randomly, all over the distant length of I-50, he or she, would almost surely need an accomplice to follow and bring them back after they ran the car out of gas. Perhaps with all but the exception of one of the locations, it would have been much too far to walk, and someone might have seen them."

"Maybe that's how they did it, they hitch-hiked and didn't care if they were seen." Suggested Joe Bobby, Current Sheriff of Benton. "Maybe they're not even from around here and no-one would recognize them by face and never make any connection with the missing person's vehicle anyway."

"Nah, too risky," suggested Sheriff Harry Luttze, Sheriff of Beaumonte. "Supposed they were picked up by the Sheriff, his Deputies, or the State Police? No, I don't think so."

17
Hypothesizing
Friday, July 27th, 2007, 2:10 pm

"Maybe they towed them out." suggested another. "Not likely, would have had to have been seen by someone, sooner or later," responded Luttze.

"So, it could be a couple of people, perhaps more. That's little help, maybe we should start talking motive, that might narrow the field down a little," suggested Sheriff Logan.

"Good idea!" said Sharkey. "Why do you suppose any two or more people would do such a thing?" asked Sharkey. "Let's hypothesize awhile."

"Now we're cooking with gas," said Mr. Keaston. "There has to be money or valuables involved here for these goons to go through all this trouble."

"Unfortunately," said Sharkey dejectedly, "We have not been able to make any case for theft, embezzlement, ransom or any other form of financial reward for what they are doing."

"O.K.," said Officer O'Brien. "Let's try to come up with some possible motives. Any way you look at it, these people in question are missing in the sense that they do not have the freedom of choice, so it would have to be considered kidnapping. Why, would these people, conspire to commit these on-going kidnappings? Moreover, why would they do it for such a prolonged time? Also, why have we not been able to identify any particular pattern for the timing of each incident?"

"Many times, people, primarily women, are kidnapped for a sexual purpose; even children sometimes," said Tom Keets. "But we have both men and women being kidnapped here. Sex does not seem to fit. Unless of course, we are dealing with some extraordinary personalities."

"How about children?" asked O'Brien, "Have any persons been under the age of 18?"

"No." replied Sharkey, "The youngest person known to be driving any of the recovered vehicles during the time they were abandoned, was Tommy Trent of Porktown, on Friday, May 7th of 1993. The eldest was 45-year-old Janet Wentz, of Bigelow, on Monday, November 27th, 1993."

"Ya know," stated another, "It would be helpful if we had all the data you have available to you, Officer Sharkey."

The others all chimed in too. They felt they could have been more prepared to help develop possible scenarios and hypothesize if they would have had the data also.

"I'm sorry," stated Sharkey. "I guess I dropped the ball, and I can see now where much of the data I didn't think I needed to share with you before-hand would have been greatly helpful. I promise this won't happen again!"

"How about some cult activity? Any reason to believe some deranged bunch of weirdoes could be doing this and perhaps using the victims for blood or sacrifice?" asked Randy Dobbs. The group reached a consensus that the cult scenario was a real good possibility. Probably the best idea yet.

"While I agree it does carry outstanding possibility, I can't accept the probability of it because there have been, at least to the best of my knowledge, no reported cult activities in the affected areas. At least not near that degree of strange behavior." Commented Sharkey.

"Well I like the idea, and I think we all should be watching out very closely to see if there might be other strange activity; activity possibly related to a cult organization operating somewhere within the boundaries of these occurrences," remarked Sheriff Randy Dobbs.

"I like the idea too," remarked Sheriff Lonnie Potts. "It would sure help to understand and explain what we have been seeing, and they would have enough members to pull it off."

"I caution you all not to jump to the cause," said Sharkey, "It is no more than a possible theory, and remember, we have not found a single body or remains."

"Where, if there are any bodies, would they dispose of so many that none have turned up in all these years?" asked another attendee.

"Millions of places out there," said Sharkey.

"Perhaps we should spend some time trying to set up some small search parties in areas and search some of the more secluded less frequented spots that could easily hide a dumped body." Suggested yet another.

"That might be helpful." said Sharkey, "Particularly if we have any newer findings. Let's make that one of our action steps."

"Any other ideas or theories?" asked Sharkey.

There were none.

"Perhaps the real perpetrator just did this to sidetrack us or slow us down and make it harder to get more people involved," said Sheriff Randy.

"But how would he, or she, or even they, know that she left town unless he knows her, and she told him." Replied Sharkey. "Let's go ask her specifically. If she let it slip to someone, perhaps he's our man."

"May just be she told someone on board, and they radioed the news back to someone at home." said someone in the rear of the room.

"I think now we're thinking just a little too far out of the box." said yet another voice.

Just before the meeting broke up, several of the attendees expressed their dissatisfaction that only the abandoned car cases were getting attention when they have been involved in other missing person cases where the scenario was different. It seemed that all the various town Sheriffs were getting beat up to some degree because they weren't turning up any clues on the other missing person issues.

The Sheriff of Porktown, Milo chimed in, "I've certainly had my hands tied following up on unrelated missing person reports for several years now. These people are just as missing as the others, why don't we include them at this meeting?" he asked.

Officer Sharkey felt his grip on the Sheriffs slipping, and he didn't like it. He needed every one of them to help him if he was ever going to solve the abandoned car capers. He had felt deeply that lack of workforce and attention to detail was the reason he had not gotten even one solid lead to date. He wasn't about to lose the men he did have as they go off chasing leads that he felt didn't lend themselves to his problem. He needed to get the Sheriffs to regroup and refocus on the major problem that he felt plagued the area. He called the men back to order and said, "The most efficient way I know of to solve a compound problem is to break the whole problem down into bite-sized parts, prioritize the various parts that make up the whole problem, and select the part that is the most serious or urgent. We can then use it as a starting point. Work on only one problem at a time. I repeat, work on only one problem at a time." insisted Officer Sharkey. "I don't know about all of you, said he, but speaking for myself, I can't effectively and efficiently problem solve or work on more than one problem at a time!"

"The abandoned car cases are by far the most important because of the public fear out there. People are afraid to travel I-50, especially after dark. Also, of course, that's where my boss wants me to put my attention! I repeat!" said he, "I want to emphasize to you that the abandoned car cases are the most important issue to work! There will come a proper time and place to address the other issues, but we cannot afford to lose our focus at a time like this. It could be catastrophic for all of us! We need to now, more than ever, keep our eyes and ears open, especially during the nighttime hours."

"But Officer Sharkey," asked Sheriff Crocket. "Do we know for sure these occurrences did all happen during nighttime hours?"

"No one but the good Lord up above knows for sure, because the cars were all recovered during daylight hours." Replied Sharkey.

"However, it sure does lend itself to that strong possibility. It seems unreasonable to believe that even one of these vehicles could have been sitting on the road all of the nighttime hours and no one reported it. No... No, I'm sure the abductions happened with-in hours and perhaps even just minutes before the cars were found."

The men were getting quite restless and were burned out. There were no critical questions or possibilities to offer. The meeting ended; it was quite productive as far as setting direction and action steps to be taken. There was a list of follow-up items, mostly questions needing answers. Several of the officers volunteered to attend to them. Randy stayed back a few minutes to help Officer Sharkey clean things up and organize the collected data.

"Everybody's too damn busy working their problems!" stammered Sharkey. "I guess I'll be working this case a long, long time."

Though Officer Sharkey was trying to sound discouraged, Sheriff Randy sensed a feeling of satisfaction coming from him. He knew Sharkey loved investigations more than buffalo wings and cold beer. This case would keep Sharkey from pounding a beat for quite some time.

Anxious to bust Sharkey, Randy spoke up and said:

"I think I kind of know what you mean Officer Sharkey, not that I've had any murders mind you, but Sheriff Keets over in Apollotown and I have had more than our share of problems, with accidents and ticketing people for passing school buses."

"May sound funny to you but with all this other stuff happening at the same time, and so often, it's almost as if it were planned that way." said Sharkey.

18
Implementing Action Steps
Saturday, July 28th, 2007

The next few days were quiet, and all the officers were thankful because they needed to try to catch up for the full day they lost attending the meeting in Oreville on Friday.

One of the action steps created at the meeting was for all law enforcement officers from the particular crime watch area to keep a separate log of all their daily job-related activities, and to include notes if anything strikes their minds as unusual, odd, or out of place. They were then to fax or otherwise send a copy to each on the list of designated names created during that meeting no less than daily. Communication was the number one thing that all attendees felt was lacking and needed to be addressed.

Officers in all districts were now paying much more attention to detail than they had before. They watched for unfamiliar, (especially unsavory looking or behaving) groups of people seen loitering or passing through town. Stolen vehicles descriptions were reported immediately. Moreover, of course, one should never devalue the rumor mill. Some people seem to know things you don't, and some people seem to know everybody else's business.

During the follow-up check done by Matt Sharkey to see how the new system was working, he was amazed to hear the various stories and rumors obtained from people in different towns. He was impressed at how well that data was relayed from officer to officer. In the past, most of the officers didn't want to be bothered with things they thought were trivial and just a bother. They pretty much looked the other way or closed their eyes and ears to things going on around them that didn't seem like it was part of their job description, and in many cases just meant more work for them. But when the word got around that officers now were more interested in finding out what was going on in their districts, and acting to make their communities safer, more and more people provided them with useful information.

19
The Unscrupulous Financial Advisor
Saturday, August 18th, 2007

One story at the top of the rumor mill lately was one that grabbed hard for Roxis' Sheriff Randy Dobbs attention. He was very concerned as he discussed this rumor with several of the other officers, primarily around the Beaumonte & Championsburg area. It centered around a shady financial advisor named Kevin Sneezelyn from Benton that everyone was telling others to watch out for. He had reportedly sold some small or worthless investments to some retirees, and they had lost most of their retirement income. They were left in a real fix. Some of his desperate clients that could get backing from their family or friends took Sneezelyn to court but were unsuccessful because he lied about so many material things. He was also said to have withheld essential data from them that would have been proof of his intentional wrongdoing in addition to a rumor that he threatened some of his clients with bodily harm if they took him to court. The unscrupulous scoundrel got away with stealing these poor unfortunate futures away from them. It didn't sit well with the proper justice served philosophy.

People were commenting on how the ancient saying crime doesn't pay, isn't a reality, and how it doesn't work anymore under today's justice system. This surely exemplified the fact that evil does sometimes pay in today's world, especially if you're someone famous or rich.

Randy and the other officials decided that off the record, they would put the word out about this no-good so it would be harder for him to score against the elderly in their towns.

Late, on Saturday August 18th, 2007, Randy received a fax stating that the remains of financial advisor Kevin Sneezelyn were found on the premises of a vacated farmland in Championsburg. He had been stripped naked and was severely tarred and feathered.

Perhaps, it was not the intent of the perpetrator(s) to kill him but the tar had been so scalding hot, it cooked his epidermal skin. In places where it was applied in unusually large and heavy gobs, the skin and even muscle had pulled away from the body. Though most of the team felt Sneezelyn got what he richly deserved, they all hoped their new way of getting the public to open up to them hadn't in any way encouraged this action.

One person Randy's townsfolk kept bussing his ear about was Randy's nemesis, Tom Adams. Tom had continued to degrade in both appearance and his attitude. Randy, who used to more or less let all this finger-pointing go in one ear and out the other, was now paying more attention to what people were saying. Randy noticed that Tom seemed to be being blamed for just about everything that happened anymore.

20
The Bedloe House-fire

Tuesday, September 18th, 2007 6:30 am

The town of Bedloe was awakened by the sound of scrambling fire vehicles and sirens. The Bedloe Fire Dept. consists of volunteers from various occupations that live in and outside of the town itself. When a fire is reported, all volunteers available, drop whatever it is they are doing. This morning they were all racing to the farm about three miles away, owned, operated, and lived in by twenty-four-year-old Mr. Brad Wate, a bachelor, and a volunteer fireman. Only on this particular some-what chilly Saturday morning in September, Mr. Brad Wate would not be racing to the fire with them. Mr. Brad Wate would not be running anywhere that morning or any morning again. It was his farm home amassed with flames that seared so high, the fire could be seen from town. It was a building that had been passed down in his family from generation to generation since being built in the later 19th century. It burned like kindling, it burned fast, and it burned completely.

Of course, everyone had hoped that when they got there, he would be alive and fighting the fire. Mr. Brad Wate would never be seen alive again. Mr. Wate had been a free-spirited individual that loved and enjoyed life to the fullest. Being very contemporary, he took what you might call the fast track; fast cars, fast women, and fast experiences. Though Brad was kind of rogue, a scoundrel, people generally liked and accepted him.

It took days for the deep embers to cool enough to conduct an investigation into the cause and look for remains. During that time, rumors and reports began to come into the Sheriff of Bedloe, Sheriff Tom Bones' office. Sheriff Bones, of course, is a member of the abandoned cars team. There were many reports of unusual activity at the farm during the evening hours preceding the fire. These activities were observed by several witnesses that had passed by the farm that evening.

As Sheriff Randy carefully read the fax sent to him with great interest, he was fixed on one particular vehicle reported. It had made his flag wave, and he decided to dig further into it. One of the cars that attracted passerby's attention was a tractor-trailer. Sheriff Randy wondered if was possible that the tractor-trailer seen at the Bedloe farm was the same one Randy saw at Tom Adams place a little while back.

Randy contacted Sheriff Bones to see if he could get a description of the observed tractor-trailer. When Randy received the reply that there was a Dixie flag on the front of it, he immediately went to Bedloe to question the witnesses himself. Unfortunately, no one could confirm that the trucks exhaust emitted a high level of dark smoke from its stacks

Randy had an extreme suspicion that the tractor-trailer parked there was the same one that threatened his girlfriend, Marge Betley, earlier. This is especially true since a group of parked motorcycles was also reported to have been at the location during the same time as the tractor-trailer was. He knew Adams had been hanging around some unsavory motorcycle gang thugs. He felt strongly that his nemesis Tom Adams was in some way involved. Randy shared his convictions with Sheriff Bones and returned to Roxi.

Sheriff Randy nor Sheriff Bones took action against Randy's suspicions as many tractor-trailers carry the Dixie flag on the front of them and many motorcycles are on the roads too.

Wednesday, September 19th

Sheriff Bones received word that the remains of seven individuals were found buried under the burnt-out debris in the farm homes basement area. Officials did not know if the victims had been in the basement area or if they had been on the floor above and forced beneath as the extreme weight of the upper levels collapsed. Further investigations brought forth evidence that suggested some illegal drug-producing lab was in operation or had been in operation in that basement recently. Sheriff Bones, though flabbergasted that something like this was going on so close to town and his, was more puzzled by the fact that neither the tractor-trailer nor any of the motorcycles were found at the scene of the fire. Bones didn't know if this was a job for the abandoned cars team or not, but he wasn't taking any chances, sent the newly found data to the team, and contacted Office Matt Sharkey personally. Officer Sharkey couldn't dismiss the fact that this case was a precise reverse of the previous cases. It did, however, invoke a strange feeling that intrigued him, so Sharkey directed all available team members to converge at the Brad Wate farm at daylight the next morning.

Anxious Officer Sharkey was the first member of the team to arrive, and it was still dark. It had been several days since the fire, but the stench of its ruin still hung heavily over the area.

As daylight broke that morning, available team members began to arrive at the site of the fire.

"Glad so many of you could make it on such short notice, thank you for coming!" said Sharkey delightedly.

"With what I know right now," said Sharkey, "This house fire could in some strange way be related to the other cases. If it is, it would be the first time we have found remains and missing vehicles. Something about it, especially at this specific time, seems more than a coincidence to me. Perhaps the cult theory has some value, and it played out here."

"Kind of puts the shoe on the other foot. Doesn't it?" interrupted and questioned Officer O'Brien from the State Police.

"Could be a very clever attempt to confuse or sidetrack us," said Sharkey. "Let's start checking things out and talking facts. If we can eliminate some of this data as being non-fact or non-essential, we will have a better focal point."

"Sheriff Bones, this has been your baby. Bring us all up to speed, don't let anything out!" commanded Sharkey.

"O.K., Has everyone read my fax sent to you?" questioned Bones.

All nodded affirmatively.

"Then I'll fill you in on what we know since," Bones said. "We know that along with the tractor-trailer, motorcycles were reported to have been seen at this location as late as 12:15 a.m. the night of the fire. We also know that when the first person on the scene arrived in the area and noticed the fire at approx. 06:15 a.m., neither were seen. Unfortunately, there was so much foot traffic, dragging of hoses and tracks from firefighting equipment, that we were unable to find any truck or motorcycle tire tracks to establish that they were here. We currently have no clue substantiating that they were driven away, loaded upon the tractor-trailer and hauled away, or even possibly

68

moved by some other means. Hell, other than the testimony of the people that say they saw them, we don't have any physical evidence they were ever here.

Naturally, we have no choice but to believe the eyewitness testimonies because we have bodies and they had to get here somehow. So, conceding that motorcycles were the transportation choice of the deceased fire victims, we still do not know who drove the bikes in or who owned any of them. Ditto the tractor-trailer. Until the identities of the bodies can be ascertained, if ever, we won't know whom to check out as possible owners of the bikes" ended Sheriff Bones.

"When do they expect to have the first I.D. available?" asked Sharkey.

"Don't know," said the Sheriff. "They don't sound too confident. I think there is a high probability that they were all burnt beyond any recognition."

"How about dental records and broken bones?" asked Lou Crocket. "Can't burn bones and teeth, can you?" he asked.

"Unfortunately, the answer to that is yes if the temperature is high enough. At least that's what they have led me to believe." Replied Bones.

A woman and a man approach.

"Good morning, Doctor Evans!" Sharkey wished enthusiastically. "I am so glad you could take the time to address us, Doctor."

"Good morning to you all too." wished Dr. Evans as she began introductions.

"This is Peter Fritsil, State Police Fire Marshal working out of Bedloe. Peter, this is Officer Matt Sharkey. He's been assigned to investigate the mysterious disappearances of people along our I-50 route. Officer Sharkey believes he has reason to suspect this incident may be related to those disappearances."

"Very pleased to meet you, Fritsil." replied Sharkey, who then did introductions with his team members.

"We would like the opportunity to look over the fire scene to see if we can unearth any new findings that might help us get a bearing on what happened here. Are you guys through with your part of the investigation?" asked Sharkey.

"I've gotten everything I could." stated the Fire Marshall.

"The rest of my job has been sent to the lab. It'll keep my experts and I busy for a while. Go ahead as far as I'm concerned. Let me know if you find anything new that you need my help with." Replied Dr. Evans.

"Do you know what caused the fire yet?" asked Sharkey.

"No, not sure if we ever will know for sure," Fritsil replied. "What we do know, though, is it started in the center of the building, most likely at or just below first-floor level. The heat damage concentrated there indicates a solid propellant."

"Are you suggesting arson investigator?" asked Randy Dobbs.

"No, no, we can't be sure of that at all. Our data suggest that maybe someone was messing around with some solid, highly flammable materials at some point in that basement. More than likely, that is what caused it. It would easily explain why so many died before they could get out and why there is so little of them left to identify. It would have consumed that dry old building in a flash!" said Fritsil.

"Sheriff Bones," asked Sheriff Lonnie Potts of Bigelow. "Do we have a number for how many Motorcycles we are looking for here?"

"Eyewitnesses differ slightly; reports suggest 4 or 5 to possibly as many as 7. The witnesses didn't focus on the number, just that it was considerable." stated Bones.

"Any reports of cult or motorcycle gang problems in the area?" asked Lou Crocket.

"I was hoping that you all could answer that question for me." Bones replied, "I haven't heard or seen a thing from anyone around here. However, highway traffic on I-50 almost always has its stream of bikers, both alone, and in pairs or groups."

"Seven bodies, possibly seven bikes." said Sheriff Milo of Porktown.

"Yes, could be, but we have to try to find out for sure, it might be a significant detail at some point in this investigation." Said Sharkey abruptly.

"Let's say they shared bikes, and that all the killed came here by way of motorcycle. One probably is Brad Wate. I think we are looking at a minimum of three different motorcycles." Said Dobbs.

"Makes sense," said Sharkey, "Let's focus on between three to seven bikes. It makes the most sense."

"You know," says Sheriff Bones, "Since this happened here, I've had a few people tell me that a similar event happened several years ago in Beaumont that I didn't know about. I even received a phone call from a news station in Denver asking me if the two incidents were related. Anybody have any information about a fire over there?" he asked.

"I think I can shed some light on that," said Fire Marshal Fritsil. "When I first heard about this fire, it took me back to Thursday, December 18th, 1997. I'm sure about the date because I went back and re-familiarized myself with it before I came out here today. I know it well, I should, it was my first major investigation as Fire Marshal. I was fortunate enough to be joined by some of the most well-known and respected fire investigators in the country. Unlike this incident, there were no missing vehicles of any kind, at least as far as we ever knew, and with time, all of the 13 deceased individuals were accounted for."

The Fire Marshal went on to say, "There was a kind of convention being held in Beaumont consisting of people highly interested in and participating in body art, body piercings, tattoos, nail, body painting, and even intentional body scarring. It was to be a huge event. People from all over the country would be there, members of the fraternity, both male and female, were meeting to show off their artwork, designs, styles, specialties, and jewelry. You know, real body artwork enthusiasts. We've all seen them around. Many were body art professionals trying to pedal their talents. Most were just the average design geeks looking for something that would set them apart from everyone else. People from every walk of life and occupation were there.

As strange as it may seem, the convention was a sellout. Places to accommodate that many people were scarce, and bookings had to be made well in advance if you wanted to have a place to stay when you got there.

Some people drove there by cars, trucks, and motorcycles. Most arrived in groups on buses.

We were never quite sure if something happened to their booking or if they just came here expecting there to be a place to stay. Anyway, there was this unfortunate small group that found there was no room in the inn and had to search elsewhere for accommodations. It appears the only place they could find available was some long-abandoned and dilapidated apartment complex above a tire sales business on the outside of town. Thirteen of the unluckiest young men and women you'll ever hear about decided they would accept the poor but only accommodations.

As one might expect, these young people partied well into the night. It was reported that they had kegs of beer and cases of liquor brought into the building for their consumption. That and perhaps some illegal drugs, had these young individuals sleeping like Rip Van Winkle; well before the time the fire started below in the tire store. I'm sure you all know tires burn very hot and rapidly. I don't know if any of them awakened in time to escape the fire, but there were no outside stairways, so the only way of their apartment was through the heavily engulfed tire store. It was an inferno, no one in the building when the fire started got out alive.

Through the bus driver, who fortunately slept in his bus, the club registry, and testimony of the building owner who rented them the apartment, the count and identity of the deceased were quickly ascertained. Forensic testing through the dental record and x-rays confirmed those findings.

The fire there, though extreme, did not destroy the evidence and bodies near as complete as the fire here did, must have had some bad stuff down in that basement!" The Fire Marshal concluded.

"In my opinion, other than the fact that they were both deaths by fire-related causes, I fail to see any obvious connection or relationship between the two events.

Right now, I'm more concerned about a possible relationship between these missing motorcycles and the missing persons in the abandoned car cases we are currently working on," said Officer Sharkey.

"You know, if there were seven motorcycles taken from the scene, that could very well be the motive for this. Especially if it were a deliberate case of arson!" suggested Sheriff Dobbs. "I've seen the bikes some of these gang members drive, and even if they weren't gang members, hell, did you ever see some of the bikes the more respectable cyclists drive? Could be upwards of $100,000 street value of these bikes. It could be that they did this to profit from the sale of the bikes." Dobbs Remarked.

"Could be, could be. If and when we find out who owned the bikes, if we ever do, we may be able to find out the makes, models, and colors, then put out a bulletin on them. Could be a real big lead!" said Sharkey enthusiastically.

Evans and Fritsil left, and the team began their investigation.

About 1:15 p.m., Officer Sharkey got a call from Dr. Evans.

"Officer Sharkey, after talking with you and the team this morning, I started to remember certain missing biker reports that came across my desk."

"Yes, I vaguely remember some myself. I didn't pay much attention to them, though, because they didn't fall within the parameters of the abandoned car cases." Interrupted Sharkey.

"I checked with Dan Tillbury at the Bradford headquarters," continued Evans, "He said that over the past several years, we had received multiple reports of missing bikers from western, northwestern and southwestern states as far east as Oakley, Kansas over to San Francisco, California. Those reports indicate the persons on the bikes were last seen or heard from by their families while either traveling to or returning from biker week in Orlando, Florida."

"Individual investigations in each disappearance revealed one obvious similarity that you might be interested in. They were all reported to have been on I-50 at some point in their travel before they went missing or were anticipating traveling I-50."

"Wow!" said Officer Sharkey "Could have merit. Do you have any idea where on I-50 any of them were when they last made contact with anyone, or how many missing bikers we are talking about?" asked Sharkey.

"Again, anywhere from Kansas to California." Said Evans. "Credit cards used by a few within that range didn't tell us any more about their locations than we already knew but might be helpful to you if you make a connection with your case. As far as I have been able to ascertain, there were reports of as many as seventeen people missing since Thursday, December 18th, 1997. Not as many bikes though. Only 14 motorcycles reported missing."

"Must have doubled up, traveling together, some of them." said Sharkey.

"Perhaps Sheriff Dobbs was right about it being all about the bikes." said Evans.

"Maybe so." said Sharkey, "But then it's about fencing stolen goods, not likely our man or men doing it, or they would have stolen the cars that we found too. Some of them were worth plenty!"

"Just thought you might like to know," said Evans as she was about to hang up.

"I'll keep it in mind, thank you again for all your help!" said Sharkey, and he hung up.

"Kind of short with her, weren't you Sharkey?" asked Sheriff Randy

"Maybe I was, I'll apologize later," said Sharkey. "We've got lots of work to do here, don't need or want any more interruptions!" Sharkey said grumpily.

"Maybe you are too eager to dump the data Dr. Evans just gave you." said Randy.

"Just what are you getting at now, Sheriff?" Sharkey snarled.

"Well, it's just that…" Randy hesitated then said, "Well… could the bodies in this burned-out house be those of the missing and abandoned car victims we're trying to find?"

"If the remains of those fire victims are identified, we'll know right away!" scowled Sharkey. "Otherwise, we are only wasting precious time speculating! Now let's get back to the job in front of us and see if we can find any real evidence."

"Just one more question." interrupted Randy. "Don't you think we should check out Tom Adams and his truck?"

"You got something against this guy, have you? There must be hundreds of trucks that match the Rebel flag description, want to check them all too?" Sharkey asked cockily. Soon, the daylight and the investigation at the farmhouse was coming to an end. Nothing of any value was discovered.

21
The Scarecrow and Cult Activity
Sunday, January 20th, 2008

Things had been relatively slow in Sheriff Randy's neck of the woods since the house fire investigation in September. That changed around 10:00 am on Sunday, January 20th, 2008. Randy's deputy, Fred Baynes stopped at Randy's upholstery shop where Randy told Fred he would be working if he needed him.

"Sheriff," said Fred, "You got a call from Sheriff Logan over in Oreville. Sounded excited. Wants you to call his office as soon as you can."

Randy immediately called Sheriff Logan to find out what he wanted.

"Randy Dobbs here," said Randy. "Hear you're trying to reach me. What's up?" asked Randy. "Got a situation here," Logan said. "Some crow hunters, Clem Jenkins and Oliver McArthur, were camped out in Farmer Nesters field late yesterday afternoon just before dark. They were awakened about midnight to the sound of screams coming from the clearing in the wooded area about 200 feet away.

When they looked out of their tent, they saw something blazing brightly in the clearing. A fire of some kind! They rushed up to see if they could help and at first thought that someone had started one of Nesters scarecrows on fire. It was still strongly ablaze as they cautiously approached. They said the smell was awful. Clem Jenkins recognized the scent. He had to pull several badly burned bodies from car fires in his many days with the ambulance crew. Both men were badly shaken when they realized what had happened.

The men became frightened, and they were afraid of what might be out there. They walked back to back away from the scene until they felt they were safe. Using their cell phone to call 911, they reported what they had found and waited for the authorities to arrive. They told authorities what they had seen and heard, and an investigation began. Someone had poured a flammable chemical all over the body and set this man on fire. Police initially thought it was revenge for some hate crime, but when they got there, they found candles burning in bottles and small, dead, mutilated animals. They now believe it takes the appearance of cult activity.

Naturally, I've already contacted the team. Officer Sharkey doesn't see any fit. But because a cult surfaced as one of the potential motives for the abandoned car scenario, Sharkey wanted me to call you personally. He said you told him about some guy named Adam's that lives up there by you. He said you might want to check this guy out!"

Randy didn't know if Sharkey was busting him or if he did want him to check Adams out. Randy figured it couldn't hurt, so he went to talk with Adams. It did hurt though and only served to worsen the relationship between the two of them. Adams denied any involvement in any cult activity and resented the fact that the Sheriff was trying to implicate him in something he claimed he knew nothing about. Especially when Randy told him, "You should clean yourself up or get a job with the carnival, I heard their tattooed man ran off with the bearded lady!"

After a few days, Randy received a fax with the details of the investigation. The victim was identified as Ben Stinson, from Orville. One crucial piece of data that the fax included caught Randy's eye. A fingerprint found on one of the glass bottles that housed a candle found at the scene belonged to one William Rapsey, from Kansas, one of the abandoned car teams missing persons.

Randy and Sharkey must have read the fax at the same time. Just as Randy was reaching for the phone to call Sharkey, the phone rang. It was Officer Sharkey.

"Sharkey here Sheriff, did you read the fax from Orville yet?" He asked.

"Yes, I did Matt. What do you make of it?" asked Randy.

"Too soon to say," Sharkey said. "But one thing I know for sure now, William Rapsey may still be missing but he sure ain't dead, and your hunch about a cult is maybe what we're dealing with."

"What do you think this says about the other missing persons?" asked Sheriff Randy.

"Don't know, it could mean anything. I suppose it could just be an isolated incident apart from the others. I'm going to try immediately to get as much background information as I can on William Rapsey. I want to see if he has any history of being involved with any cults." Said Sharkey.

"While you're at it Matt, you might try to see if he had any priors for fencing items like motorcycles or perhaps dealing with the sales of used cars or bikes." said the Sheriff. "He might have a market for such items, and it could be how they're funding their activities."

"Good idea!" said Sharkey. "By the way," he further asked, "How did you make out talking to Adams?"

"Guy hates me! He claims he has no idea what I'm talking about and says he never was in Bedloe on the night of the fire or ever belonged to any cult. Claims he doesn't like cults either. I don't know for sure Matt but the fire in Bedloe, a cult killing in Oreville, and all the abandoned car cases from these other places. Some of these incidents took place just too far away from Roxi. Makes it hard to believe he could have been involved. Sure, he drives a rig, and he goes through or past most of these towns, but he has a schedule to keep. How could he possibly do anything like this?" answered Sheriff Dobbs.

"Maybe with the help of a whole lot of other people, like cult members, for instance." Shot back, Sharkey.

"Well, we can believe what we want, but until we can get some proof, we are powerless to act on any of our beliefs." reminded Randy.

"And that's exactly what we need to do, find Proof!" shouted Sharkey. "Keep an eye on this guy, anyway, will you?" he asked. "I'll keep in touch."

During the days following, word somehow got around about suspicion of cult activity in almost each of the towns the abandoned cars team was operating in. What a mess! Every little bit of seemingly unusual happenings was blown out of proportion. There was enormous finger-pointing, and suspicions of cult-like behavior targeted almost all young people and especially people who looked a little different than the others. No one was above suspicion. Law enforcement officials didn't have a spare minute in their day. There was nothing but worry and mass confusion.

This had undoubtedly thrown a monkey wrench into the abandoned car team's goal to get the people to open up to them. Suddenly the information gathering plan that had been working so well had turned into one massive pain in the butt for the team. They were taking so many calls and trying to sort through them, that they no longer knew or had time to handle the ones that were important to them. No progress was being made. Everyone was going in too many different directions all at the same time. Follow-up items from their direction meeting were now sitting there with no one having the time to follow-through on them.

22
No New Leads
Sunday, March 23rd, 2008

A message was sent out from Sheriff Milo Really, Sheriff of Porktown. A car was found abandoned on highway I-50 inside the Porktown limits. The car fit the M.O. of all the other vehicles that the team was involved in. Officer Matt Sharkey immediately issued an order for every available team member to report to the scene of that suspected crime. Officer Sharkey reminded everyone of their commitment to make themselves available and get involved immediately if and when any other abandoned car incidents occurred.

As each official arrived at the scene, Sheriff Randy briefed them as he knew the situation to be. He assured them that he immediately checked the car at the radiator area, the hood, and even reached under the car to feel the catalytic converter which he felt would probably maintain any heat the longest. The team did an entire and extensive search of the area. However, as feared by Sharkey and the rest of the group, there was no indication that the engine had been run recently and every aspect of the incident fit the elements of the other events. Sharkey immediately called the town's newspaper and those from the cities nearby. He called the new stations, both radios, and T.V. and was pleading with citizens far and wide to report if they have seen anything in or around the area the car had been found. Though Officer Sharkey wanted to, he hesitated to say anything about possible cult members around the area because of the terrible panic the mention of cult activity had been causing the communities.

A few days after this latest incident, the report came in from the forensic specialist at the state police crime lab and mechanics that had examined the abandoned vehicle. It was just like before, identical situation, no evidence, no leads. The assumed driver of the car was identified as 27-year-old Oliver McArthur from Delaware. A medical supply salesman and part-time bodybuilder that had won several titles. He had no priors and no history of sales other than those of the medical field were linked to him. There was nothing questionable or immoral. He had no cult attachment or following. Sharkey and the team were no closer to solving these mysterious disappearances than they were before. This again found them further behind in their everyday duties because of the time they contributed to this fruitless investigation.

23
The Clairvoyant
Wednesday, April 22nd, 2008

In April that same year, Matt Sharkey received a call from a Dr. Stephen Clock. He had a doctorate in Parapsychology and the supernatural and was one of the leading, most renowned Parapsychologist in the country. He told Sharkey that he and a clairvoyant friend he jokingly described only as (The Medium) had been quite interested in these mysterious disappearances for quite some time and that he had only recently found out that Matt Sharkey was the lead detective overseeing the investigation. He told Sharkey that he had the utmost confidence that he and (The Medium) could be invaluable to them in solving these cases. He felt this way primarily because of and due to a large amount of subject matter that remained after each event. He felt that he and (The Medium) would be able to receive visions and sense helpful, tell-tale things that others can't, and possibly even be able to communicate with the spirits of the victims, if in fact, they are departed. He offered to be of assistance if the department wanted them.

Officer Matt, of course, didn't have much faith in all that, as he called it, hocus-pocus non-sense and wanted to ignore their offer and write it off as just someone trying to profit from the misfortunes of others. However, he told them he would have to run it by his superiors first and that he would get back to them.

Surprisingly enough, when Sharkey's Captain heard about the proposal, he lit up like a three hundred-watt lightbulb and was unusually excited about it. The captain wanted to have more detail, like how much it was going to cost the department, when it would happen, how long it was going to take and what kind of exposure it was going to get. The captain liked exposure, especially if it helped him look more effective.

Sharkey got back to the doctor, and the doctor said that they would not be working for money, but what they did want was exclusive rights to the story. Proceeds from the story or possibly a movie that might be made, and a document from the State Police Crime Lab stating that they had been very instrumental in solving the mystery.

Sharkey shared their requirements with his superiors, and after ironing out some of the wrinkles in their demands, Sharkey's superiors agreed to have them come and be of assistance.

The doctor had one other requirement to be met, but that he did not want Sharkey to share with his superiors. It was the date and time of their arrival, which, was supposed to correspond with Doctor Clock and (The Mediums) supposed vision that another abandoned car and missing person occurrence was to be fulfilled. They wanted to be there for it to have the freshest visions and feelings available to them. They were quite specific that they wanted no one in the entire police force, except for Office Matt Sharkey himself, to be privileged as to when, how, or where they were going to arrive. This request was also based upon a premonition the doctor had that someone in the law enforcement ranks was somehow involved in the disappearances. Sharkey did not share this last requirement with his superiors or team as requested.

Officer Sharkey went along with the unusual requests but took significant exception to their claim that a fellow officer of the law could be involved. He anxiously awaited the day they predicted to come, so they would see how wrong they would be.

It was Tuesday, May 6th, 2008 at 6:55 a.m. on the day that Dr. Cooke and (The Medium) were to arrive. A call came into the Sheriff's office in the little town of Justice where Officer Matt Sharkey was just awakening in the hotel room where he stayed the night. He was to meet with Dr. Clock and (The Medium) at 8:00 a.m. in Sheriff Lou Crocket's office.

It was another call that fit the abandoned car and missing person profile. With anyone and everyone being a suspect or at least a person that might have specific details helpful to solve these cases, Sheriff Crocket gave firm instruction to the officer driving the informant that had already left the scene. He was driving east on I-50 as he made the call to the Sheriff to turn around, return to the vehicle, and wait there for him to arrive. He further warned him not to touch anything and if anyone else stopped at the scene, to keep them away from the vehicle and surrounding area until he arrived.

As Sheriff Crocket prepared to leave, he sent out an alert to the team. The team had implemented a new system, a new way to get the notice of an abandoned car and missing person alert out to all members that might be available to respond. Perhaps, not in the vicinity of their fax machine, and to reach still others that might be somewhere out of the range of cell phone service at any given time. The new system required all members first receiving the fax alert to immediately begin phoning the other members until all were informed. All Sheriff's offices were instructed to transmit this data out to their Sheriff's radios. The new alert system the team had devised saved the Sheriff valuable time, and with sirens blaring, he was able to get to the scene within minutes!

The Sheriff followed protocol and did all the duties decided upon by the team to ensure consistency of actions and increase the probability of finding any useful data or evidence to help solve these mysteries.

Officer Sharkey got the news as soon as he arrived at the Sheriff's office around 7:30 a.m. The code for an abandoned car and missing person incident had just arrived by fax. He was so overcome with the news and the fulfillment of Doctor Clock's prediction. He had to sit down and compose himself before he could think clearly and decide what to do. "It couldn't be!" He thought. "How could they have possibly known?" he wondered. The phone calls were starting to blare on his cell phone and at Sheriff Crockets office phone.

Sharkey didn't know what to do. He had a strong impulse to rush to the scene himself just as fast as his aging legs and his aging car could carry him. This certainly was the closest he had ever been to an actual incident. He wanted to go, but how could he? He was there to meet Doctor Clock and (The Medium) who would surely want to get to the scene as soon as possible also. He thought to himself that this would be the perfect opportunity for the supernatural geeks to get the new signals or vibe's they talked about. That is if they really could deliver as they said they could.

Then, suddenly, Officer Sharkey started feeling somewhat incompetent. He had been advised that an incident would happen today, he had pretty much known around the time it would happen, probably at night, sometime with-in perhaps 12 hours before the car would be found, as all the other instances were. He also had the location pretty much narrowed down to the Justice town limits. He began to feel scared when he started to envision the scenario that would be playing out at 8:00 when they arrived. There was no way to stop them from coming at this late point in time, and they would only want more than ever to be here now to cover the most recent occurrence. Sharkey sat there dazed, shaking his head from side to side, wondering, just wondering.

Officer Sharkey now wholly forgot about his duties and the case. He soon became a clairvoyant himself. He could see himself stammering to explain himself. He could see his peers laughing at him and making jokes. He could hear the captain hollering questions at him like, why didn't you do something to prevent this? Why didn't you increase the number of patrols in the Justice portion of I-50? He could see himself getting either discharged from the force, pounding a beat, or even facing dereliction of duty charges. He could see the team losing respect for him and no longer willing to jump through hoops for him as they once did, that is of course if perhaps, he was allowed to stay on the case. He could read the headlines in the papers (Key law enforcement officer fails the citizens). His picture and name all over the newspapers and television, even the world news. Poor State Police Officer Matt Sharkey was coming unglued. He was shaking in his police issue loafers.

Then, to top all of that off, shaken Sharkey began to wonder if he could be held legally or criminally negligent by the victim's family.

All the panic mentioned above really only lasted seconds or perhaps a minute or two at best, but it must have seemed like an eternity to Officer Sharkey who was drawn back to reality when the alarm on his wristwatch went off. Officer Sharkey's mind wasn't as sharp as it once was and he had been having a hard time keeping track of time with all that has been going on, so Sharkey started putting his memory and schedules into his sophisticated wristwatch. The alarm was to remind him of his 8:00 a.m. meeting with his guest if he forgot.

Doctor Clock and his friend were running late it was now 8:15 a.m. and they had not arrived. Sharkey was more impatient than ever he could hardly contain himself. He paced the office floor back and forth, back and forth! "Where are they? Where are they?" he murmured to himself. "Why weren't they calling to let him know they were delayed?" he wondered. Unfortunately, Sharkey did not have a cell phone number to reach them and hesitated to call Doctor Steve Clocks office because they were not yet that late in arriving. Sharkey wanted badly to be at the recently abandoned car scene to see for himself if he could perhaps notice something all the other officers had not in the past.

When Sharkey could not contain himself any longer, he left word with the deputy to instruct the geeks when they arrived about the current findings. He instructed the deputy to either bring them out to the scene himself or make arrangements for them to be brought out. Then Sharkey left to involve himself in the investigation at the crime scene.

Sharkey knew he was the only law enforcement person there that knew who Doctor Steve Clock was and what he and his friend did. He also was the only person that knew the doctor and (The Medium) was coming at this point. Sharkey and the geeks were the only people that knew an abandoned car and missing person event was predicted to occur at the time and location this one had.

Sharkey arrived at approximately 9:05 a.m. and while being greeted by several team members inquired what the team had discovered to that point.

"Hello, Sheriff Crocket!" began Sharkey. "Please tell me you've found something this time!" he pleaded.

"I'm sorry, Officer Sharkey," replied Lou Crocket. "Nothing new yet, same old, same old. We're waiting on an inquiry to tell us who owned the vehicle. Then we will try to ascertain who was driving the vehicle. I was on this very quickly!" Lou stated. "I immediately checked for temperatures and looked closely for fluid drips under the vehicle. A forensic specialist I talked with a few weeks ago told me that sometimes they can place a time or length of time, or how long ago something happened by how long certain fluids take to dry on different surfaces. There were no leaks, at least any that I could tell they were ever there."

"How about the area around the scene, did you check it closely?" asked Sharkey.

"Of course!" replied Lou. "I roped off the area as you see it now. I know it might have been a little bit overkill because of the median separating the eastbound and westbound lanes, but still, I diverted traffic coming in either direction off of the highway's pavement areas up to about 500 feet from the scene in both directions, just in case. As help arrived, we stopped every car traveling east or west before they approached the scene asking them if they had seen anything that might help. We also asked them not to stop as they continued through the secured area and to ensure they don't litter any items that might contaminate the scene."

"Wow!" said Sharkey. "I'm impressed, we have got to pass those tactics on to the rest of the team."

Just then, an incoming message on Sheriff Crocket's clip on radio receiver stopped Officer Sharkey dead in his tracks. The news was, "We have identified the vehicle as belonging to a Stephen Clock, a doctor from Phoenix, Arizona." said the voice over the radio.

Officer Sharkey didn't know whether to mess himself or go blind! He felt he had won the amnesty lottery of the decade. He could easily talk his way out of this horrendous mess he had gotten himself into now, he excitedly thought! You could hear his heels clicking together as he jumped for joy!

Trying very hard to control his feeling of rapture, Sharkey resumed his conversation with Sheriff Crockett and other team members that had gathered to assist the investigation.

"Any witnesses?" questioned Sharkey.

"No, no witnesses again!" replied Lou. "I did hold the person that discovered the car, but he doesn't have anything new or different to add."

Sharkey couldn't help it, but really didn't care about the evidence this time. His mind was entirely on the political art called C.Y.A. (covering your ass). He was focused on how he would skirt specific issues and questions. He knew he would have to admit very soon that he knew the victim. However, he knew well something that the others didn't know, and that was the fact that there were likely two or perhaps even more victims, if the doctor had brought others with him Sharkey didn't know about. He did not even know for sure if Doctor Clock and (The Medium) were traveling in the same car together when this happened, if either person told anyone where they were going, or who they were to meet with.

Sharkey didn't even know what the real name of (The Medium) was. He had to be very careful about what he did and didn't say so that it wouldn't catch up with him later on, or it could be catastrophic to his career and pension. Sharkey thought carefully about it and then admitted he knew who the driver was.

"I can tell you who the driver was, or, at least I assume, that it was the car's owner Doctor Stephen Clock that was driving the missing vehicle when it went missing. He is a practicing and well-renowned Parapsychologist from Arizona. He is a clairvoyant that ironically was on his way to Justice to meet with me to try and use his skills to help solve these mysteries." said Sharkey.

"Why was he coming to Justice?" asked Sheriff Crocket.

Officer Sharkey had to be very careful about how he answered that question. It could be the $64,000.00 question that could blow his career. Sharkey quickly thought about it and said, "The doctor stated to me over the phone that he had had visions about some of the abandoned car and missing person activities and associated the town of Justice with his visions. He was not sure what the visions meant, only that Justice was tied to them somehow. He was bringing along at least one other associate that I only know by the title (The Medium). I assume his colleagues gave him that nickname perhaps because of the great new T.V. show called The Medium, but I really can't say for sure. I don't know which one came first the chicken or the egg, so I just never questioned the name to him.

I don't know if Dr. Clock and (The Medium) were traveling together in the same vehicle. If they were, perhaps he too is missing. Anyway, the good doctor thought that with the help of his friend and associate, they could find a fit with the town and the vision that would be helpful to us in solving the abandoned car cases." said Sharkey.

"Maybe he was predicting his demise and helping to write his epitaph. I was to meet him and his counterpart this morning at Sheriff Crockets office. I waited as long as I could for them, but when they didn't show and didn't call, I came out here and made arrangements for them to be brought out here when they arrived."

"How come I didn't know anything about this?" asked the Sheriff. "I didn't even know you were in town!"

"I'm sorry Lou," said Sharkey, "Apparently, It's the way the doctor likes to do business. It was a prerequisite to his assisting us." replied Sharkey "He mentioned that too many apples spoiled the whole barrel when I asked him why he didn't want me to tell anyone. I guess he thought it would litter or contaminate their supernatural highway. I'm not sure if they told anybody else, or for that matter, if they were to meet with anyone else while they were visiting Justice."

"Do you realize this makes you a suspect Sharkey?" exclaimed the Sheriff.

"I hadn't thought about it that way, but I guess you're right, I guess it does, doesn't it?" said Sharkey.

Sharkey had not given thought to the fact that he might be under suspicion, a person of interest.

Now he began to have new fears about this change in the game.

"Are you arresting me, Sheriff?" Officer Sharkey asked. "Because if you're not, I've got a job to do and I need to do it while things are ripe!"

"Let's get the job done. Then we can discuss this," replied Sheriff Lou.

Officer Matt went about his duties, but his thought was on finding evidence that he didn't do the misdeed rather than proof of who did. His mind was on what he was going to tell the detectives that question him about the disappearance. He knew that several of his peers knew or would believe he had a motive to carry the investigation out so he wouldn't have to return to the beat. However, would they think he could do this, or believe perhaps, that he could be involved with others that did it for some personal gain of his own? Could he be working with the cult that got so much attention lately?

Fortunately for Sharkey, it wasn't as bad as he thought. Gruff as he may be on the exterior, most people that knew him had a great deal more respect for him then he believed. It was down deep where it counted and was hidden mostly by his lack of people skills or his lack of willingness to use them with his peers.

Sharkey was given the benefit of the doubt and did not get the push to discard him from public service that he expected. Hotel security cameras were installed recently because of all the cult driven fear that had been driving away the customers. However, they were now aimed in the hotel's hallways, dining room, entrances, and surrounding parking lot to help ensure the safety and security of patrons. The cameras showed the only times Sharkey left his room after he arrived at the hotel, and they sufficiently accounted for his visits away from his room. This and the fact that the only other person seen accompanying him during that time was a woman he met at the hotels dining area. The woman, Joanne Basker, testified that she spent the entire night-time hours with Sharkey in his hotel room after they left the bar.

The cameras were a godsend for Sharkey, but that left the obvious question; if Officer Sharkey was the only law enforcement officer privileged to the vital information about when Doctor Clock and his friend were going arrive, then, just what precisely were they going to Justice at that particular time for? Moreover, who else were they going to visit?

Part of the directions given Sharkey by his superiors was to try to find out whom else, not associated with law enforcement knew about

Doctor Clock's plans to visit Justice. Additionally, there was the obvious task to look for motives for Doctor Clock's disappearance.

Officer Sharkey spent the better part of two weeks away from his primary tasks, being in Arizona where he turned up nothing substantial enough to arouse even the least suspicions. However, did find out that Dr. Clock's friend and associate did travel with him that day, and was also missing.

Eventually, the only answer, the most probable reason, that fit the facts as they were known, was that Doctor Clock and (The Medium) later known to be David Brannur also from Arizona, were just the two unluckiest people to be alive that fateful night. They were merely the victims of a random selection by a person or persons.

Officer Sharkey couldn't help but believe that it helped to prove a more specific time for that particular incident. He felt sure that the doctor was timing his arrival for close to the time of the meeting, and if so, the abduction must have happened shortly before sunrise. He felt that the car had probably just passed the point of cooling off to be unnoticed. He did not want to have that happen again and issued directives to the team members and all other State Police Officers that were to be operating within the disappearances vicinity. This directive stated that they were to be issued heat temperature sensing equipment.

They were instructed to force entry to the engine compartment if possible, to take a temperature reading of the engines block, manifold, motor oil, transmission fluid, and anti-freeze fluid. If entry to the engine compartment was not capable without special tools, officers were instructed to safely get the temperature reading from any potentially accessible point on the vehicle. Perhaps from underneath the car and breaching a water hose, the radiator, or oil pan.

Once fluid temperature for any or all parts requested was obtained, and the time the temperatures were taken were noted, the vehicle then would go through testing in a similar environment. Using the new approach would prove valuable even if the fluids obtained for testing had already reached the ambient temperature around them, as it would now be known as at least that long.

Officer Sharkey now feeling like a new man, publicized the directions and steps his team was taking and in any local town conversation, it was not unusual to hear the term (The A.C. team).

Because of his team's great attention to detail, cleverness, and ingenuity, Officer Sharkey was assigned the State Police helicopter he requested for flying surveillance of highway I-50 sort of like a military reconnaissance mission, and that would get him to the scene of any future cases much faster!

Sharkey was also assigned seven more officers to assist him, one of which was a helicopter pilot. Sharkey assigned him 11:00 p.m. to 7:00 a.m. duty which he staggered through the week so as not to allow anyone to know his flight-plans. He was directed to fly I-50 between the towns where incidents had happened and watch for stopped cars with their lights left on that looked like they might be in one of the travel lanes. He was instructed to touch down and investigate immediately if there is a likely-hood the vehicle meets the team criteria.

People living in and traveling through the reputed towns began to feel safer now. Most people believed that if the police can't find them to arrest them, at the very least their new efforts would discourage the perpetrators.

The A.C. Team members were feeling pretty good about themselves also. They were working very well together across town and county lines for the betterment of their town's people and community.

Working together, side by side as often as possible, as a now-notorious team of diligent crime fighters, they had created many new ways to help solve this complex issue, and America loved it.

Sharkey said to himself with a smirk on his face. "Well they were right about one thing, there was another occurrence when they said there would be! How do you like that?"

It was to be a short-lived moment of jubilation, despite all the changes and precautions, the additional force and even the helicopter, the results would stay the same.

Office Matt Sharkey, during a brief moment of hopelessness, shook his head back and forth and said to himself,

"No one is ever going to catch this guy!"

24
The Chopper Critique
Friday, August 1st, 2008

The A.C. Team received another abandoned car alert. This time in Apollotown. Officer Randy Dobbs was the first team member to join Sheriff Tom Keets at the scene. Randy got there even before the helicopter patrolman Jan Corning did as he was on the far end of his patrol perimeter. Randy and Tom had already taken and documented the ambient air temperature and had just been successful in breaching the vehicles hood latch. The engine felt cold, but they proceeded to receive, read, and document all the required vehicle component temperatures.

Off in the distance, another helicopter was heard approaching. The present team members thought it was Sharkey, and someone commented, "What does that guy do, sleep in that bird?"

It was not Sharkey, but a news station owned and operated helicopter nosing in for a scoop. Sharkey did not arrive until hours later. Sharkey made up a lame excuse for not being there sooner, but most of the team members felt he was probably caught off guard because he was so sure he had scared off the perpetrators and the occurrence was unexpected; at least so soon after the new changes were implemented.

The temperature readings were sent to the crime lab as soon as they were taken. The vehicle was found at approximately the same time as the others, just about daybreak. The conditions were the same as all the others. Looking through the locked door windows, they observed that yes, the light switch was turned on and the lights were not burning, indicating that the battery was drained.

The team members wondered why the pilot had not seen it stopped on the road lane and put down to investigate it as he should have passed the area approximately 20 to 30 minutes before it was reported found.

The pilot stuck firmly on his answer that he had not seen vehicle lights stopped anywhere on the entire strip of I-50 that he was patrolling.

Officer Sharkey instructed each of the responding team members and the person that found and reported the vehicle to clear their schedules and meet at Sheriff Keets office the next Monday at 10:00 a.m. to critique their latest response.

Monday, August 4th, 2008

"Greetings everyone," began Sharkey, "I asked you all here today to review our response to last Friday's abandoned car and missing person event. First, I want to apologize for not being there sooner. I'll be the first to admit I let my confidence get in the way of my readiness. Until this case is solved, we must all try not to put ourselves in situations where phone service or availability is compromised and be able to respond in a minute's notice! Sheriff Keets and Sheriff Dobs, I want you both to know that I appreciate you both being minute-men.

That said, let's get on with the business at hand. I'll bring you all up to speed on current revelations and then we'll see if there are any steps we can take to help keep our pants up if we have another incident.

The recovered vehicle was owned and operated by a Mr. William Smidlap from Oreville. He never came home from working second shift at The Billings Interior Cabinet Manufacturing Company about 30 minutes away in Justice. Mr. Smidlap had a history of coming home very late at times, and his wife went to bed without him when he didn't come home at his usual time. She didn't know he wasn't home until we, by phone, awoke her after his vehicle was found. No one remembers seeing him at any of the bars he usually frequents. According to his time clock entry, he left through the company gate at 11:45 p.m., no one has been reported to have seen or heard from him since.

This time, we did find something we had not noticed before. We can't say whether or not it means anything for sure, but there was a strong odor of perfume detectable in the vehicle when the crime lab opened the locked doors. A trained canine was brought in to whiff the interior and odor retaining objects from the car. Those same objects were bagged and transported to the lab. Both the gathered objects and the animal may be used to help identify any reported missing female individuals or individuals that may have also been in the vehicle at the time its occupant went missing.

Next, the subject of the vehicle components temperature findings.

Every temperature gathered was at a reading consistent with the outside temperature at the time of the readings. Lab test on the abandoned vehicle reveal it would have taken five to seven hours for all components to have reached the ambient temperature level under the same conditions found at the time of the reading, with data given us from the United States Weather Bureau for the range of time from 11:00 p.m. to 7:00 a.m. This data puts the time that the engine last ran to be somewhere between 11:45 p.m. and 1:45 a.m. that night. This doesn't solve our case, but it is new data and potentially important data. It is not my intent to put anyone on the spot, but I do want everyone, especially those team members that were not present at the scene to hear from all of you about your experiences with this event.

Jan Corning, if you don't already know is the chopper pilot that is flying surveillance over the troubled areas of I-50. Jan, will you fill us all in on your duties and what you saw?" asked Sharkey.

"Be glad to," said Corning. "I've been a pilot for The State Police for 30 + years. I flew combat missions during the Vietnam war. My job is to fly random watch over I-50 during the hours of darkness. I do not have a relief pilot, so I fly only 5 out of 7 days a week. I use my own best discretion as to what days of the week I fly to switch my schedule around enough not to develop an apparent pattern that the perpetrator(s) might pick up on.

On the night of Friday, August 1st, I was on active duty. That night, like most nights, it was very dark and near impossible to see anything on the highway that wasn't lit up by its lights, another vehicles light, or pole lights which there are very few of and very far between. To draw the least attention to myself in the hopes of catching the perpetrator(s) off guard, I only shine my powerful light on something that in one way or another gets my attention. Sometimes cloud cover makes it impossible to see anything more than a hundred feet away. I try to pay particular attention to weather projections to plan my flights." He continued.

"Because it was a clear night, and some visibility was afforded me because of moonlight, I was able to fly lower than I usually do. Though still very difficult to make out objects that aren't lit, I was able to, in areas not shadowed by trees or some of the higher mountain ranges, see more than normal. I might be able to believe that I didn't see the car without its lights on, but I know I would not have missed it if it had its lights on. I logged flying the air space above where the abandoned vehicle was found at 11:57 p.m. as I flew west and then again at 1:10

a.m. after I U-turned over Roxi and flew east. I believe that places the time that the vehicle was abandoned at some time between 1:10 a.m. and the labs' estimate of 1:45 a.m. I would like to know how long it would take to run that vehicle's battery down with the lights left on. It might be helpful data." asked Corning.

"I'll see if I can get the lab to do that test for us!" said Sharkey.

"Another thing that still puzzles or bothers me," said Corning. "I want you all to know that I firmly believe that I would have seen that car sitting where it was found at least one time during my several runs back and forth over it. I feel it's just not likely that cloud conditions could have been bad enough not to have seen it on that particular night. Makes me wonder just how good our gathered data is."

"The lab says it was cold, I don't know any other way to explain it," said Sharkey.

"There's been too damn much publicity about the chopper flights!" said Sheriff Keets, maybe full fly overs makes it too easy or gives too much time in between for this event to happen if someone is watching for you. "Would you consider more erratic flights?" he asked.

"I've already been considering doing just that." Replied Corning.

"Sounds like we're doing some good here," said Sharkey.

"How hard was it for you guys to get that hood opened?" asked Sharkey.

"Piece of cake!" replied Sheriff Randy. "Plastic grill ripped right away; we were able to trip the release once it was out of the way."

"O.K.," said Sharkey, "Let's wrap this thing up and get back out there. Good work!" Declared Sharkey.

25
Those Left Out
Thursday, September 18th, 2008

Things were about to take a shift in public attitude. No one can underestimate the lack of gratitude the public can have for its civil servants, especially where the loss of life is concerned. For quite some time there was a faction that appeals were falling on deaf ears. These were the families and loved ones of the persons other than abandoned car victims that were missing or unaccounted for.

There were many unrelated missing persons cases over the vast number of years since the first abandoned car and missing persons case occurred back in February of 1992. I guess it was all the attention the media was giving to the unfortunate car cases, and it ruffled the feathers of the others that felt swept under the rug.

Officer Sharkey was having one of those days like we all experience from time to time. His alarm clock didn't go off because the power was out. He woke up 20 minutes later than he had planned. No electricity and no hot water for his morning shower. He made a quick drive-thru for coffee on his way to work, though he was rushing because he was running late. Hurrying while trying to fasten his seat belt, he spilled the hot coffee on his lap. Not a napkin or paper towel to be found in the entire car! He comes into the State Police station, and everyone was staring at him. Not because he was late, but because he was grumbling and mumbling loudly to himself. He arrives at his office, and guess who was there waiting impatiently for him? You guessed it. His boss Captain Swantler, and some new faces Sharkey had not seen before. One look was that of a beautiful young woman with a face that could melt your heart! Don't forget poor old miserable Sharkey was still dripping and had a large stain still on his suit where he spilled his coffee earlier. Certainly not one of his better days!

95

"Good morning Officer Sharkey!" said the Captain, not questioning his tardiness. "I'd like you to meet inspectors Jill Launette and Leonard Bates from the Federal Bureau of Investigations, Missing Persons Division." Officer Sharkey greeted his visitors, and embarrassedly tried to explain his appearance, stating that he always keeps another suit in the closet in his office for just those kinds of emergencies. He asks for a moment to change and returns promptly.

"Inspectors Launette and Bates are here to speak with you about the high number of disappearances reported to them by a citizens group called H.U.F.T.N. (help us find them now). This group is made up of some of the very same people you have become familiar with as you have been investigating the mysterious disappearance of their family members. However, most of them are people and faces you might have never met or seen except, perhaps on one of the many news reports."

"But why the F.B.I.?" interrupted Sharkey, "These cases are out of their jurisdiction," he questioned.

"Not entirely!" replied the Captain. "The F.B.I. has reason to believe that at least some of these cases are happening across state boundaries and might be tied to the bodies found near-by of severely mutilated persons believed to be from the drug violence communities in Mexico. That brings them into the picture."

"Inspectors, why don't you fill us in on what you know and what you want from us, and we will see what we can do to help you with your investigation." requested the Captain.

Inspector Launette took up the baton and ran with it a while then passed it off to Inspector Bates.

"The F.B.I. has been swamped with missing persons reports recently." She said, "It's not that we don't ordinarily get many requests from friends and families asking us for help finding their missing loved ones, we do, and it's not that these requests just started coming in. Lately, it is pretty much on-going."

"Ordinarily our hands are tied, and we direct the callers to contact their state law enforcement officials for help and follow-up. However, H.U.F.T.N. members, which are a group of citizens angry that their needs aren't and haven't been getting the attention they feel they should be, have brought to our attention some specific new revelations that weren't identified by anyone else before. At least as far as we know."

"The F.B.I. has been interested in the abandoned car and missing person issue much the same as you all are, however, though we have followed the happenings and progress we were never given the green light to go ahead. Mostly for the reason you have already stated Officer Sharkey. Of course, we are not here to imply that you haven't been doing your job, we admire the progress you've made to date, and we are not even sure whether your missing person cases and our missing person cases even belong in the same tiki-hut together. However, data provided by H.U.F.T.N. presents us with an issue that deserves and requires our attention, so we are here to compare notes so to speak and help each other if possible."

"What are the new revelations and specifics you speak of?" inquired Sharkey.

"I'm pretty sure you wouldn't have a great deal of knowledge about isolated disappearances as your focal point is and has exclusively been incidents that deal with and fit the criteria specific to abandoned cars found, and people missing, and that's O.K., we understand that. What now stands out with several of the isolated missing person cases is that the tracking of victims' credit card usage has proved to move back and forth between and across state borders. All this during the timeframe identified that the owner or driver was last seen or heard from till the missing person reports were filed. In most cases, the credit cards were never found or used again after a missing person report was established.

"But why does that bring you here to this location on I-50, were they used in this vicinity?" asked Sharkey.

"Vicinity yes, same towns? No." replied inspector Bates. "From what we gather, the credit card usage is not the same towns as your incidents, but other, usually smaller and less significant towns or townships within proximity of an abandoned car and missing person town. A few more notable incidents that cross state lines only pass through your vicinity, but because of that, are more responsible for us being involved. Our concerns are not only because we have this sizable group of citizens that are unhappy campers, but we have discovered data that may indicate that some of the missing persons this group wants us to find, may very well be responsible for some of the abductions. Some are persons of interest in other crimes."

"What kind of data are you referring to?" Sharkey asked inspector Bates.

"Fingerprints and reported sightings," Bates replied. "Sightings not only of a reportedly missing person but of vehicles matching the license and description those owned by some of the missing persons."

"This is getting too confusing!" interrupted the Captain. "Let's just cut to the chase. Give us some supporting examples and fact, lots of facts!"

"Let me share a more recent fact or two," began Inspector Launette.

"Fingerprints found at the scene of an attempted abduction in Newton, Kansas on June 11th, 2008 belonging to Architect John Beasley, of southern California, reported missing October 20th, 2007. A car description and license plate number verified by witnesses at the attempted abduction scene matched the vehicle John Beasley owned and was reportedly operating when he was last seen on October 11th, 2007. John Beasley, of course, was and is one of your abandoned car and missing persons victims.

"Yes, I recognize the name," said Sharkey.

Moving ahead to August 29th, 2008, we received a report that Mr. Beasley was frequently seen in Trinidad, Colorado, by a person that identified him through his missing persons photo."

"Blood and fingerprints of a group of three youths from Garden city, Kansas, one male, two females, reported missing October 19th, 2008. Found inside a crashed and stolen automobile in Fallon, Nevada, on April 26th, 2009."

"Last seen, March 9th, 2009. A minibus is full of possibly illegal immigrants suspected of peddling drugs from Amarillo, Texas to Salt Lake City. Though under random surveillance, disappeared just prior to a sting being conducted, somewhere between Championsburg and Apollotown, your well renowned abandoned car and missing persons playing field."

"O.K. got the picture. I guess if I were in your position, I'd be looking closely to see if there was some tie between cases too," said Sharkey. "To be perfectly honest with you, I've heard or read the reports you speak of at one time or another, but really never felt any connection. Still, don't! However, I'm willing to try anything if it helps either one of us with our cases, what do you suggest?" asks Sharkey.

Both groups spent hours looking at data, sharing facts, looking at pictures of persons,and vehicles trying to find that one piece of overlooked data that would produce a lead. They pretty much came up cold, and neither law enforcement group was feeling the initiative had been worth their effort. Sharkey and the Captain for that matter started to put up their defense shields and became less receptive when Inspector

Bates made a remark they felt jabbed at them when the Captain asked them what they wanted from his people in the future and what they might do differently to help the issues at hand.

"The very fact that you refer to your cases as abandoned car and missing persons and not the missing person(s) and abandoned car is sending the wrong message of priority to the citizens of these and for that matter to anyone that might have plans to travel through one of those towns."

"Complaints we are getting is that State Police officials are out looking for the cars of missing people and not persons that are missing!" Inspector Bate said snidely.

"It is how we classify and differentiate our duties in these matters!" said Sharkey defensively. "We don't have the resources to work all the various types and kinds of missing persons reports," blared The Captain. "Hell, half the time these persons aren't even really missing. Drunken stupors, fights with their spouses, kids run away, I could go on forever. We need to be selective to have a clear focus. It's hard enough just trying to maintain the momentum going forward with the distractions our cases are plagued with. Man-power is short, we depend heavily on the sheriffs of these small communities, and their hands are full."

"We will keep the info you shared with us and help by keeping our eyes out for the things you portrayed as possible links, but we can't promise you that we will pick up responsibilities that do not fall on our shoulders of charge. We have our job to do, and you have yours." the Captain was finished.

Inspector Launette trying to repair any bridge damage,

"Perhaps we are all allowing our feelings to run away with our words. We are all under a great deal of strain, and people have expectations that are sometimes a little too high. Let's all remember the basics of law enforcement, and though we may take a glance outside the box from time to time, the truth is always right there in front of us. Some facts will help us solve these mysteries, and we have to find them!"

The meeting ended, and because of the clout The F.B.I. has, the Captain and Sharkey both felt beat up on!

"Almost 40 years on the force, 40 painstaking years, and I can't remember one other time that I felt so overwhelmed. I just haven't been able to get a clear shot at this problem. There is always something that pops up unexpectedly when I think I have the solution in sight. There have been so many things over the last few years. I don't think there are enough officers in the whole country to properly address all the issues in time for them to be helpful." said Sharkey dejectedly and expecting some understanding and sympathy from the Captain.

"You've got to do something Sharkey!" said the Captain sternly. "This is getting ugly. Not suitable for either of our careers. This is taking too long! Too damn long! Do something!... Do something, even if it's wrong... do something and do it now!

Poor old Officer Sharkey! Hell, he didn't know what else to do, and he knew it. He had spent all his official and political bullets. He was as perplexed as everyone else. He only had silver bullets left but couldn't find a werewolf to save his shabby soul. Sharkey secretly believed that the Captain was starting to believe the circulating rumors that he was delaying the prosecution of this case to buy him time away from pounding the beat again.

26
The Flood
Tuesday, January 6th, 2009

It was Tuesday, January 6th, 2009. The new year had started a little warmer than most, and a cold front had chased a bad Pacific storm front south enough to severely threaten the small town of Roxi and its neighbors. Flash floods have always been one of the most unnerving threats this area had to offer. Heavy rains were not uncommon and flood pathways were pretty well known as places to stay away from when it storms.

A storm as powerful and destructive as the one forecast to hit Roxi had hit the area three times in the past 15 years and left many people dead in its aftermath. In 1993, five youth from Championsburg drowned when their car got swept away and stuck underneath a ledge of a flooded quarry. By the time the storm ended, and the floodwaters had receded enough to recover the bodies, they had long washed away. None of the bodies were ever recovered. It was believed that at least one of the youths was able to get their door opened before the raging water would have forced them to shut fast. Authorities acknowledge that with the door open and the vehicle stuck fast, that the bodies were probably sucked out by a vacuum force much too great to resist. At least if they had stayed with the car, their bodies would have been recovered for a decent burial.

In 1999, three also young souls drowned as they tried to forge a flood pathway in their S.U.V. and got upended in more than seven feet of raging floodwater. Long extending roots from a large, storm fallen tree, encapsulated their vehicle holding it and them under the stormwater for several hours. None were able to escape the Houdini like predicament. Their bodies were taken to The Roxi Funeral Home for a decent funeral.

In February of 2006, a recently married couple returning home to Roxi by car from their honeymoon in the beautiful Pocono Mountains and not knowing about the storm's severity, came upon a stopped and damaged vehicle occupied by two injured young women also from Roxi. The storm, as it began, had some powerful wind gusts that had broken a large and hefty branch of off a big old oak tree. It fell directly on the roof portion of the automobile crushing it and its occupants immediately. The car was blocking the road in the direction the young man and woman would have needed to go to escape the quickly advancing, and unknown treacherous storm waters. The unexpected deadly torrent was coming upon them, and though in all likely hood the two young women in the damaged car were probably killed instantly, the honeymooners didn't know it and stopped to help. They all had new accommodations at the Roxi permanent housing cemetery.

The weather service was using every media outlet at its disposal to warn townsfolk as well as incoming travelers about the storm and its potential hazards. Flashing lights were placed at sites along highways, and even lesser-traveled roadways to bring attention to areas known to have flooded in the past.

On one such road traveled a mini van driven by a Mr. David Belcan loaded with ski equipment and five poor souls who thought they were going to have a nice early winter ski vacation in the high snowy mountains of Denver. Friends remembered their expressions of jubilation that they were leaving their rainy winter behind and going where the air was cold, and the snow was deep and soft.

A young couple by the name of David and Donna Belcan who owned the mini van had invited three close friends to go skiing with them. David Belcan was not the type of individual to monitor his cars or its components health. Not only did he not have snow or all-season tires on a vehicle he was planning on driving into winter mountain terrain, but he had a tire with a slow leak that had lost significant air pressure. It had not been so noticeable before it was loaded down with gear, supplies and approximately 750 to 800 pounds of people.

As the latecomer finally arrived now ready to depart for the ski lodge, everyone had to rush through the torrential downpour to get to the car, covering their heads and hair from the rain in a fashion that no one noticed the far much lower tire. The vehicle did not ride, feel, or respond as usual, and David Belcan commented about it shortly after they got underway. The others diminished his concerns by explaining it was probably just because of the extra weight and the stormy winds.

Visibility was abysmal, neither David who was driving, nor any of the other passengers saw the recently posted flood warning signs. Then, just as the van entered the flood pathway zone on the only road out to the main highway, the tire ultimately failed, de-rimming itself. The car lopped heavily towards the drivers side as if a spring had broken. The van could go no farther. The heavy rain was coming down in sheets, and the rain was ice cold. No one wanted to venture out of the weatherized vans security to change the tire and decide to wait until the storm either stopped or slowed enough to do the necessary task. As they waited and the rain didn't break or even let up a bit, and no other cars had come along, they started to realize that if they ever wanted to get to the lodge, they needed to do something about getting the flat tire changed.

Money not being a problem as they were quite well to do, Donna suggested calling for road service to send some other poorly paid, low soul out in the storm to change their tire. However, there was no phone service in that locale. Perhaps the rain played a part in that too. Eventually David and one of the passengers decided that they better get busy as it would get dark early because of the heavy rain filled clouds and fog. As they opened the rear hatch door, they realized that the spare tire, tire iron, and the jack were buried deep under all of their ski gear and vacation supplies. They worked feverishly to unload the van where the tire and jack were as the remaining young ladies inside complained about the rain being blown inside and about how cold they were getting. Through the clatter of the storm, a roar was heard that sounded like the water going over the brink at Niagara Falls. Within mere seconds, the thunderous wall of rushing water engulfed the tire changers forcing them into the van through the hatch opening as the water stormed in, slammed the hatch closed and washed the vehicle and its occupants down the flood pathway.

Instead of going skiing, they visited the areas only weather permitting, water ride, "one life each," no height limit requirements. So yes, included with the package were accommodations at the Roxi permanent housing cemetery.

Sheriff Randy always works extra hard during a flood and its aftermath, as he pulls double duty at the funeral home. Along with Randy's Sheriff responsibilities, he moon-lights preparing local victims for burial. It's money he depends upon to supplement his income because of the meager Sheriff earnings he gets from the town. The Sheriffs other side-line businesses were not being very profitable lately because of the severe recession the country was going through, and every dollar counted.

27
Randy Unavailable
Monday, January 12th, 2009

Monday, January 12th, 2009, another abandoned car and missing person report came in. There had been three other incidents since the William Smidlap incident in Oreville on August 1st of 2008.

None of the last three events had brought the A.C. Team any closer to solving any of the cases. Most of the Sheriffs were now going through the motions when they had to respond, and fewer were taking the time away from their busy schedules to respond at all. The talk was common amongst them that the person or persons that were executing these kidnappings, if that's really what they were, would never get caught. Not unless the hand of fate stepped in and somehow tripped the perpetrator(s) up.

Law enforcement officials were dumb founded; they couldn't see how it was possible for the incidents to continue with all the preventive measures they put in place and how they were no closer to solving the matter. There were all kinds of stories going around explaining what must be happening, from that of some supernatural phenomenon to alien visitors from distant planets whisking these people away. All of which seemed to make more sense that the logical abduction theories the authorities were employing.

However, this case in Porktown would prove to be different from all the others.

Officer Sharkey arrived by helicopter expecting the same old, same old. As he approached the members of his team that did respond, they turned anxiously toward him, and Sheriff Milo excitedly said, "We got heat Matt, we got heat. All components tested showed temperatures at or near the average operating temperature for a vehicle cruising an interstate highway. I lucked out! It must have just run out of gas when I came along. The battery was still up, and the lights were on."

"Did you see anyone?" asked Sharkey enthusiastically.

"No.," replied Really.

"What time did you find it, was it still dark?" asked Sharkey.

"It was shortly after daybreak, maybe 20 minutes ago or so."
Replied, Sheriff Really.

"Car seems to be favoring the edge of the road towards the shoulder, did anyone move it?" inquired Sharkey. "Of course not!" replied Really. "Find anything else unusual?" asked Sharkey.

"Well, kind of," replied Milo.

"First standard transmission as far as I know," he said.

"What gear is it in?" asked Sharkey.

"We won't know that until they get the door open at the Garage."
Replied the Sheriff.

"I... I don't know." Started Sharkey, "I don't like it! There's something that doesn't feel right about this to me."

"Anybody saw any motorcycle gangs or other undesirable groups coming out here?" asked Sharkey.

All the members replied that they saw no unusual people or groups of people.

"Still hanging onto Sheriff Dobbs cult activity theory, Matt?" asked Sheriff Tom Keets.

"Just checkin'... just checkin', that's all…never can tell." Replied Sharkey.

"Where is Sheriff Dobbs anyway... anybody see him today?" asked officer Sharkey.

"Couldn't make it Matt. He asked me to tell you he's busy with the flood problems in his neck of the woods." Explained Keets.

"The flood was a whole week ago, what's he got to do with the flood now?" Matt inquires.

"Guys probably just beat!" said Keets. "From what?" asked Matt.

Sheriff Keets went on to explain to Officer Matt about Sheriff Randy's duties at the Munson Funeral Home, how hard it has been for both Randy and himself trying to make ends meet with the recession and the inflated prices of everything. He told officer Sharkey about how hard Randy works trying to build up his other business interests and how he hopes to retire into them when he is no longer the Sheriff of Roxi.

"Sheriff Randy had a lot of new clients at the funeral home because of the flood," said Keets, "But never question his dedication to his badge. He's a good man to have around when you need help!"

Sheriff Keets could feel that Officer Sharkey was not too pleased that Sheriff Randy did not respond, though it was a far way to go. Sharkey grumbled to himself when he heard about Randy and the funeral home. Keets himself had searched for a reason not to go and questioned whether it was worth it. He hoped he didn't get Randy in any trouble with Officer Sharkey.

By late that same day, much of the results from the investigation of the found vehicle being done by the crime lab had come back in. Officer Sharkey had been on edge waiting. The car was owned and operated by Mr. Gus Laurelson, a day trader from Atlanta, Georgia. His wife had reported him missing while on a trip to the casinos in Las Vegas, Nevada. He was said to have been carrying a large sum of money when he left. The money was unaccounted for. The engine temperatures were confirmed as were stated to Sharkey by Sheriff Milo Really. A partial fingerprint on the key did not match the driver but was unconfirmed. The transmission had not been left in high gear. The driver's wallet was unaccounted for, and no change, belt buckle, watch, or wedding ring were recovered.

The report was enough for Officer Sharkey to realize that he now had another problem; it was apparent that they had one or more copycat abductors. It looked as if someone was using the abandoned car and missing persons scenario to cover up thefts and possibly even murder. Officer Sharkey decided to shelve all the data subject to this case for the time being and to turn it over to local law enforcement as a potential abduction with the intent of a robbery and murder. Officer Sharkey hoped that this would be an isolated incident. He faxed the A.C. Team the acquired data to keep everybody up to speed on what was happening. He encouraged everyone to disregard the current happening as not to affect their direction.

Additionally, on the fax Officer Sharkey sent to Sheriff Randy, he told him that he had missed him at the scene of this latest incident, understood that he had had a hectic schedule, but reminded Randy of his commitment to be one of his Minutemen when the need arises.

28
The Discovery

Sunday, November 7th, 2010 8:30 am

The relationship between Sharkey and his daughter Sara had been deteriorating. She had distanced herself even further from her father lately and called him less frequently since she told him about meeting a motorcycle riding free-spirited slime-ball nick-named "Slice" who had recently joined their pack of bizarre, bothersome, brummagem.

Sharkey could tell by the way Sara spoke of him that she had sparks for Slice and sparks always spelled more trouble. Officer Sharkey wanted to call and talk with Sara much more than they did, but it was Sara that still called Sharkey because she didn't have a cell phone and no home phone for him to call her on.

Sara had always called her father at least once a week if for nothing less than to check in so Sharkey wouldn't worry so much about her. Sharkey hadn't heard from her for almost five weeks, had no idea where to look for her and was a nervous wreck worrying that she took off somewhere with Slice. Sharkey feared that Slice might have done something terrible to her! The only thing he did know was that the last time he talked to her, she was still with that weird cult-like bunch she had been with for a few years. All the recent talk about cult activity had Sharkey even more concerned.

So as if things weren't bad enough for poor old miserable Officer Matt Sharkey already, now rumors have been circulating throughout the team members that Officer Sharkey had fallen deeply behind the eight ball with his captain and other superiors. They were getting bombarded with calls and letters from people from all the towns involved. The latest abandoned car and missing person vehicle that was found belonged to a son of one of Sharkey's highest superiors best friend. It was 19-year-old college student named Bernard Benninger who was traveling home from his college where he stopped to top off his gas tank. There were no other charges on his card after that. If it weren't for the fact that the missing boy's car turned up on I-50, no one would ever have even had any idea where he disappeared. Now it was Sharkey's problem, and he was catching the be-Jesus from his boss about it. Sharkey was once thrilled because the abandoned car and missing person cases were hard to solve and took much time, keeping him from pounding a beat. He was now fearing for his job or at least afraid he would be pulled off of the assignment and put where he would not be doing investigations.

If you think Sharkey was cranky before, you sure didn't want to get in his way now. He was biting the head off of everybody he met.

He blamed everybody for his failure. He was sleeping like a wall-street investor during the great depression, and that didn't help matters. The confusion of this case was eating him like cancer. As hard as he tried, everything he did was always to no avail, there was never any significant evidence, there were no leads, and he was damned if he could come up with anything new to try. Of course, everything fell squarely on his shoulders and like the brave public servant that he was, he reluctantly accepted the blame. He was feeling lower than a rattlesnakes belly in a wagon rut. Not unlike Sisyphus, of Greek mythology, Sharkey was getting pretty tired of pushing his stone up the hill many times, only to have it keep rolling back down on him again and again and again.

Sharkey's biggest concern was that he might lose his pension. Naturally, he could not retire without it. Moreover, like most law enforcement officials, he hadn't been able to save much money on his meager earnings. Officer Sharkey held on to only one possibility, and that was that perhaps Sheriff Randy Dobbs was right in his suspicions that all that was happening was cult driven. Officer Sharkey also sensed that this cult group, if they were behind these happenings, might be the misguided group of weird youths his daughter was hanging out with and they may know something about where his daughter Sara was.

Officer Sharkey had heard about Sheriff Dobbs taking time to work at the funeral home and wanted to get the Sheriff to rethink his priorities.

Because the other law officials didn't give much credence to the idea of cults operating in their areas, officer Sharkey decided to pay a visit to the only Sheriff on his team that did, Sheriff Randy Dobbs from Roxi.

The real reason Officer Sharkey wanted to visit Sheriff Dobbs was that he was so concerned about his suspicions that his daughters new idol (Slice) was either a gangbanger or a devil worship cult leader. Either was equally bad.

Because of his need to do extensive traveling, Officer Sharkey had been assigned a state vehicle to use. Sharkey had grown to feel very comfortable in the older car he had been driving for a few years and declined the offer of a new one when the offer was made.

Sharkey had recently been having braking problems on and off with his car, which the mechanics at the garage were having a hard time solving because it was intermittent. They had changed several parts out, but the problem was still there from time to time. The car had an automatic transmission, and sometimes when he went to stop, especially if the surface was slippery, the cars front wheels would lock up and the vehicle would tend to slide forward like a sled. He could not steer out of the way of things when this happened, and he came very close to having a couple of rear-enders recently.

Mechanics at the shop believed the problem lied within the metering valve, a combined dual-purpose valve that controls the amount of hydraulic pressure going to both front and rear wheels of a car, and particularly crucial during emergency stop situations.

Sharkey had his plausible idea about what was going on with the brakes. He felt as though it had something to do with the airbag system, because the problem started immediately after he had an extremely hair-raising experience caused by the deployment of his airbag when he hit a particularly deep and unusually lengthy pothole. He was lucky he was able to stop his cruiser safely. He expressed his concerns about the incident to the mechanic by merely stating: "I could have been killed!"

Officer Sharkey had pretty much learned to live with the brake problem, but it was getting worse. Sharkey had told the mechanics that he didn't think the brake problem has gotten worse, but that he had sensed the throttle was not working correctly at times. He said that sometimes the engine stayed at a too fast idle when he took his foot off of the accelerator. The throttle worked as designed when the mechanics tested it, and they replaced the worn floor mat thinking that it might be obstructing the pedal at times.

Officer Sharkey feeling under pressure, didn't have any concern for the vehicle braking problem. He thought he could handle it and he started to Roxi for a visit with the Sheriff.

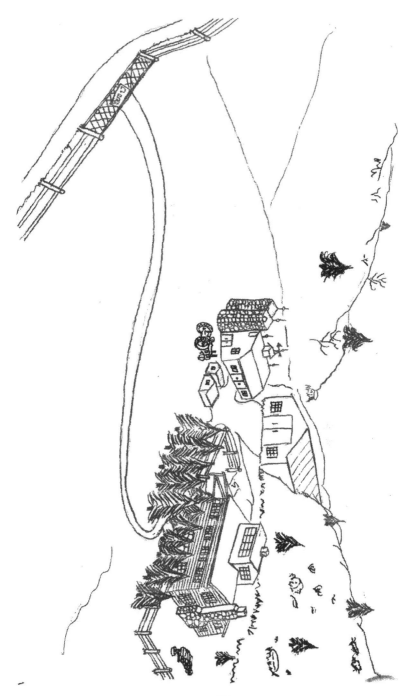

When he arrived in Roxi at the Sheriff's office, neither the Sheriff nor the Deputy was at the site. After all, it was a Sunday morning, and Officer Sharkey didn't bother to call ahead of time.

Officer Sharkey got the directions to the Sheriff's house at his farm and started there to talk to him. This particular area where Sheriff Randy lived was going through a freezing period, and there was about a half-inch of fresh snow on the ground. Sheriff Dobbs farmhouse, where he stays when he's not in town, was about five miles away off of the main road.

It set at the foot of a long, downhill, but very well constructed and smooth driveway that was kind of shaped like a tilted "*S*." The roadway turned to its left just in front of the house's large pine tree hidden side yard. It continued in a half circle to the front of the farmhouse, also in the area was an old barn, an old large structure, some smaller structures, and a relatively new large pole barn type structure. These were the buildings in which Randy did his side occupations; upholstery and taxidermy.

Officer Sharkey started down the long driveway with the intent of merely following the road until he saw the house because the "*S*" turn part of the driveway could be seen coming down the hilly driveway.

Officer Matt could see a grove of pine trees that appeared to run in single rows on both sides of the driveway just inside the first left turn of the entrance as he started down towards the buildings. However, Officer Sharkey could not see and had no way of knowing that there was a large truck vehicle parked just into the turn partially blocking the lane and wholly hidden from view.

Sharkey, who was admiringly looking around at the beautiful country winter scene and not having his mind on his driving and the well-known brake problem, was accelerating a little too fast for the weather conditions. When he neared the lower end of the driveway while coming into the first turn and was getting ready to turn to his left, he suddenly saw the vehicle completely blocking the portion of the lane he was favoring. Ordinarily, if driving at a more reasonable speed for the conditions one could swerve and go around the truck, but Officer Matt momentarily panicked and slammed on the brakes. With his foot not appropriately positioned on the brake pedal and his brake pedal going down closer to the floor because of the brake problems he was having, he inadvertently activated the accelerator throttle with the side of his shoe sole, the engines RPM's increased and the car sped up!

Because of the faulty valve, the braking system did not work as it should have but locked only the front wheels that slid like a sled on the freshly fallen bed of snow and the back wheels continued to be driven by the engine and transmission. Sharkey pushed on the brakes with all of his might, and of course, the side of his foot was pushing harder on the accelerator. The big Chrysler just kept plowing forward slithering between two of the towering pine trees branches that lined the house side of the driveway. It drove through the wooden rail fence that ran along the length of the narrow side yard area on that side of the colossal farmhouse. Continuing across the small side yard where it impinged and crashed through the wall and shuttered window of the house, coming to a stop with the vehicles front end buried into the home halfway up to the cars windshield.

Fortunately, officer Sharkey was uninjured, but the car and the house was a different story. Sharkey turned the ignition key off and the engine shutdown. All much too late! Sharkey was afraid he might have killed or injured someone. He scrambled quickly out of the car and crawled over the hood of the vehicle while forcing his way through and under the part of the wall that was now lying on and against the vehicle. He apprehensively looked around and under the car and saw no one.

Sharkey was so relieved. Before Sharkey's eyes, because of the weight of the now severely damaged structure, the house almost wholly sealed itself around Sharkey's cruiser. As he stepped back for a better look, he couldn't believe he was able to get inside in the first place. Fear and adrenaline had played their part. Sharkey now wondered how he was going to get back outside and into his car. There was very little light in the room as all the other windows were shuttered and locked to prevent burglars from entering when the Sheriff wasn't around. Sharkey heard the sound of what he thought might be the large truck that was outside moving around.

While looking around the walls of the dimly lit large room with the light fading more each minute, the collapsed building seemed to seal itself even more and engulfed the automobile. Officer Sharkey turned to face the inside of the house and was preparing to call out to anyone who might be in the building. He suddenly noticed some framed pictures on one of the walls that had caught his attention. Something seemed strangely familiar with the images. He stepped closer to the strange framed articles hanging on the walls. It was much too dark to make out the finer details of the pictures. Sharkey removed a framed photo from the wall and took it close to the part of the room that his car was still letting in some small rays of daylight. There, holding in front of him was a framed photograph of an automobile.

The included artwork was like that of a collage. It displayed a persons picture, name, and date beneath it. There was a drivers license, a written article with print too small to make out in the poor lighting, and what looked like photos of inked body artwork.

Suddenly Sharkey cringed with realization, as his eyes scanned the lowermost right-hand corner picture in the frame. It was a picture of a dead, tattooed, naked man. Sharkey recognized the face and name as that of one of the abandoned cars missing persons. Included, was a newspapers headlines clipping about the missing person that only the most massive printing was readable in the darkness.

Officer Matt Sharkey swallowed hard! He suddenly summed it all up and realized he may now be in a den of wolves. He was reasonably sure he had stumbled upon the people responsible for at least some of the missing persons from the abandoned car cases. He didn't know if they were kidnappers, murders, or both. They could even be cultists. He felt the need to be ready to defend himself. He threw the framed collage-like picture on a couch that was covered with a dust cover. As he replayed the not too distant last several frames in his troubled life, Officer Matt began to feel heart-stopping fear! It was authentic. The courageous crime fighter had remembered that in his haste to get out of his car so quickly after it hit the house to see if anyone was hurt, he left his holster with his gun in it, on the front passenger seat of his car along with his badge and cell phone. Matt dug down really deep to contain his fear; he knew to panic at a time like this could be fatal.

Officer Sharkey's self-preservation instincts kicked in and he began searching in the near dark conditions for something he could use as a weapon if the need arose. He felt along the walls for a light switch for he feared he could be jumped from behind by someone in the dark, at any minute. He thought surely; someone must have heard the crash. He felt only rectangular-shaped holes in the wall where it seemed like light switches once were. After being unable to find anything suitable for defense, his next instinct was to get out of dodge before someone returned. He tried unsuccessfully to open the few doors he was able to find in the darkness.

Suddenly, a dimly lit light came on in the center of the ceiling of the room. A door opened, and he heard footsteps hastily approaching through the doorway. He thought to himself, "How could I let myself get caught in a situation like this? Possibly my greatest opportunity to capture the perpetrators in the biggest case of my life and not only am I not offensive, but I'm also defenseless!" He compared himself to one bullet, Barney Fyfe.

A lone, tall, figure entered the room, approached him rather quickly, however non-threateningly and asked excitedly,

"Are you all right?"

By the sound of the intruders voice and as Sharkey's eyes focused on the tall man, he recognized him as Sheriff Randy Dobbs of Roxi. The reassuring tone of Randy's voice and the face of one of his formerly most trusted A. C. team members soothed Sharkey's fears.

He thought to himself, "He's not acting as if he were hiding something! Maybe I'm jumping the gun here. There must be some other possible explanation for what's going on here." Then he replied to Randy's question: "No, no, I'm all right." He said.

Not knowing earlier what was happening and who he was dealing with for sure, Sheriff Randy had activated his body cam that had the capability to record both voice and video when he first heard the crash. The device would continue to record as things worked themselves out. Randy always uses the audio function but when on duty, he only uses it to protect himself from any possible false, accusatory, and liable statements. He only records what he says and turns it off when others speak as not to violate any privacy laws.

Sheriff Randy recognized Officer Matt by that time too, and asked a jumble of questions: "Matt, that's you? This is your car? Was anyone else with you? Was anybody hurt?

Officer Matt, still trying to sort things out, and reluctant to provide any information that might make him even more vulnerable, thought to himself, "He doesn't appear offensive, maybe I've been looking at this all wrong, besides what difference does it make. He'd soon find out I lied." replied as he inconspicuously tried to get between Randy and the collage he had removed and placed on the dust cover covered couch behind him. All this in an attempt to hide it being there from Randy and said,

"It's me Sharkey. No, no one else, thankfully no one got hurt!"

"What the hell happened?" asked Sheriff Dobbs inquisitively.

Officer Sharkey replied with his jumbled answers, "Damn Car! She got away from me, I couldn't stop! The damn thing just kept sliding faster and faster till I hit your house. I've been having brake problems, but I never thought I'd pile her up. Damn brakes again! I tell ya, I just couldn't stop her. Couldn't steer her. The harder I pushed on the brakes, the faster she slid on the snow. My mechanic is sure gonna hear about this. Guess I was going a little too fast.

Officer Sharkey thought very fast and hard to come up with an answer that might help cover up the knowledge of his revelations, and replied, "Cult activity... maybe devil worshipers! I wanted to talk to you in person about all the rumored increased cult activity going on in the A.C. team sector lately. I think you may not be telling me everything you know, and I need answers. I tried to call you and let you know I was coming, but I couldn't get through to you."

Sheriff Randy noticed the framed picture sitting on the covered couch. Officer Sharkey saw him eyeball it and knew the façade was up. Who would make the first move?

Officer Sharkey figured he played his cards this far. He would be silent and let the moment play out. Randy had similar thoughts. The room fell silent for what seemed like forever to Officer Matt, for from where he stood, though still at a distance, he was capable of seeing all of the framed collages on the walls that made up the large room. As he gazed and scanned each framed phenomenon, his faded former fears became rejuvenated.

Officer Sharkey's feet were stopped in their tracks as if being held by Gorilla glue. He couldn't have run if he had to. His tired, bloodshot eyes were popping out of his balding head! His mind was racing like a turbo engine. He couldn't believe his eyes. You could see the question marks surrounding his head like hornets around a disturbed nest. He tried in vain to hide his overwhelming fears as he tried to digest and diagnose what he saw, maintain his composure, and subjugate the situation.

Matt Sharkey, though unarmed, took solace with the thought that Randy, if he was any threat to him at all, evidentially didn't know that he didn't have his gun on under his lapel. Matt felt confident that if Randy had found the gun on his front car seat before he came into the room, he would have certainly seen his badge and would not have acted so surprised to know that it was him when he went into the room. Of course, it could have been a clever ruse. However, he intended to play this all out while attempting to inconspicuously, eventually draw Randy outside and close enough to make a desperate grasp for his weapon if necessary.

The silence broke when Randy said, "Matt, you look like you saw a ghost! I guess you and I need to have a nice long talk about those memorials on the walls."

"Memorials?" questioned Officer Sharkey. Memorials of what? Are they cult-related? What aren't you telling me?"

Randy invited Sharkey over to a wall so he could see each entire collage and read the written articles that were included with the many gruesome pictures. Randy remained quiet for a short while, while Matt indiscriminately stopped directly in front of several of them, examined the images, and read the written documents as well as he could with the dim lighting. His tired old eyes didn't help matters any. They were collages of various designs and colors with the potential to be cult or devil worship related. As he looked closer he saw that they were all reproductions of inked body art designs as one might find in a flesh design catalog, but the reproduced artwork seemed to match the artwork on the body also seen in the collage. Accompanying the artwork were drivers licenses, other forms of identification, and written documentation containing names, dates, and places. Many of the collages included pictures of automobiles. This primarily interested Matt because, for most of those, he made a correlation between the vehicle type and the name and recognized them to be those of abandoned car and missing persons case.

Sharkey only skimmed some of the collages as they were plentiful. While it became much clearer to Sharkey what each collage represented, he became more obfuscated about what they were doing in Randy's large old family farmhouse. Who created them and why? Of course, the big question was who was responsible for the demise of the victims shown in each collage.

"These are intended to be viewed as memorials to the individuals that contributed the specimens that the artwork you see was created from." Said the Sheriff. "The included epitaph for each served to provide a small synopsis about each contributor."

Much to Officer Sharkey's surprise and dismay, Sheriff Randy did not seem at all appalled by the artwork but seemed boastful as if he had created them.

"And just who was the epitaphist?" asked Sharkey.

"Isn't it obvious who made these masterpieces?" said the Sheriff.

"You're not going to try and make me believe that you had

anything to do with this, are you? It's inconceivable, why it's imperceptible, you, you're impeccable! It would be duplicity on your part! Come on now, come on, the jokes over." Said Officer Sharkey.

"Things are not always as they appear," said Sheriff Randy.

"Randy, what's going on here? You do know something about all those missing persons from the abandoned cars you haven't told me about, don't you?" begged Officer Sharkey.

"Lots." Said the mysterious Sheriff.

"This is your place, isn't it, Randy?" asked Officer Sharkey.

"Yes, this is the farmhouse I was born in and raised in. My Great Grandfather and my Grandfather built it.

"Do you live in this house now, or do you live in town?" asked Sharkey.

"I live in many places." Said Randy.

"Now, just what do you mean by that?" asked Sharkey.

"I stay where I am when I am there." Said the Sheriff. "I have a place that I bathe and sleep in town. I have a place that I bathe and sleep in the new large building here on the farm. I have a place that I can bathe and sleep in my truck too. I am always on the go when I run out of gas or get the opportunity, I sleep wherever I am. I never sleep a full nights sleep as everybody else does, I have just too much to do and too little time to do it all."

Trying to sound as if he is still in control and unafraid, Sharkey says, "See, I told you to get more rest, didn't I. No wonder you always look like shit warmed over when I see you," said Sharkey.

"Why don't you use the farmhouse as your residence?" asked Sharkey.

"I cannot," said Randy. "This building is a memorial; it's sacred grounds."

"Now you're talking like you're from some ancient Indian tribe, are you Indian?" asked Sharkey.

"No, it's not sacred burial grounds if that's what you're getting at." said the Sheriff.

"Stop messing with me, Randy." Said Officer Sharkey, "Is this a memorial to your lost loved ones, your family, or what?" He asked.

"Their kind of like my family, I guess," said Randy. "We do reside here at the farm together. The many collages you see represent them and is intended to honor their contributions."

Officer Sharkey taking time out from being afraid, only because he is dumbfounded says, "You've got me thoroughly confused; I got off the train a few stops ago." Complained Sharkey, "Back up and help me get on again." he asked.

29
The Confession, Part "1"
Sunday, November 7th, 2010 10:15 am

Officer Matt Sharkey had just found Sheriff Randy with insurmountable evidence to at least incriminate him in the abduction and deaths of dozens of missing persons. However he was having a difficult time believing that his trusted friend and law keeper could take on such a persona.

"These memorials pieces, the collages, are my masterpieces. I constructed them all by myself." Randy, half proudly and half somewhat embarrassed or ashamed, replied.

"I guess I'm glad in a way this happened, and you caught up with me, surely an intervention," said the Sheriff. "I have needed someone to talk to about myself for a long, long time. Moreover, I suppose divine intervention had to play a part if I was ever going to be discovered. The devil has imprecated me; he has given me dark, evil, and elusive talents. Wait, while I turn on more lights, and we'll make ourselves comfortable, and I'll tell you everything. You've surely worked hard enough trying to stop me to deserve the whole story and all the facts!" said the now criminally exposed Randy Dobbs.

Randy, followed closely by Officer Sharkey, goes out through the steel door he had opened to gain entrance to the room. Would it be perhaps the only chance Officer Matt Sharkey has to escape? Officer Matt thought about making a break for his car, but it was too far away. He was already too old and too slow. Randy certainly was much younger, faster, and stronger. He decided to keep up the charade that he possessed his firearm and was in control.

"See this door and lock?" Randy asked, "They're both made of such extremely hardened steel, no file or hacksaw blade could scratch them. If you don't have a key, the only way to get into that room we were just in, is the way you accidentally did." said Randy. "Shutters and locks on the windows too!" Randy added.

Randy turned on the other light switch and invited Sharkey back inside.

"Make yourself comfortable on that dust-covered sofa over there, just sit right down on the dust cover, you won't hurt anything," said Randy.

Randy sat on another dust-covered chair in front of Officer Sharkey. Sheriff Randy Dobbs decides to tell Sharkey the whole story.

"Perhaps it's best if I start right from the very beginning." Said Randy.

"I grew up right here on this farm, this house we're standing in was built by my family many, many years ago. Living here growing up was some of the happiest times of my life. There was lots of work to do, and we all helped each other. As a child, I didn't have much playtime, but I got much enjoyment out of doing things with my father and my grandfather. I've learned so much from them.

It all started one day so very long ago when I was helping my father prepare a body for burial at The Munson Funeral Parlors morgue. My dad worked there as often as there was work for him to subsidize the meager living he made working on our farm. I know it's a strange sort of setting for a child to be brought up around. However, I looked at it as just a natural part of life, and by helping my dad there at times, I was learning some new skills. I was helping my father get done sooner so he would have more time to do things with me.

On that particular day, I remember it as if it were just yesterday. It was Thursday, January 4th, 1990. I was 14 at the time and my dad and I brought in the body of a local man in his early 40s' named Brent Weisburger. He had died unexpectedly from a heart attack he suffered after he got excited while watching a professional wrestling match at the local Catholic Youth Center. As my father was getting the instruments he needed ready, I removed the man's clothing, and I saw this tattoo he had on his upper left arm. The design of the tattoo was nothing I would consider unique. However, something happened to me at the very moment I gazed upon it. It was as if the devil himself had entered my body and ripped out my soul. I didn't know what was happening to me. A feeling of lust came over me matched by no other feeling I've ever had in my entire lifetime. I felt love. I felt the passion. I felt evil. I felt the most active kind of lust and desire any person could imagine. Sort of like a vampire lusts for blood, I guess. I was enamored by a thing, not a someone. The lust was insatiable!

I had always felt I was a God-fearing, kind, honest, respectable, loving, and caring, young man. I still somehow feel like that un-possessed person I once was. However, I know I must not be, or I wouldn't have ever done, always do, and have the overwhelming desire to do the un-Godly terrible things I have done.

Strangely, I feel no remorse. I don't feel bad because I do them. I can honestly tell you I don't want to stop or be stopped. I would never have given myself up if you hadn't caught me this way. A moratorium was never an option. I feel an overwhelming degree of satisfaction when I am successful in executing my plans and acquiring another specimen. I look at these collages and relive the experiences. With each new picture, my pleasure is increased. Kind of like a hunter's trophies, I guess.

I knew I was unique, and though I knew no matter however clever any evil doer is, he always gets caught sooner or later. Though I knew I had to do my best to be mutable to prevent detection, I knew someday my day would come. I prepared for that day and my legacy, which I was always sure, would be unlike that of anyone before me, and hopefully after me. I kept a log or diary if you prefer, and a list with names of contributors, dates, times, location and manners of death. I saved keepsakes, clippings, or other pertinent details about each contributor I call artifacts. I preserved and adequately utilized every specimen that I felt gave the best honor and recollection to each contributor, and placed them in my Special Donors Memorial, of which, you have only seen a small portion of. I will show you the rest later. I did not do any of this for the notoriety, fame, money, or the glory. I honestly wish I had never become possessed. I am proud of my work and my accomplishments. No one else has ever had what I have here, and for the sake of all humanity I hope and pray no one ever will again!"

"You speak of your victims as a specimen. You've lost me here. Explain," commanded Sharkey.

"I will in due time. First, I will brief you on my methods." Offered the Sheriff.

"Many of my local specimens were acquired at the Munson's morgue in Roxi, where I, over the many years, continued part-time work as a supplement to my current job as Sheriff and each of my previous jobs. I made it a priority to be available to prepare any incoming patrons that had or likely had tattoos that could be easily hidden by their departure dress. I made it my job to inconspicuously know who in the town and surrounding area had tattoos and who patronized The Munson's' Funeral Parlor and on occasions the Scarlet Funeral Home in Apollotown."

And, yes I did my gruesome part to prestigiously provide preferred customers that I knew would wind up at Munson's or Scarlet's. I thought feverously and constantly about methods that would make untimely deaths look like strokes, heart attacks, and especially accidents. I am responsible for several drownings at flood pathways, lakes, ponds, and even a few at the beach. There were many potential contributors at those locations."

"You got off by killing people just because they had tattoos?" Questioned Sharkey, shocked and surprised.

"No, not by killing them. I prefer to call it harvesting. Murder for the sake of watching someone die was usually not a motivator, though I did sometimes seek a level of retribution or justice against some of the worst and most unsavory tattooed contributors."

Randy tells Officer Sharkey a story about the return of Arthur Owind, the child rapist at the beach.

"Do you remember back in July of 1992, when a little five-year-old girl name Tammy Chilks was abducted from a children's amusement park and raped at a Nevada beach several hundred miles from Porktown by a hippie type slime-ball,Porktown resident named Arthur Owind?" asked Randy.

"Yes, as a matter of fact, I do. I remember thinking at the time that it could have been my daughter. He got caught and went to prison, didn't he?" Sharkey asked.

"He only got ten years for ruining that little girl's life!" answered Randy angrily. "Do you remember what happened when he got out of jail?" asked Randy.

"No, I guess I missed that part. What happened?" asked Sharkey. "Tell me about it."

30
Awful Arthur Returns
March 2003 – December 2004

Randy fills Officer Matt Sharkey in on what transpired after evil Arthur Owind was released from prison.

"It was Thursday, March 7th, 2003. The system supposedly rehabilitated the child rapist that raped innocent little Tammy Chilks on July 23rd, 1991. The now, a thirty-one year old ex-convict named Arthur Owind was released upon the world by the prison system. He did serve a full term as he frequently brought attention to himself by associating with some of the prison's worse guests, using drugs, undesirable conduct and attitude.

A probation officer named Montgomery Twain was assigned Arthur Owind. He arranged housing for Owind and got him a job at a metalworks plant as a swing shift guard. Arthurs home mailing address, place of employment, and address were required to be reported to the probation office.

At first, he started reasonably well and got acquainted with some of the other guards and production employees. Arthur appeared to be doing a good job. Only his employer knew of his crime and prison time and saw no reason to share this with the other employees.

Then after about one week, the landlord of the apartment that Arthur was staying at asked to speak with him and his probation officer. He told Arthur and Montgomery Twain that somehow a few of his other tenants with children had heard about Arthur's past, they were frightened of him and very upset. They were threatening to move out if Arthur stayed. Arthur would have to look for a new place to live. Arthur told Mel Ryan, a newly acquainted friend, and an employee where Arthur worked about his predicament. Mel told Arthur about the half home apartment that he had for rent in the home that he owned, Mel lived in the other half alone. It would be a good fit as Mel was single and there were no couples with children close by.

Arthur moved his stuff from the apartment at the address registered with the probation office to the new address. Both Arthur and probation officer Mr. Twain were supposed to register Arthur's new address with the probation office as a convicted child molester and sex offender. Later that evening before Mr. Twain, who was 64 years old, had the opportunity to make the address change with his office, he became very ill. The victim of a stroke it appeared. Arthur was told what had happened, that Mr. Twain was not expected to recover and that the Probation Office was taking a wait and see approach before appointing Arthur, a new probation officer. He decided to keep the change to himself and hope that he would fall through the cracks of the system as happens so many times with child molesters and sex offenders. Arthur did provide his employer with the new address, a requirement for call-ins and other notification needs.

When no one from the probation office contacted him for many months, Arthur began to feel confident that he was lost somewhere in the shuffle. This was bad because Arthur began to feel free to do as he liked and much less under control of the system and authorities.

As Arthur was shopping for groceries one day, he noticed a pretty little girl name Chelsea Knott, that closely resembled his former victim, Tammy Chilks. From the very moment evil Art saw little Chelsea, the vision of her haunted Arthur relentlessly, and it seemed to have power over him. Each time he saw her, he could barely contain himself. Until one day, feeling he was out from under the thumb of authorities, Arthur weakened, gave in to his temptations and followed her and her mother to their home.

Evil Arthur began to devise a plan to kidnap the little girl from her home. After being incriminated and incarcerated so quickly and easily by the identification his prior victim, little Tammy Chilk, made of him, he planned to have his way with her, kill her, and burn her body in the incinerator where he worked so no evidence would be found. Getting the girl to his apartment and then getting the body to the incinerator would prove challenging to do without being seen. Arthur would have to wait for the opportune time. Evil desires were consuming Arthur, then one day his friend and landlord Mel Ryan who still lived next door to him in the other half of the house he lived in, sparked an opportunity. He told Arthur that he was going back home to visit his family in

Tucson for a week and asked Arthur to take care of the place and tend to the coal furnace that heated both halves of the house. It was early spring, and some nights were still cold.

The opportunity evil Art was waiting for had arrived. Arthur arranged his shifts at work so he could be off to do his evil deed. In the dark of night, Arthur was able to quietly jimmy the lock on the back door of the little girl's house as she and her mother slept soundly in separate rooms. Within mere minutes, he had forcefully and inconspicuously abducted little Chelsea from her home and held her helplessly captive in his bedroom. It was Friday, March 28th, 2004, one year since he was released from prison as rehabilitated. One year and a little girl's lifetime?

Afterward, Arthur placed the body and blood soiled clothes and bed linens in a durable plastic garbage bag. He took the remains and evidence into the building's other half-basement where the furnace was located. Arthurs half of the dwelling had no access to the furnace area, so Arthur had to use Mel's' key and enter the basement through Mel's apartment.

Arthur was afraid the odor of a burning body in the home's furnace would arouse suspicions. Arthur removed the coal from the corner of the coal bin, placed the bag deep into the edge of the container, and covered it entirely with the coal leaving it well hidden under and within the coal pile. This would do, he thought, until he could sneak it out and into the incinerator at work.

However, when a police investigator, Lieutenant Jim Plowe, a close friend of Chelsea Knotts mother heard of the abduction, he quickly became involved. He became intent with bringing the perpetrator of this heinous crime to justice as soon as possible. He immediately called for a list of potential child molesters or sex offenders that are registered within 5 miles from the scene of the abduction. When Lieutenant Plowe got the requested list of names, he asked for information on the background of each of the individuals. He very quickly found many similarities between little Chelsea the now missing little girl and evil Arthurs former victim, Tammy Chilk. Arthur Owind lived and worked within an area that encompassed the home that little Chelsea Knott lived.

Because the investigation was taking place during regular daytime work hours when most people are at work, Lieutenant Plowe went directly to the business where Arthur Owind worked to find and question him. When he was told Arthur Owens was not at work, he obtained the address where Arthur lived from the business's records. He immediately called to make ready a search warrant to search Arthur Owind's apartment. He and Officer Bill Galli stopped at police headquarters on the way to the address Lieutenant Plowe had already obtained from Arthur Owind's employer to pick up the search warrant.

When they arrived at the residence, an unpleasantly surprised and frightened Arthur Owind would not let them in. The door was broken down to gain entrance. Mr. Owind was forcibly restrained, and the entire contents of the house were searched from top to bottom. Substantial evidence was obtained to show and prove that Mr. Owind did have the abducted child in the bedroom of his apartment.

Lieutenant Plowe did a great job! Or did he? It would take months for the trial to come about. As Mr. Owind's defense council began looking for any improprieties that they might find to help their case, they found a terrible mistake had been made that would severely hurt the prosecution of the case. Even though the error was intentionally caused by the defendant' deliberate attempts to conceal his whereabouts.

In Lieutenant Plowes haste to bring the murderer to trial, he never checked the search warrant for the address it contained before he broke into Arts apartment but went directly to the address provided by Arts employer. The warrant was for a search of the residence evil Arthur lived at before his most recent move.

The judge, with his intent to make sure evildoers rights come before those of their victims, ruled immiscible all the evidence gathered at the residence where the little six-year-old helpless girl was brutally tortured, raped, mutilated, murdered, then thrown away like a bag of garbage.

This ridiculously irrational ruling, plus the fact that a body was not found allowed the obvious repeat offender to be found not guilty because of inconclusive evidence. Blind justice or blind judges?

It was the second week of an unseasonably cold December when outrage filled the community that Chelsea Knott had lived her short life as the verdict came down. The smirks on murderous Arthurs face as he walked out of the courtroom, knowing he had just gotten away with murder tore family members hearts apart. Many vowed revenge as they cursed the justice system and the judge. The court provided Arthur protection as he left the courthouse grounds.

Ironically, fate does sometimes play its cruel tricks on the innocent.

Because of the icy weather conditions, Mel Ryan, Arthurs friend, and the landlord was burning more coal than expected and before a new delivery would have helped hide little Chelsea's remains for another undetermined amount of time. Mel pushed his coal shovel into the pile of coal to stoke his furnace and discovered the body and all the evidence needed to have convicted evil Art for his most heinous crimes. This discovery happened less than ten hours after the jury found murderous Arthur Owind not guilty because of lack of admissible evidence! Incompetent, incompatible, inappropriate double jeopardy rules allowed evil to trump good again! One ruling that appears not to be ambiguous, when if it were, might stop things like this from happening. Ever wonder why the laws and rules that protect evildoers from prosecution are always unambiguous and those that could prosecute them seem always to be ambiguous?

Monday, December 20th, 2004, just ten days after being found not guilty of the murder of six-year-old Chelsea Knott. The remains of Arthur Owind were found off the edge of a lonely country road just inside the Orville town limits. Police claimed it a revenge killing and believe he was skinned while still alive, causing a deserving, painful death. Both hands and his head were missing, supposed to have been done to hide the identity of the victim. A positive I.D. was made of the remains through current medical x-rays of Arthurs previously fractured ankle associated with his arrest for the rape of little Tammy Chilk back in 1991.

31
The Confession, Part "2"

Sunday, November 7th, 2010 11:10 am

"Are you implying, that you had something to do with the gruesome death of Arthur Owind?" inquired Sharkey.

"Yes, I took that devils life! Moreover, I made him suffer! He screamed, boy, did he scream!" replied the belligerent Sheriff.

"Her Uncle Bill and I were good friends. I met him years ago when he first came to my taxidermy shop. He invited me to his ranch to hunt with him, and we've been hunting together since. He took the murder of his niece very severely as did the rest of her family that I met and grown fond of over the years.

Little Chelsea used to call me Uncle Randy. I liked that. I knew I had to do something, or her uncle would do something foolish. He wanted Art to pay for what he did, and it was killing him to see Owind, running around loose because of a legal technicality and probably looking for another potential little victim.

Bill made no attempts to hide how he felt and had made serious threats about his intentions to see that Owind doesn't ever get the chance to do it again. He spoke out loud about how he would do it. Skin him alive and dispose of his identity to castaway any evidence that might prove authorities' suspicions of himself."

"By doing it the manner your friend said that he would kill Owind, didn't you only make him the prime suspect?" questioned Sharkey.

"Yes! It was all part of my plan. I wanted Bill to have the satisfaction of Owind's death and mutilation as he would have had, if, he had done it himself. There was no way to prevent him from being the primary suspect, so, I waited until Bill, who was an instructor for a business that teaches problem-solving courses around the country, went away to Iowa for a two-week class. There would be a whole classroom full of students that would place him in Iowa before the last time Owind would have been seen and during the entire time for which he disappeared and was found. It was foolproof! Sure enough, the local authorities came looking for Bill as soon as the body was found. They still suspected that somehow, he had something to do with it, but could never prove anything, after all, he was innocent."

"Did you ever tell Bill you did it?" asked Sharkey.

"Of course not! I didn't want to in any way incriminate my good friend. I sure would have liked to though!" Dobbs said.

"Do you suspect that he suspects that you had a hand in it?" asked Sharkey.

"Not really, lots of people would have wanted to see Owind suffer and die for what he did!" said the Sheriff.

"So, help me get this straight, you killed Owind to punish him for what he did to that little girl?" asked Sharkey.

"In that particular case, punishment and retribution played a large part in it, he deserved what he got!" declared Randy. "I took pleasure in what I did that time and one other time too, but usually I just basically did what I had to do to get specimens. Owind was a great contributor; he had magnificent specimens!"

"A large part, you mean you more did it so that you could look at or photograph his tattoo's too? Did his tattoos' give you sexual gratification, or what?" inquired Sharkey.

"No, Matt, I'm afraid it cuts much deeper than that knife does," Randy replied.

"I became infatuated at terminating people with tattoos, especially those with multiple tattoos. People with full-body tattoos made me scream uncontrollably inside! I wanted their specimens the most and had to be extra careful not to diminish the quality of the specimen. Nothing would stop me! After I killed them, I would find a multitude of ways to make them disappear, but only if I felt there was little chance their body would wind up on the slab at the Munson's Funeral Parlor morgue in Roxi.

"I did my collecting religiously, (if you'll pardon the expression) I didn't want to miss out on any potential opportunities. The few times I did miss a chance to collect a specimen, I was sick for days over it! Severe depression!"

"There you go with that specimen talk again. When you say specimen are you referring to your victims?" Sharkey asked a little confused.

"No!" replied Randy, "My... (he hesitated) victims, to coin your phrase, were contributors."

"What are you referring to when you use the word specimen?" asked Officer Sharkey again.

"Tattoos." Replied Randy.

Officer Sharkey shakes his head for a second and says, "Let me get this straight... when you say specimen you are referring to your victim's tattoos, which you refer to as contributors tattoos, is that right?" asked Sharkey.

"Now you're catching on Sharkey." Said Dobbs.

"Please continue." Sharkey pleaded.

"As I had started to do way back in July of 1990 when I was only 14, I would surgically remove any contributor tattoos that could be hidden beneath their clothing as I was prepping their body for burial. When they were on display at the funeral parlor, no one could see that they were removed, and my secret was buried with the contributor's body."

"But... suppose there was a reason some had for the body to be exhumed, you would have been exposed." Said Officer Sharkey.

"As an employee of the funeral home, I would be informed if there were ever a need for any of my contributors to be exhumed for any reason. There was a very slight chance that might ever happen, but if it did, I would cross that bridge when I came to it, and if I couldn't find a way to hide the revelation, I would get out of Dodge, Quickly!" explained Randy.

"For other contributors that I would deliberately allow for their specimen riddance body to be found, I had to orchestrate how, when and where I wanted them to be discovered — discovered in a way that it did not attract attention to the fact that the contributor had once had tattoos that were now removed. I would cleverly harvest the specimen and then inconspicuously mutilated the area on the contributor it had occupied in a fashion that no one could conceive that one was ever there and removed. "

"You refer to the surgical removal of the contributors tattoos as harvesting specimens. Is that correct?" asked Sharkey.

"Affirmative," replied Randy "But I prefer to say that I harvested the contributor as one growth from a crop in the massive fields of society, and then collect the specimen from that contributor as a yield of that crop. I know it may be hard for you to understand my thinking and logic, but just think of it like perhaps cutting or harvesting a stock of Brussels sprout for its tiny cabbage-like heads, an ear of corn for its kernels, or even like taking the juice from an orange that's been taken from a tree."

"Suppose one of the victims' family knew the victim had a tattoo(s) located on the body in the spot where you so cleverly mutilated that part of the body?" asked Sharkey.

"You already know the answer to that Question Matt! It never was an issue as families don't like to look at the dead body of their loved ones. They may look at the face to identify their kin if necessary, but that's as far as it ever gets, I was always careful not to damage the face in these type of instances, so the family didn't have any reason to identify the kin by tattoos or scars" said Randy.

"I've always supposed that there might come a time or two that someone other than a family member might be familiar with these people and their body-art drawings, but I figured they would all lend credence to the fact that the reason the tattoos were not there was due to the accident. Even the investigators and examiners never questioned it. They never even made an issue of the fact that all my contributors wore body art. I guess during their investigations, it never came up. It didn't stand out as a difference, lack of cross-referencing those kinds of facts and data with other cases, I guess." Dobbs said smugly.

"I've created and kept a book of all my contributors. I've also recovered some keepsakes from each contributor. They're to be used with each contributor's display. Probably be worth some real money to somebody, someday!"

"I notice you don't like to use the word kill, does the term bother you, make you feel bad, make you feel sick, perhaps?" asked Sharkey.

"No, I just prefer to sugar coat that part of it as I explain my actions to you," Randy explained.

"But you do like to use the word contributor to describe your victims, don't you?" asked Sharkey.

"Don't try to psychoanalyze me, Matt! Do you want the story or not?" asked Dobbs defiantly.

"I'm sorry...please continue, but let's get to the abandoned car stuff." inspired Sharkey.

"In due time!" responded Randy, "There's much, much more that you need to hear first for all the pieces to fit together correctly and so no parts are left over when the puzzle is finished."

"How did you find the time to run your taxidermy business, your upholstery business too, be the Roxi town Sheriff and still commit all these gruesome acts, didn't you ever sleep? No wonder you looked like dog poop in a pile every time I saw you." Questioned Sharkey.

I already told you I didn't sleep as other people do. This is why I didn't have enough hours in my days to get the things done I wanted or needed to get done!" said Randy abruptly.

"I was feeling so overwhelmed and tired; I feared I would develop health issues that might jeopardize my ambitions and aspirations. So, I farmed the taxidermy work and upholstery work out to a couple of businesses about forty miles north of here. A place where things were quiet and separated from the rest of the world, and all that was happening in it," replied Randy Dobbs.

"I visited each of the shops that I eventually chose to represent my standard of excellence in both fields. When I felt confident that the quality of artistry coming out of the two distant businesses would not compromise my business values and lose me potential future customers, I employed their services on a full-time basis." Said Randy,

"It was a great ruse, and it helped to keep up the appearance of active business for each of the businesses. The underwriters never knew what happened to their products once they left their door. I hired unrelated carriers to do pickup and deliveries. The customers were all shills and never suspected a thing. I had a powered gate; you must have seen it as you entered at the top of my long driveway, with a closed sign on it that I closed when I didn't want anyone coming to the farm or my businesses. I had most people drop off taxidermy work and smaller upholstery items at the Sheriffs Office, and they would pick them up there as well when they were ready. They knew I was busy with many needs and realized it was more convenient for everybody involved and they appreciated it. The drop-off and pick-up service at my shops, for large upholstery items like couches, were by appointment only."

"Because of the impenetrable gate, over time, most customers knew they were wasting their time to drive over or try to drop in when it wasn't scheduled business hours. I tried to have certain normal business hours each week if I could. Let me try to get back to the beginning, jumping around like this might make me leave some important details out," said Randy.

"Of course, I'm not going to go into full detail for all the incidents that I'm responsible for, hell, it would take forever, but... you'll get the drift.

My collecting specimens from contributors from places other than the Munson and Scarlet Funeral Homes morgues, started in Oreville in July of 1991. This was about the same time as that Arthur Owind was assaulting little Tammy Chilks at the beach in Nevada. I was desperate to find more contributors. I had so many needs to meet. The funeral homes in Roxi and Apollotown were much too limited, and if I wasn't careful, it could trip me up. I always pictured the ideal contributor was the one with the largest and most tattoos to offer. Design and colors were of particular interest to me for some special needs I had, but mostly I just needed lots and lots of tattoos. Tattoos of various designs, shapes, sizes, and colors.

I started imagining the types of individual that might best meet my contributors criteria. Certain types of people are more drawn to body art than others. Very few people that get tattoos want to or try to hide them. Kids sometimes do, if they don't want their parents to find out, but most people want them to be seen and to be identified by them. When and where they want them to be seen and whom they wanted to see them was another part of the equation. Some are primarily for tattoo club member prominence, acceptance, appreciation, and identity. Some are spouse or sex partner specific. Some are for flaunting at the beach or poolside. Some are more all-purpose. Some are for purely obnoxious reasons to antagonize the portion of the population that find them offensive. Some are for gang markings, fear purposes, and to intimidate. Some are for promotional and attraction reasons as with dancers or sideshow entertainers.

Tattoos and motorcyclists are kind of synonymous with each other whether or not the group is peaceful or threatening. Some are even worn by gangbangers to exploit death by some of their members hands, such as tiny teardrops around the eyes. I wanted them. I wanted them all! No one was to be excluded or turned away from my Special Donors Memorial.

I was pleasantly surprised as my escapade expanded that there were so many more people that had inked body art than I ever could have imagined. Where I once thought people that had tattoos were the exception, I found it be just the opposite, especially where I went shopping for them, but then again, the old saying goes, 'If you want to bag a bear, you have to hunt where the bears are.'

Once my potential donors criteria list was completed, I next had to figure out where these special contributors had the highest probability to be found. The beaches and pools were a cinch, the others not so simple.

I started to patronize places that attracted all of the various classes of potential contributors. I staked out hundreds of tattoo shops with-in at least a one-hundred-mile radius of Roxi. It was well worth my time; I was able to identify dozens of highly qualified and desired potential contributors. I quite often recruited a donor as a result of a visit. Mostly, it was just a matter of opportunity and timing. Clever disguises, careful preparations, planning, execution, and guts were the key to my success. However, this kind of recruitment was often quite messy and would result in too many unexplainable missing persons cases. This usually happened if I took too many applicants from any one area, with any sustainable frequency.

Naturally, I couldn't just harvest the specimen and allow the otherwise intact rest of the contributing donor to be found or it, of course, would have sparked a specific manhunt. A search that would have sparked tremendous fear in the hearts of and give warning to all tattooed persons in those areas and would have made it near impossible to sustain the growth of my gatherings."

"You said there was one time other than Arthur Owind that you took pleasure in killing someone, elaborate on that instance... please," asked Sharkey.

"Well, now you've interrupted me again. I would have gotten to it eventually, but all right, I like to talk about this one, anyhow!" replied Randy.

"It began taking shape in 1987 when I was still a youngster. My Grandfather, who was also my best friend in the whole world, next to my dad, of course, hired a Financial Advisor Named Kevin Sneezelyn, who was a registered securities broker-dealer from Benton."

"I read about that guy!" said Sharkey astounded, as he interrupted Randy momentarily. "Killed in Championsburg not too long ago... tarred and feathered, wasn't he?"

"That's the guy," said Randy. "I wasn't old enough to understand very well what was going on at that time, and I was only around 11 or 12 years old, but I remember well the face and voice of Sneezelyn.

Grandfather was very ill and called me aside. He told me that he had invested some money in a bank certificate, especially for me the day

I was born. Lord knows, that our family could have used that money to help pay bills many times over the years, but no one other than grandfather knew about it, and he wanted me to have it someday for college or a business. Moreover, he kept this important detail to himself.

Grandfather confidentially hired Kevin Sneezelyn to invest the money from those bank certificates wisely for him. Grandfather even told him what companies he wanted the money invested in, and he put both his name and my name on the forms as owners of the portfolio. Grandfather wanted the funds to continue to function and grow exclusively for me after his death that he knew was imminent.

Grandfather told no one about this except for me. He then swore me to secrecy and made me promise not to interrupt the fund's growth in the future to more or less, bail out the family during bad times. He wanted me to do as he had done. He said we always managed to find a way to get through the difficult periods with-out relying on the investment, and if knowledge of the investment were privy to others, it would have only served as a crutch. The family wouldn't have explored alternative ways to dig themselves out of that financial hole they get stuck in from time to time.

He explained a little about how investments work to me and the importance of not touching the money that has been intentionally set aside for a specific purpose, such as retirement, illness, weddings, and college. I understood and could appreciate the value of his teaching and the generosity of the investments he had made for me. Fortunately, or unfortunately, I'm not just sure which, Grandfather stopped short of telling me what to do with the investments, such as occasionally meeting with Sneezelyn and making changes if necessary.

He instructed me to always get to the mailbox before anyone else and if there was any correspondence bearing the names of the investment company, Sneezelyn, or funds within the portfolio, to grab them before anyone saw them to avoid any questions and to protect the secret. I always did just that. Till the day's mom and dad died, they never knew.

I guess the investment company and Sneezelyn never knew Grandfather died and the correspondence from them continued to come in his name. All those years, I just opened the mail and reviewed the funds progress and growth of which most of the time, I was pretty pleased with.

I had been hearing these rumors about elderly and disabled

investors over in the Championsburg area being deliberately duped by their financial advisor, whom I thought was working out of Championsburg. It was believed that the Advisor had run a successful business, but then he began to spend more than he was earning, so he devised an ingenious scheme to pilfer money from his clients funds and began to perpetuate the thefts.

His clients had too much trust in him as he seemed sincere, personable, and was very convincing. His honest exterior hid his devious and dishonest interior. No one ever did any independent research of their investments or Sneezelyn. They wrote checks and other bills of the note directly to Sneezelyn instead of the financial institute and never once attempted to verify any of the monthly account information he sent them, just as he knew they would.

He also sold hundreds of thousands of dollars worth of inappropriate annuities to other old, retired and even handicapped persons. Investments that were not suitable for those who need and are using their investments at the time the annuities were bought. He fraudulently told them lies about how those annuities worked and how their purchase would affect them in their retirement years. He knew because the annuities were ambiguous, none of these elderly and sometimes poorly educated suckered clients would ever catch on. For the vast majority of the people, he had supposedly bought annuities for, he never actually purchased them for his clients. However, he created his own fictitious but authentic-looking annuities using purchased software on his personal home computer. He did this by cutting and pasting useful to himself letterheads, signatures, and text from copies of various real documents from the few actual contracts that he did purchase for some of his clients before he got too greedy and hand-carried them to his unsuspecting clients. Though his hoax was not very sophisticated, and more opportunity oriented, it worked very well.

These poor old folks were left in a real fix. Some of his more desperate clients that could get financial help and backing from their family or friends took the sleaze-ball Sneezelyn to court. He showed absolutely no remorse for what he had done and denied everything. Those folks were unsuccessful because he lied about so many important things, and had his ass cleverly covered. He was also said to have withheld important data from them that would have been proof of his intentional wrongdoing. He threatened some of his clients with bodily harm if they testified against him in court. The unscrupulous scoundrel got away with stealing these poor unfortunate futures away from them.

The plaintiffs couldn't get one cent from the insurance company representing the financial institute Sneezelyn worked for because of the not guilty verdict.

Many of them were put out of the very homes they built and lived in most of their lives because they could not afford them or the taxes anymore because of the failed securities. A few even took their own lives because of the emotional trauma and severe depression.

I loved my Grandfather with all my little black heart, and I could see his face in theirs every time I saw one of these poor souls. I felt terrible for them, and I needed to do something to protect all the elderly and disabled people in the area. I decided to execute the justice and punishment the courts would not rule on that bad dude, to stop him from doing it to anyone else ever again.

As fate would have it, as I began looking into these rumors to find out whom the villain was, I was astounded to find out he was the same financial advisor Grandfather hired almost 20 years before, and I also found out that Mr. Kevin Sneezelyn wore a few tattoos. After that horrific discovery, learning about the inking's, and knowing how he defrauded all these other poor old souls, I got worried about my investment. It suddenly occurred to me that I hadn't had received any correspondence from the financial company in Grandfathers name or my name about the investment for quite a long, long time.

I had been so busy it never occurred to me that something may be wrong. I examined an old statement to find the companies phone number. I didn't call Sneezelyn because I didn't want there to be any calls from me recorded on Sneezelyns phone call record, for the obvious reason. I called the finance company and inquired. I was told that about one year prior, Grandfather was listed as deceased and the account had been closed out and cashed out by a Randal Dobbs, whose name also appeared on the account.

One didn't have to be a genius to figure out who used my name and who had my money. Of course, I could have gotten the authorities involved and had a pretty good chance of getting a conviction that might have sent him to jail for a while. However, I figured I probably would never get my money back that way, and, besides, I would have only solved my problem. He would still be free again sooner or later and would probably pick up where he left off before he was caught, and even worse, I would have drawn attention to myself, making it more difficult to stay excluded if I decided to delete him from the population later on.

I found out where Sneezelyn lived in Benton. I set up my surveillance. I quickly learned about his habits and timetable. Very early on the morning of Saturday, August 18th, 2007, while it was still dark, I visited Mr. Sneezelyn at his home in Benton. I intended to abduct him and induct him into my Hall of Famers. I felt there was little chance of getting the money he owed me without in some way, exposing and incriminating myself. I was very pleased to be wrong after I had abducted him and took him to that field in Championsburg, and, told him what I think of and do to people like him; he started to cry like a baby. He wanted, he begged me for sympathy and mercy. Can you imagine? Like he ever had any mercy on those poor souls he screwed over!

Slimy Sneezelyn told me he had money and that I could have it all if I let him go, he promised he wouldn't tell anybody what I was going to do. I told him it didn't want any of his wonderful funds, but he kept begging.

'No... no... I've got cash!... I can give you all the cash... all the cash I have.' He pleaded. I asked him how much he had and where it was. He had it stashed in a safe in a fake wall in his bathroom back at Benton. At first, he wouldn't give me the combination to the safe saying that he thought I would kill him anyway if I knew. He quickly changed his mind after I painfully started harvesting the first specimen, and he saw the hot tar I had waiting for him slowly coming to a boil. The hot tar erased any evidence that there were ever any tattoos on his arms.

I figure I made out pretty good on Grandfathers investments after all. Authorities never did find that hidden safe in his bathroom. They were too focused on it being a revenge killing, instead of a robbery. They were half right. However, truth be known, he died from terminal greed and self-inflicted stupidity!

Damn shame he didn't have more tattoos." Finished Randy.

"What did you do with the money?" asked Sharkey.

"It just went back into the kitty, more or less. I reinvested most of it. Used some to buy things I needed."

As Randy spilled his guts and the many minutes it took him to do so, Officer Matt Sharkey began to feel more at ease. He was trying to bring up the courage to ask the one most important to him, question.

He was in no particular position to ask it because it had a high probability of having an answer he didn't want to hear, and it might cause things to escalate.

"Is anyone else involved with the abduction and murder of these so-called contributors?"

For the time being at least, Matt would continue to play things out, still hoping for the climate to cool a little further and that one possible opportunity he needed to regain control.

As you probably can tell by now, Randy is not one to get excited quickly. His imperturbable nature was making it difficult for Sharkey to gauge him. He was calm as he always was. Soft-spoken as he ever was. No symptoms were indicating even the slightest fear in his voice or on his face. The only passion he displayed was related to his devious deeds, which he seemed incapable of only scanning the surface of when he revealed the nature of each victim's fate. Sharkey knew he was dealing with someone, unlike anyone else he had ever had to deal with, but it was much graver even than that. Sharkey was dealing with a being, a being that possessed a nature the world had never known and had to deal with.

Strange as it may still seem, Officer Matt Sharkey couldn't, (that is if you take away the fear of the unknown, ordinary and distinct sense of survival) really, down deep, feel fearful of Randy. For some strange and unprecedented reason, Officer Matt still thought he could trust Randy and that he wouldn't hurt him. However, it was such a peculiar feeling somewhere between that of almost a false sense of security mixed with that sense of total trust. He couldn't feel contempt or hate, or even a dislike for Randy. He felt more like he wanted to help him as a parent might want to do when their child does something really out of character.

"Randy," said Sharkey, "You know you're not this evil character you're telling me about. I know it, and you know it too. You've told me as much yourself earlier when you said you almost wished this evil mind possessing desire never came over you. Something strange really must have gone haywire someplace, a short circuit in the old noggin or something like that and it probably happened like you said when you saw your first tattoo. You were so, so very young, and to be in a place like a morgue at your age, could have been the catalyst that set you off. It's not your fault when these things happen; society cannot hold that... that... the imperceptible person accountable for their actions during the time their mind was on the fritz. You can be fixed! It's a simple matter of finding out just what happened to you, so they know what to do to fix the problem. It's been done before, and I want you to know that I'll help you in any way I can."

"That's very gracious of you, Matt, and I do thank you for your concern," said Randy. "But as I told you before, I always knew it wasn't right, but I didn't want to fix it."

Officer Matt, sensing he may at this point, be overplaying his hand, decided to take the conversation to a different level.

"You told me you... how did you put it? (paused Sharkey as he looked at the page of notes he had been taking,) Oh, yes, here it is, you said, I did my gruesome part to prestigiously provide preferred customers that I knew would wind up at Munson's or Scarlet's." Then again you talked about your being responsible for several drowningss at flood pathways, lakes, ponds and even a few at the beach. You want to elaborate on that a bit?" asked Sharkey.

"Alright," replied Randy. "Come over here a minute, and I'll show you a sort of ledger that I keep." Randy opened a drawer on a gorgeous and ornamented cabinet, in the center of the north-facing wall. He pulled out a multi-page document and opened it to a particular page.

"Look here, Matt," Randy instructed.

Randy dropped his finger down the page till he got to Sunday, 7/18/1993.

"These five persons are flood inducted contributors, or donors if you prefer." Said Randy.

			Contribution	Method	Collected	
Sun.	7/18/1993	Edward Kasmarinski	Multiples	Shot	Roxi, flood	Championsburg
Sun.	7/18/1993	William Wright	Multiples	Shot	Roxi, flood	Championsburg
Sun.	7/18/1993	Nick Beltraws	Multiples	Shot	Roxi, flood	Championsburg
Sun.	7/18/1993	John Simonsini	Multiples	Shot	Roxi, flood	Championsburg
Sun.	7/18/1993	Marcus Yogaurt	Multiples	Shot	Roxi, flood	Championsburg

Officer Matt Sharkey had many of his questions answered in just a fraction of a second as he saw the booklet listing and the five names Randy specifically showed him.

"If you follow each name from left to right, it serves as a simplified log of my acquisitions." Said Randy.

"The left column represents the day and date the contributor or donor... whichever term you prefer, in the column to its right is who was plucked for harvesting. The very next column, to your right titled (Contribution), reflects the number of specimens harvested and sometimes the location on the contributor the specimen was eradicated.

This next column, titled (Method), gives reference to the manner the relinquishing of the specimen occurred.

The column titled (Collected), indicates the location the plucking happened, and finally, where the contributor lived."

"You're telling me these presumed drowned youngsters were shot to death by you?" asked Sharkey puzzled.

"That's a harsher way of putting it, but yes," replied Randy.

"How could you have hidden that fact from the authorities?" asked Matt.

"Their bodies were never found and were presumed drowned and washed away after the vehicle they were riding in got stuck underneath a ledge of a stone quarry during a flash flood," replied Randy.

"I think I remember that." said Sharkey, "But how did you ever get their bodies out of that flooded car?"

"I got them all out safely just before the vehicle slipped, turned and wedged under the ledge," replied Randy.

"You saved them to kill them? I don't understand!" said Matt.

"Gosh, I wish you would refrain from using that word." Said Randy, "It was all for the cause. When I went to save them, I didn't know that each one of them would meet the criteria of a donor for my special Donors Memorial. Then I saw their drawings, a perfect opportunity had revealed itself to me. To not act would have severe ramifications with my disposition. I could not put myself through such distress! I was glad I did what I had to do; they all were prime specimen carriers."

"Were there other flood-related contributors?" asked Sharkey.

"Yes, but not the way you think," explained Randy as he turned the page and pointed. "These three contributors right here, on Monday, November 8th, 1999."

Mon. 11/08/1999	Garego Montinni	Multiples	Drown	Roxi, Flood	Roxi
Mon. 11/08/1999	Rita Montinni	Multiples	Drown	Roxi, Flood	Roxi
Mon. 11/08/1999	Luigi Savianos	Multiples	Drown	Roxi, Flood	Roxi

"They all received their honors posthumously." Randy turns yet another page, and says, "As did two of these four contributors here, on Saturday, February 11th, 2006."

Sat.	2/11/2006	Lilly George	Multiples	B.F.T.	Roxi, Flood	Roxi
Sat.	2/11/2006	Bruce George	Multiples	B.F.T.	Roxi, Flood	Roxi
Sat.	2/11/2006	Rhoda Ringo	Multiples	Drown	Roxi, Flood	Roxi
Sat.	2/11/2006	Tanya Ringo	Multiples	Drown	Roxi, Flood	Roxi

"During the fierce storm that produced the flooding, I found the two Ringo sisters that I knew lived in Roxi while I was out on patrol. They were seriously injured after a huge tree branch fell on their car. I had long admired their potential specimens and seized the opportunity to recruit them. I figured that if I didn't, they might survive their injuries. I was confident they would wind up at Munson's. I had just returned to my police car after their induction, when the unfortunate but criteria fitting Belcan couple also from Roxi, came along and stopped to help them; only seconds before a wall of raging water came out of nowhere and swept them both away. They were found washed up in a field five miles away when the floodwaters receded. All four were brought to me at Munson's."

Randy flipped another page. "These five especially unfortunate contributors, were all-natural, posthumous donors." Declared Randy.

Tue.	1/06/2009	Donna Belcan	Multiples	Drown	Roxi, Flood	Roxi
Tue.	1/06/2009	David Belcan	Multiples	Drown	Roxi, Flood	Roxi
Tue.	1/06/2009	Manny Lopez	Multiples	Drown	Roxi, Flood	Roxi
Tue.	1/06/2009	Martina Lopez	Multiples	Drown	Roxi, Flood	Roxi
Tue.	1/06/2009	Angela Do'little	Multiples	Drown	Roxi, Flood	Roxi

"Haven't all your contributors, received their place in your special (Donors Memorial) posthumously?" asked Sharkey.

"I simply mean by more natural means." explained the Sheriff.

"Are the contributors you told me about related to the lakes, ponds, and the beach in this ledger too?" asked Officer Sharkey.

The Sheriff turned back to the first listing page and said, "I wasn't category-specific, and I didn't put them in alphabetical order either, mostly it's by dates, but if you just look under the method and collected columns, it pretty much gives you that information."

The cold calculating Sheriff starts on the first page and speaks of each collection.

"Remember," he said, "For all my contributors that have the term drown by their name, their stalks were at some point found. Then, they were either taken to The Munson Funeral Home morgue or The Scarlet Funeral Home where I would eventually harvest their contribution. Their enrollment had to be done in a manner that there were no visible signs of foul play."

Randy points to the name below on the list.

Mon.	7/04/1994	Mary Speck	Multiples	Drown	Home, pool	Roxi

"Take this first one, Mary Speck for instance," Randy started.

"Young, vivacious, beautiful, and tan. I followed her from the Tattoo Parlor to her home one evening. She had just made a purchase and was very pleased. It was a hot day and as soon as she arrived, she dropped her clothing and took a swim. I don't know what she did for a living, but she had a lot of time on her hands. She sunbathed every sunny day from 11:00 a.m. till at least 1:00 p.m. I made up a nice paper plate of what appeared to be a partially eaten but spoiled fish dinner, crumbs and all. Wearing a disguise, just in case I was seen, I slipped into the pool yard unnoticed. I rendered her unconscious and enlisted her with-in seconds by helping her into the pool. I left the platter on the table next to her drink where she was sunning herself and snuck away. She came to visit me at Munson's latter that same day. Authorities, including myself of course, concluded that she became violently ill after eating that spoiled sandwich and drowned while out of control in the pool."

"How did you render her unconscious?" asked Officer Sharkey.

"The same way I always do," said Randy. "I compress one or both of the carotid arteries on the sides of the neck. It quickly restricts and interrupts the flow of blood and oxygen to the brain. I am well-schooled as an officer. I leave no marks or welts."

"What about these two women?" asked Matt, as he pointed to these next two names, lower on the list.

| Wed. | 7/26/1995 | Alice Dankos | Multiples | Drown | A-town, pond | Apollotown |
| Wed. | 7/26/1995 | Milly White | Multiples | Drown | A-town, pond | Apollotown |

"I used the same method," replied Randy, "Not difficult when it's at a pond. Just have to scout well and make sure there is no one else around. No one ever questions it. Those things have a way of happening. No apparent marks, scratches, or bruises. No one questions it. Same for these," said he.

| Wed. | 7/16/1997 | Larry Mourry | Multiples | Drown | Roxi, lake | Roxi |
| Wed. | 7/16/1997 | Lana Tuush | Multiples | Drown | Roxi, lake | Roxi |

"And these too," said Randy.

Fri.	6/26/1998	Jane Mullins	Full body	Drown	A-town, pond	Apollotown
Fri.	6/26/1998	Jacki Mullins	Multiples	Drown	A-town, pond	Apollotown
Fri.	6/26/1998	Bob Raulston	Full body	Drown	A-town, pond	Apollotown

"These next three are a little different," said Randy.

Sun.	8/06/2000	Billy Bonete	Multiples	Drown	Roxi falls	Roxi
Sun.	8/06/2000	Jenny Braids	Multiples	Drown	Roxi falls	Roxi
Sun.	8/06/2000	Tony Miller	Multiples	Drown	Roxi falls	Roxi

"The two young men tried to blindside me, must have sensed something. Got to give them credit, when I saw I couldn't get to them in a bunch, I pulled my gun and ordered them to get together. They moved directly away from each other, both at the same time, leaving me in the center. Hell, I knew I couldn't shoot. It would have resulted in three more missing people. I couldn't have that.

So, when I jumped the Miller boy, the Bonete boy jumped me just as I had subdued his friend. I had to leave some impressions on him, so I sent him and his friends for a ride over the falls. Their oars were both very old, and they probably shouldn't have even ventured out with them, especially in a dangerous area such as the falls. I broke one in half quite quickly and threw the top part in the boat and the bottom part in the stream. It was assumed they got too close to the brink and tried frantically to row away when the old weakened oar broke. They were all much more peaceful when they came to pay me a call at Munson's that evening." said Randy.

"Did you ever encounter anyone that didn't allow you to use the carotid artery approach?" asked Sharkey.

"No, I'm quite good at it. It's quick, and once I make full contact with a victim from behind, there is nothing they can do to prevent being overpowered."

"I did have an "almost" one time though," he said. "I had this grand plan to enroll a young farmer from Roxi named Jim Whittin, see...right here on the list." Said Randy Dobbs as he moved his index finger into position on the page.

Wed.	8/06/2003	Jim Whittin	Multiples	Fright	Roxi, barn	Roxi

"Jim's taunting of his bodacious inked artwork was just about more than I could stand. I had to have him for my memorial. I knew he was doing some repair work on his high barn roof, must have been up to over 30 feet. Naturally, I couldn't get up there without him seeing me, so I hid in a shadowed area between his silos and waited for him to come down. I intended to render him unconscious using the usual technique and was successful with. I was then going to carry him up to the highest part of the barn roof and drop him headfirst to the concrete part of the cattle loading dock below. After I put him into the usual temporary sleep, I walked away from him to do a visual and ensure there was no one around to see me and reposition the ladder for the heavy load I had to carry up it.

I was about 60 to 70 feet away from where I left him lying on the ground when out of the corner of my eye, I noticed some movement. He had somehow recovered from my subduction and was running full tilt away from me, heading toward a field area on the other side of the barn where some migrants were hard at work harvesting crops. He was already a good 120 to 130 feet ahead of me and just entered the clearing where the workers could see him. He was screaming as loud as he could."

I knew I couldn't shoot him. The shot would only draw more attention to him and I would be seen running from the area. I didn't know what to do. I didn't know for sure if he could recognize me or not. I was getting pretty damned scared! I should have clobbered the bastard with my steel bar that I usually use for securing enrollment in my memorial. I didn't know what to do and thought my jig was up. Then suddenly, while running, he went crashing to the ground like a whitetail buck shot as he was leaping over a fence.

I carefully glanced one-eyed like around the edge of the barn to see if anyone heard his screaming or otherwise took notice to him as he ran away. I think every damn picker in the field heard him and was rushing to his aid. I slipped away while the slipping was good and quickly returned to my office waiting to be notified about the incident. I couldn't figure out how the hell he ever revived so quickly from the carotid maneuver.

I was afraid of what the farm labors may have seen and especially what they heard. I hoped the farmer was dead, but that seemed too much to hope and ask for.

Less than a half-hour later, I received the call about him and followed the usual protocol to respond to it. I was afraid out of my mind that I might be recognized and or identified as the perpetrator. I maintained my candor and began questioning the witnesses. Fortunately for me, none of them understood English, and I had to use a translator to interpret what they had to say about their experiences. They saw no one but him and thought he had taken some frantic seizure. I was pretty sure I was off the hook and boy was I ever relieved!

It wasn't until about two days later that I was able to piece together what had happened and why my carotid maneuver was insufficient. It appeared that the farmer, though young and healthy-looking on the exterior, suffered from a history of strokes related to a disease that caused a narrowing of the vessels that maintain the blood and oxygen flow to the brain. Jim did pretty well most of the time, because for some reason, the disease only affected the carotid artery on one side of his neck.

The narrowing of the carotid artery is because of plaque buildup inside the artery reducing the flow of blood. So, to help prevent any more strokes and potential disability, the Surgeon performed an artery-opening procedure. This is where a section of metal mesh type is placed inside the damaged or restricted portion of the carotid artery using a catheter.

Not knowing that Jim had the stent procedure and with my impeccably rotten luck, I applied pressure to the side of the neck where the stint resided, and I must have only been able to produce a portion of the usual results allowing him to recover much, much faster. Unfortunately for Farmer Jim and very fortunately for me, my maneuver dislodged some plaque that was forming a clot at or near the place I applied pressure. As he ran excitedly to get away, and his heartbeat frantically going, the dislodged clot rammed itself fatally into the blood supply going to his brain. This permanently and thoroughly cut off his blood supply and dropped him in his tracks never to get up again. The blood to the other side of the brain was insufficient to sustain him. The cause of death was ruled natural causes due to complications of a failed stint.

I was off the hook and had a paying customer at Munson's as well as a new specimen contributor for my memorial. All's well that ends well," said Randy poetically.

"This next contributor was one of my most desirable inductees. He was harvested similar to the other drown category contributors. Mr. Wesson received honorable mention, for the full suite of the specimen he donated. Not only multiple designs, shapes and sizes, but a multitude of colorings." said Randy enthusiastically.

| Fri. | 6/07/2002 Matt Wesson | Full body | Drown | Roxi, stream | Roxi |

"What does the B.F.T. under the method column mean for this group of people?" asked Officer Matt as he pointed to a group of names on the list.

"Good question!" replied The Sheriff, "For these next five young men and women, I had to work extra hard to convince them to enroll. When I have larger numbers of potential contributors, the carotid artery approach is not always the best approach for everyone and sometimes just not practical. In such cases, I invoked character, dignity, and honor upon the contributors by employing the Royal dubbing method. Perhaps I was a little heavy-handed as I dubbed them, thus the B. F. T. designation for blunt force trauma.

I always plan these ventures during the time of year that hunting season is not in to reduce the probability that I may be observed picking my crops from nearby woodlands. I also designate the ideal locations, like steep mountainsides, heavily brushed areas, and places that are heavily laden with poison plants to further reduce the potential for on-lookers.

"I chose to crash the contributor's speed boat into the log pier to eliminate the clues provided by my dubbing method. I got a little wet as I jumped from the ship just before its crashing, but it's all in a day's work."

Wed. 8/11/2004 Jeff Bradock	Multiples	B.F.T.	Roxi, dam	Roxi
Wed. 8/11/2004 Jock Ridges	Multiples	Drown	Roxi, dam	Roxi
Wed. 8/11/2004 Chelsea Swath	Multiples	B.F.T.	Roxi, dam	Roxi
Wed. 8/11/2004 Cindy Cobler	Multiples	Drown	Roxi, dam	Roxi
Wed. 8/11/2004 Irene Shemanic	Multiples	B.F.T.	Roxi, dam	Roxi

Turning the page, Randy continued explaining his methods.

"This one, Mr. Wilkens, another typical drown category contributor." Said Randy.

Thur. 8/04/2005 Jason Wilkens	Both Arms, U &L	Drown	Roxi, Pond	Roxi

"There's not much to tell you about him; he was an easy acquisition and drew little speculation about his demise."

Pointing yet farther down the page, Randy said,

"These next two contributors were recruited at the beach in Mallard."

Thur. 7/05/2007 Steve Bittur	Full body	B. F.T.	Millard, Beach	Millard
Fri. 7/06/2007 Calvin Hawthorne	Full body	B. F.T.	Millard, Beach	Millard

"They were the result of a police officer convention I attended, being held on the beachfront. Instructors were invited to show new methods of subduing criminals. The public, beach-going, passers-by were invited and encouraged to observe the training to enlist public support and confidence. I noticed two different full inked, body design laden men that routinely flaunted their art endowed bodies as they trolled for spectators. They were not together and I got the idea they resented each other by the fact that they had to compete with each other for attention. I noticed that they both passed by a huge dumpster at a boardwalk eatery as they came to and left the beach. I observed the business's utilization of the dumpster, and it was only occasional. The dumpsters were labeled for pick up on Mondays, after the busy weekend business.

In the early evening before the last day of the convention, I plucked Mr. Bittur as he unsuspectingly walked by the dumpster, leaving him well hidden from view behind the building. I was confident that no one was going to linger around the horrible smell of the dumpster because of the scorching weather.

After the eatery closed, everything went dark and the boardwalk was near empty. I waited for the boardwalk security vehicle to pass, drove up to the dumpster, placed the contributor in a body bag, and loaded him into my trunk. I purchased two dozen bags of ice and placed them in the trunk. Then I parked my vehicle in a cool area of the hotel parking lot. In the early evening, the day the convention was over, I repeated the procedure with Mr. Hawthorne and returned to Roxi.

The rest of these enrolled contributors were by the usual drown routine." Said Randy, "Got them all one at a time, no trouble."

Sun.	6/28/2009	Aron Strealy	Multiples	Drown	A-town, pond	Apollotown
Sun.	6/28/2009	Dorothy Strealy	Back, Upper	Drown	A-town, pond	Apollotown
Mon.	6/27/2010	Tom Ryan	Multiples	Drown	Roxi, Stream	Roxi
Mon.	6/27/2010	Bob Ryan	Both arms, U.L.	Drown	Roxi, Stream	Roxi
Mon.	6/27/2010	Alan Zapotipchi	Multiples	Drown	Roxi, Stream	Roxi
Mon.	6/27/2010	Dolores Zapotipchi	Waist, thigh	Drown	Roxi, Stream	Roxi
Mon.	6/27/2010	Eileen Dupre	Posterior	Drown	Roxi, Stream	Roxi

"There is this one other one, back here, though," said Randy, as he rifled through the pages. "I tried a little different approach to her. It was an extremely hot beginning for May that year; many people opened their pools early. It was the first time I saw this young lady, Eileen Dupre," Randy points to her name also.

Thur.	5/08/2008	Eileen Dupre	Back, posterior elect.	Home, pool	Roxi

"She got married and left Roxi about four years ago. She had since gotten a divorce and moved back to Roxi to be near her folks that lived only a few houses away. I was in the Roxi Plumbing Supply Store when she came in wearing a skimpy bikini bathing suit to buy a part for her pool pump. Here come those crazy feelings again! She was decorated like the park on the Fourth of July! Every design was so beautifully colored.

I didn't want to do it. I didn't. I knew her parents well, and she had just moved back home. How could I? I asked myself. I felt bad just thinking about it. I seldom felt remorse, or for that matter, any feeling except for that of gratification when I was successful. However, as bad as I felt, I knew I would eventually feel a thousand times worse if I did not act!

In disguise, I approached from the rear of her yard that was all woodland, basically to case the area and observe her activities so I could plan my strategy for later. However, when it became apparent how easily I could recruit her immediately and without having to make a return visit, I decided to act.

I could hear the music immediately as I was approaching the pool area and thought to myself, 'Good, it's loud, very loud... It will help cover any noise I make.' I was fortunate that she didn't have a dog. Dogs are my biggest barrier to home recruitment.

I cautiously peered over the fence, and I could see her lying there just on the other side quietly sunning herself. Her eyes were closed. I didn't know if she was sleeping or not. I was able to come within six feet away from her and where she had her radio plugged in without being seen. The radio was only about four feet from the pool. I found a long thin branch that was long enough and strong enough to push the radio into the pool. I only waited a short while when Eileen decided to take a dip in the pool.

Mrs. Dupre would be wearing considerably less revealing clothing when she next entertained guests at her new short-stay home."

Officer Matt Sharkey could feel the arrogance and lack of remorse the Sheriff had for this unfortunate young victim and said,

"You really can be a [son of a bitch], can't you Randy?"

"I'm sorry, Matt. I sometimes do get a little conceited about my work, but I did warn you I don't feel the remorse you probably expect from me," said Randy.

"Are you ready to tell me about the abandoned car and missing person involvement yet, or do you have any other, possibly more amusing stories to tell me?" asked Sharkey.

"I have lots and lots to tell you, but perhaps I just tell you about some of the more unusual happenings." said the Sheriff.

Sheriff Randy Dobbs turns a few pages until he gets to 2005, he places his finger next to five names dated 6/30/2005, and says, "These five young contributors unexpectedly bestowed their contributions upon me up on Caterpillar mountain in late June 2005."

Thur.	6/30/2005	Walter Hawkins	Multiples	Fire	Roxi, woods	Roxi
Thur.	6/30/2005	Ben James	Multiples	Fire	Roxi, woods	Roxi
Thur.	6/30/2005	Jim Reshper	Multiples	Fire	Roxi, woods	Roxi
Thur.	6/30/2005	Ron Eurell	Multiples	Fire	Roxi, woods	Roxi
Thur.	6/30/2005	Joe Rieely	Multiples	Fire	Roxi, woods	Roxi

"There was an alert out about a deranged killer that had attacked and killed a young couple in the Oreville area, and the State Police had tracked him to within approximately a 50-mile radius of Apollotown, which meant he could be with-in the Roxi town limits. my jurisdiction." said Sheriff Randy Dobbs.

"The heavily wooded area on caterpillar mountain, a mountain with wandering boundaries that make it look like a caterpillar from the air, was where he was expected to be. He was said to be heavily armed and extremely desperate to avoid going back to prison. A search was on to try and flush him out.

As I patrolled a highway near that vicinity, I saw a jeep with three young ladies and two young men alongside the roadway. I stopped to be of assistance and warned them about the fugitive that could be in the area. I asked them what their trouble was and found out that the jeep had overheated. The vehicle had cooled down and one young man was putting water in the radiator. I asked him how far he had to go, and he said they were heading back up to Tobins point where they were camping by the riverbank. I saw that all but one of the five youngsters, that ranged between 18 to 21 years of age, (at least for as much as I could see,) had sufficient body art to qualify as a contributor. I was concerned and bothered about the young lady that appeared to be without contributor credentials. I am strongly averse to harvesting even one non-contributor as it seemed sinfully wasteful.

That fact and that I needed to patrol for the fugitive, was holding me at bay. Besides, devising a way to harvest so many contributors and not leave a bunch of suspicious bodies lying around is not an easy thing to do, especially at a time like this. I was not adequately prepared to make the bodies disappear, and even if I were, that would only create more future hardships for me as I continued my crusade. So, I was just letting this opportunity pass, at least for the time being.

When the young man that was the driver began to get into the jeep, he took off his tank top that exposed the designs on his upper and lower arms. He also had a magnificent specimen on his back that mesmerized me and instantly made me realize I would go into a terrible deep depression frenzy if I passed up this fantastic opportunity. Maybe...just maybe, the other girl had a hidden tattoo. The jeep had cooled down by then, I wished them all well, and they drove off.

I noticed a strong smell of smoke as I got back into my cruiser. I thought I had smelled smoke on and off earlier throughout the day but dismissed it as probably from campfires. I looked up into the mountainside and saw huge bellows of smoke off in the distance; flames were also visible. I was going to call it in, but I didn't want to reveal my coordinates. The woods were extremely dry for there was a drought at the time.

I drove quickly towards Tobin's landing where I kept a small boat that I used for fishing. I strained to think of a way to collect those specimens without it being obvious that it was not by natural causes.

About halfway there, I heard a call over the police radio that the entire Apollotown side of Caterpiller Mountain was heavily engulfed in flame and a sudden wind shift might seriously endanger Apollotown. A massive fire-fighting effort was being executed to control and contain the fierce blaze. The wanted fugitive was named culpable for the fire. Authorities claimed he set it to interrupt and sidetrack the search for him.

That was the break I was waiting for. It gave me a great idea. I knew that the firefighting officials would employ their firefighting resources entirely on that side of the mountain. They would let the Tobins landing side burn itself out or to the river.

Once I got to my boat, I rowed about 100 yards from Tobin's point, went ashore, and waited for opportunities to induct each of the new contributors. To help cover my actions, as I subdued and rendered each inductee unconscious by compressing their carotid arteries. I drug four of them, the two young men and two young girls into their tent, made a fire, and sealed off the openings of the tent. After they were fully inducted and desired specimens were removed, I carried them one by one into a nearby grove of pine trees that had a deep bed of very dry, fallen pine needles. Spacing them inconspicuously away from each other was done so it would look as if they had been fleeing the fire when it came.

I baptized the confirmed non-contributor in some deep water until she resisted no more and haphazardly put her on a large log; knowing she would soon fall off and drift down the river. I overturned their boat and sent it drifting down the river to make it look like she overturned and drowned. I didn't have to hide any specimen removals with her, so I used the opportunity to help disconnect any possible link to inking's or other body art.

The fire spread up the mountain range just as I had anticipated. Days later, when the donors stalks were found, they were completely obliterated. There was never a question of foul play. However, an autopsy was performed on one well to do contributor, and it was determined that the cause of death was by asphyxiation, from smoke inhalation during the fire.

I always had to think very fast and act very quickly or my opportunities would slip away! It would almost always be easier to take the contributor to the Memorial. However, it would then be listed as another missing person. So, I always had to juggle my harvesting between various methods, abductions, murder, and accidents. That would draw less attention to each other and serve to confuse and mislead all of the various officials that were in any way involved. It would especially tie up their time so they couldn't spend much time on any one case.

Well, Matt, the time has come for me to get to the heart of the subject closest to your own heart, the abandoned car and missing persons cases," said Randy. "We can always come back to the other cases later if you want."

"That sounds like a good idea to me!" said Officer Sharkey, who couldn't wait to hear about the unfortunate car cases.

Officer Matt Sharkey had already heard so much and saw so much, he really could have used some time just to let it all digest. He was still perplexed about things, primarily because of some of the strange terminology Sheriff Randy Dobbs from Roxi was using to describe his victims and his actions.

Matt had thousands of questions going through his mind as he listened to Sheriff Randy to tell his adventurous stories. Though he was very much afraid to ask them because they could lead to specific ramifications and complications he did not feel adequately equipped to deal with at the current time. He also thought it might interrupt the process Randy was using to inform him of his escapades.

Officer Sharkey was a skilled interrogator, one of the best the State Police had. He always got the best results. However, he had still used some very heavy-handed and intimidating tactics to do so. This however, was not that kind of a situation. He was the one that was being intimidated and he didn't like it or know precisely how to handle it. This was a vast and utterly unchartered ocean he had to swim, and he didn't know how many sharks were in the deep waters with him.

To this point, taking the wait and see approach had at least seemed to be working well for him as he waited patiently for things to play out. However, it bothered him down deep, not knowing if he or Randy, or even possibly someone unknown to him was the one in charge.

This was the part of the puzzle that most perplexed Office Sharkey. Though somewhat comforted that Sheriff Randy did not use the words, we or us as he discussed his dastardly deeds to this point, Matt was completely insecure that it would be the case moving forward. He was also feeling anxious about the fact that no one had seen his car protruding the house by now and investigated it. Sheriff Dobbs continued to behave non-threatening and displayed the persona of someone subdued and relinquishing. He gave Officer Matt no reason to believe otherwise. Officer Matt, at least temporarily, shrugged off his fears and listened attentively as Sheriff Randy Dobbs from Roxi began to answer his most intriguing questions.

Officer Sharkeys throat was as dry as a desert, and his voice began to reveal that. However, as much as he wanted to ask Randy for a drink, he felt he was risking ingesting some poison or drug that would incapacitate him. Therefore, he kept quiet about it hoping at some point he would be directed to someplace where there was a natural water source or even a water fountain. He was getting pretty hungry and to complicate matters even worse, he was now starting to feel undeniable pain between his shoulders and in his neck. Symptoms that are usually synonymous with that of whiplash. Until now, he hadn't realized that the crash had caused him any short or long-term complications. His concern was primarily for anyone that might have been in the way of his car when it crashed.

32
Explaining the Abandoned Cars
Sunday, November 7th, 2010 1:45 pm

"In a little while Matt," said Sheriff Randy, "I'm going to go outside with you to show you the many things I'm going to tell you about now, so you can get the same picture in your mind that I have. There is much to see and much to tell, so I guess I'd better begin. I feel much more comfortable in this setting, talking to you alone."

Officer Matt took that as a preliminary statement of submission from Randy.

"Matt, I took the time to tell you about myself, my life and my family as I did, because it was important data for you to know how the pieces fit together as my account of happenings progresses," stated Randy. "You pretty much know [The who I am] now and have a pretty good start on [The what I am]. I'm hoping at this point, that no matter what you've heard me say, and or may hear me say, for some reason, you won't hate me. I feel that's the way it's been to now and I hope that stays the same case when I'm done."

Officer Sharkey did not respond.

"While gathering contributors," started Randy, "For my specimen harvesting, I was becoming more and more fueled to produce with each new specimen I added to my collection.

Since I started collecting, one of my main fears and concerns was that I would be stopped before I could complete a worthy Special Donors Memorial and Contributors Archive. I was feeling some days like the wolf was already at my back door so to speak. I knew I would be creating a lot of business and concerns for authorities long into the future. I felt that all the various authorities investigating the magnitude of strange occurrences I was and would be responsible for, would very soon make a connection between their victims and the fact that they all were walking inked body-art displays. I had to come up with and implement an on-going, and continuous diversion to ensure that never did happen.

I devised what I felt was an ingenious plan... the perfect plan, that would when implemented, derail any current and on-going investigations. I knew it would take many years to perfect and have this plan come together in a way that would create a confusing and fictitious timeline for my activities. The real meat and potatoes of my plan would all come in time, but I had to be very careful because my mother and father were still alive and living at the farm with me at that time.

The plan as I had envisioned it was to build a special collection and diversion vehicle, a truck, and a huge building to house the many things I needed to build and use for my plan to be successful. It would require a great deal of time, work, and money. I eventually got the money to build my truck, buildings, and tools from an insurance policy Grandfather had left to the family when he died in 1987. My mom, my dad, and I all got a third of it.

I also got money from an insurance policy when my Mom died in 1994 and again when my Dad died in 1995. I was financially sound for a person my age; I only really took the jobs I had then and especially the Sheriff job in 1996 to appear normal to those around me. The Sheriff job was what I guess you might, in my case, call a devil send. It was a natural fit for my plan and made it work beautifully, more productively, and much easier.

I initially spent all my night-time hours, weekends, and any other time I could get away from my daytime jobs, doing nothing but building my building, preparing for my acquisitions, and building tools. As time permitted, I worked on my own unique specimen related artwork, some of it you've already seen.

"Was that the huge building I saw across the way when I entered?" interrupted Sharkey.

"Yes, and it's special too!" replied Randy. "The mountainside on its north end, isn't just any old mountainside. It's part of the mountain that was owned by The Mc'Nullty Coal Company that mined coal from it for almost a century. Thought the old abandoned coal mine flooded way back before I was even born. It has several dry levels. All of it, at least to the best of my knowledge anyway, is unknown to any living person other than myself. My grandfather told me about it before he died in 1987. He was resting against the sloped side of the mountain one day after the land on that side of the mountain was purchased by his father, and while the mine was still in operation.

Grandfather could hear the miners talking to each other inside the mine. He never told anyone about it but me. I built up against and right into the mountainside. To the rest of the world, it is just a side of a mountain. The few miners that might have even suspected that the mine was so close to the surface died in the terrible mine explosion that flooded the rest of the lower mine tunnel on the very day that Grandfather told me about the voices. Yes. It that very same day, several miners were dead, and the mine was closed forever because it was thought to have flooded all the tunnels. I had always been curious about that tunnel he heard the miners in.

As I planned to build the huge building to house my trucks, I wanted to excavate about 40 feet into the mountain, stopping at what was my properties border with the mine. I would use the part of the building that was built into the side of the mountain as a cold cellar. Much to my surprise, I got the answer to the age-old question I had always had about the condition of the mine after I broke through the short surface separating the mine and daylight. The surface tunnel was not in any way altered or damaged by the explosion, and, it was bone dry! Getting a strong light, I explored the whole upper two tunnel levels. They were both very wide, and very high, much larger than I could have comprehended before I saw them with my own two eyes. Both were completely dry and in excellent condition. The tunnels below that level were filled with water as was the two large access shafts leading deep into the mine. I was profoundly hysterical when I found stacks of unused steel bars and rods of various sizes all leftover.

When I built my building, I did all the construction at the mountain end myself to hide the facts about the mine. I built a 12-foot-high by 16-foot-wide secret revolving door in the passageway leading from the north end of my building, into the first level tunnel of the mine. The door was designed, built, and installed to look like a turn-style on the end of the building for working on large vehicles. It was so inconspicuous that I was able to confidently hire a crew to complete the rest of the frame shell, roof, and siding. The builders were none the wiser.

Now that the building was built, all the workers had left for good, it was time to get the building furnished with the appropriate tools and start building my brainchild truck."

"Brainchild truck?" questioned Sharkey with that all so now familiar confused look on his face.

"Yes, that's what I said!" snapped Randy, unhappy about another interruption.

"Fortunately, for me anyway, he said continuing, I am multi-talented when it comes to being a craftsman, and I was able to do all the work that needed to be done myself. So no one would ever know I designed, developed, and possessed the devices I created.

Naturally, my plans primary objective was to enroll new contributors.

I would build a one-man operated enclosed box truck type vehicle, capable of hiding a vehicle inside it, yet hydraulically capable of operating like a rollback flatbed truck.

However, unlike a typical flatbed, my truck would be equipped with airbags, kind of like a city bus that lowers, or kneels and makes it easier for the elderly and disabled people to board. You've seen them.

My truck uses both the airbag system and a specially designed and constructed cam drive to reduce the steepness of the loading bed. It is state of the art technology and design. It would have to be able to move into various positions many times faster than that of a typical rollback, and it would have to automatically raise and lower the load bed door.

The truck had to be capable of much higher than normal acceleration rate and top speed. It would have to be capable of going long distances without refueling if necessary. It would have to operate without leaving any kinds of oil, water, gas, hydraulic oil, dripping, surface scraping, or otherwise obvious evidence. It would have to be and look inconspicuous. It would have to look identical to another vehicle that I would use for my Taxidermy and upholstery business so as not to draw attention to my movement of it on and about the roads and highways. It had to have four-wheel drive, for if it got stuck at an inopportune time, it could have serious consequences. The two trucks would have to never, ever, be seen together.

It took me several months, but using some bought materials and lots of the steel found leftover in the mine, I was able to finally design, build and test the perfect vehicle for my needs.

It has a programmable onboard computer that when activated like autopilot, would lock on a vehicle stopped anywhere in front of it, take over control of the truck from me, begin to reduce speed, pull directly in front of a stopped vehicle, very quickly, stop and reverse direction.

Simultaneously to, and near the end of the load bed positioning sequence, special suction-type holding cups are extended backward, out toward the vehicle's windshield. The cups attach themselves to any size or shape windshield by strong vacuum pressure. Unbelievable as it may sound to the novice car thief, the windshields are more than adequately capable of withstanding the amount of force necessary to pull the vehicle onto or push the vehicle off of the slightly elevated load bed platform.

As you now well know, I preferred to do this method of harvesting during the night-time hours, making it harder to be seen as there is much less traffic then. I installed dark out lighting, similar to that of military vehicles, making it difficult to be seen when I want it that way, and still enough lighting to function adequately.

It was vital for me to know when traveling at a speed of 65 miles per hour, and activating the onboard computer, exactly how long it took from the time the vehicles system locked onto the stopped automobile, until the car was loaded entirely and underway. So, I installed an automatic timing device that reads, records, and resets itself automatically. I have averaged only 32 seconds. The average would be lower than that, but I had a few initial bugs to work out. Sounds incredible, doesn't it? Vehicle drop-offs work similarly, but much easier and faster. From the time I physically stop the truck on the right lane of the highway, to the time I am back up to 65 M.P.H after a drop off is completed, I am averaging only 18 seconds.

I have patented both the idea, device and the procedure, (Without the enclosed box of course,) for obvious reasons. Made a bundle!" Randy bragged.

"Well, that's all very good for you, if you're running a night-time towing business. I know all this hoop-la is leading somewhere, how does all this fit with the abandoned car cases?" asked Sharkey.

"Backing way up again," said Randy, "I began to take advantage of any infrequent and random opportunities to plant the abandoned car scenarios. At night, when both mom and dad were soundly sleeping, I would slip away from the farm and drive to a town far away from Roxi. I told them I had work to do in the already existing buildings on the farm, so if they awoke and looked for me, they would not be concerned.

I would, while in disguise, visit some of the late-night establishments in the area where I went and engage in conversations with clientele. I would ensure that the subject of inked body-art would come up. If the potential contributor passed that stage of my criteria, I would find a way to leave the establishment with them, usually by asking for a ride. As quickly as possible, once we were away from the crowd, sometimes even before we got into the person's car, I would overpower and subdue my benefactor. Once in control, I would help them into their trunk, drive to the nearby place that I parked my vehicle, pluck the contributor from the field of society, [if they were still growing at that point], and then quickly harvest the specimen(s) they so generously donated and put them on ice.

I kept a small, but very fast minibike that I altered to travel longer distances on a tank of gas, in case the need arose, in the trunk of mine. I would displace the minibike with the contributor's now worthless and useless stalk. I would lay down and spread out another large plastic tablecloth in the trunk of the soon to be abandoned vehicle. This was to keep from leaving any traces of potential evidence behind when I was done with the vehicle. Fairly easily, I would throw my minibike into their trunk.

I would then drain or siphon all but half gallon to gallon of gas from the donor's vehicle. Putting on a disposable paper pair of overalls, disposable shoes, hair covers, and rubber gloves to ensure I left no forensic evidence, I would drive the procured vehicle on the interstate until it ran out of gas, coasting to a stop in the right-hand lane. I would always be very observant that no vehicles were trailing close behind me or coming in the other direction as the vehicle reached the expected time that the engine would stall.

Leaving the lights on, the shifting lever in drive and remembering to lock all doors, I would place change, belt buckles, and other items on the driver's seat as I exited the vehicle closing the locked doors behind me. I would then very quickly remove the mini-bike and the tablecloth from the vehicles trunk and drive the mini-bike back to my vehicle.

After I successfully reentered the interstate, I would return home unnoticed and store my gathered specimens in a specially prepared environment.

I only worried about leaving the evidence in the abandoned cars because I wanted the search for it to buy me time and take the focus off of my other ventures. Though I hated to do it, every once in a while, (very infrequently,) I took non-contributors to help keep the investigators from focusing on people with tattoos.

Officer Matt Sharkey was feeling very much more comfortable now. He was reasonably sure no one else was involved, at least at this point, or Sheriff Randy wouldn't have needed the mini-bike.

"So now, are you telling me that using this specially made truck vehicle is how you pulled off some of the abandoned car capers?' asked Officer Sharkey.

"No, not some," replied Randy, "After the truck hit the road for the first time, I used it for all the rest of the interstate recruitments."

"I think I understand the method of operation you employed, but why all the trouble and expense of the truck when the procedure you explained seemed to work so well?" asked Sharkey.

"The above procedure was very cumbersome and unreliable. It put me at too much risk and was limiting. One operation with my new truck and I knew I would never go back to the old way again — no more driving for many miles on a mini-bike, sometimes in the rain or frigid weather. I was no more trying to get the contributor to give me a ride. No more rushing to get the job done." replied Randy.

"Run me through a more typical truck abduction." asked Matt, "So I can get a clearer picture."

"I had performed twelve plucking's before I became Sheriff," said Randy. "Nine were using the mini-bike and one was by way of hitchhiking where I drove the contributor's vehicle to my farm. I never used that approach again. It was stupid, but it happened as an opportunity presented itself unexpectedly, and you know how I can get when I miss a chance. However, I could have sacrificed everything. Two were with the truck.

Once I was Sheriff, everything went much easier and smoother. Before then, I would load my car onto the truck and drive to a location that I wanted to perform harvesting. I swapped locations at random, on a whim, and sometimes because I didn't want to saturate any one area.

To remove or decrease the potential of being seen recruiting a contributor, I would find out where the person was planning on going when they left the nightspot. I would leave before they did, drive in the direction they said they were going, park the truck and unload my car. I would then pull next to the highway and wait until I saw headlights approaching and pretend I was having car troubles. As they closely approached, I would stick out my face so they would recognize me and stop to help. I would overcome them, take control, and have them open their own cars trunk. I would hand them a sturdy rubberized blanket and tell them to spread it down on the floor for them to lie down on and to cover themselves with because it may be a while till they are found, and they might get cold. This served to make them feel more reassured that they weren't going to be harmed, and they eventually climbed into their trunk. Afterward, I, using various methods, would pluck them from the vicious rigors of life's worrisome field.

I would then relocate my vehicle to a less conspicuous location and drive the soon to be charitable donor's car to the area where my acquisition truck readily awaited my return. In approximately 30 seconds, the donor's vehicle was loaded into my truck, and away I went back to the safety and security of my newly constructed specimen collection and processing building back at the farm.

Whether I was at the farm building or in the enclosed bed of the truck closer to where the vehicle was absconded, I was fully equipped to prepare the vehicle for drop off on the interstate. As soon as I was ready or when I desired, I picked the place on the interstate, stopped, and my truck did the rest. It was fast, it was clean, and it was fun!"

"You said once you were Sheriff, everything went much easier and smoother for you, tell me how please," asked Officer Sharkey.

"As I'm sure you gathered as I was telling you the story so far, finding a potential contributor was way too much work, and too time-consuming. It sure cut into my "Z" time! Once I became Sheriff and had my police car, the interstate virtually belonged to me and my ideas. I could pull my potential donor's car over at will and pluck qualified donors without drawing undue attention.

"But how on earth did you know the individual that you pulled over had any tattoos at all? Most of the people you [plucked,] were businessmen of sorts and wore suits and ties. Anything other than the face, head, and possibly some neck tattoos would have been covered up by their clothing?" asked Sharkey inquisitively.

"Very simple," said Randy, "I pulled many cars over, almost every driver on the interstate is speeding at least a few miles over the speed limit. I was doing my job. Of course, much of the time, I was doing it in a locale in which I didn't have any jurisdiction. I had to make it my business to know where my counterparts in those areas I visited and patrolled were at all times.

I had a close call one very dark early morning when I pulled a potential donor over in Benton, and he tried to shoot me when I approached his drivers door. I was fortunate the guy couldn't hit a battleship with an ocean. If he had killed or even injured me, the memorial would not be what it is today.

I shot and justifiably killed the much sought after fugitive driver that had a list of wants and warrants a mile long. However, I couldn't call it in because I wasn't supposed to be where I was when I stopped him.

Fortunately, or not so fortunate again, I'm not sure which, because upon a search of his body, I found not a single tattoo. It would have been a waste of my time, but then I got the idea to put the truck to good use in another way. I loaded up his vehicle, which by the way was stolen in Lansdale, and in about an hour, drove he and his car back across the Roxi town limits where I called it in and claimed credit for his capture. It sure helped at election time."

"You got sidetracked Randy; you never answered my question." reminded Officer Matt.

"Oh yeah, sorry Matt," said Randy, "Now, where was I? Oh, yes, now I remember. Of course, as a rule, I generally didn't have any idea about which drivers did and didn't have any tattoos when I pulled them over. Naturally, there were those times when through just plain luck, I would find out I stopped someone that I knew had inked body-art through some unique circumstance such as the time I finished this guy, Leonard Quisko."

Randy places his finger alongside the name of a 2002 contributor.

| Sat. | 8/31/2002 Leonard Quisko | Multiples | Shot | Beaumonte, Hwy. | New Mexico |

"You might remember Lenny, he was quite active in water sports, and they used him in many beach commercials promoting family visits to several of the areas inland beaches. He had a tremendous physique that sported many very colorful and decorative inked body designs. I met him once during a stay at a winter lodge several years ago."

"You're starting to stray again." reminded Sharkey.

"Sorry again." said Randy, "I don't mean to go on like that. Anyhow, like I said that was just plain luck."

"Typically, I induct the new contributor as soon as possible because I had a bad experience one time and I don't want to take the chance that something like that might happen again. However, in this particular instance, I only incapacitated my former acquaintance and brought him back here to show him what I was doing and how he would so nicely fit in with the rest of my artful contributors. We chatted for hours, and I wished at the time that I didn't have to pluck him. I think I came a little close to having some remorse for that induction, but I soon got over it."

Officer Sharkey was a little rattled by that exchange of words as false confidence was a fear he had that Randy might be doing with him!

"Randy!" said Sharkey as he gave the Sheriff a get back on track stare, "Tell me about the bad experience you mentioned then get back to answering my question about how you knew which travelers had tattoos, please!"

"O. K, bad experience first. Once, after I had made a typical stop and gone through my usual routine, I suddenly noticed a flash of light in a wooded area only about 100 yards from where the future donor and I were standing. I didn't know who or what it was. So, instead of using my noisy pistol, I unsuccessfully attempted to induct the young man with a tire iron. I had believed that my attempt was successful and quiet, but when I opened the trunk about a half-hour later, he was waiting for me and unsuccessfully attempted to liberate himself from my clutches. It wasn't the attack that prompted me to take more positive measures, but the fact that he could have cried out or banged on the trunk lid at a very undesirable and impromptu time. Now, getting back to your question, finally!" Said Sheriff Randy

"For the random car instances, it was a no brainer, I didn't need to know if the driver had any tattoos to pull a car over, but I did need to know to make a collection. So, after I made what appeared to the driver as being a routine stop, I would ask for their license and registration and tell them to wait in the car while I checked for wants and warrants. Naturally, if the stop wasn't in my jurisdiction, I wasn't interested in making an arrest. I would return to my cruiser for a minute or so as if I was calling in. Then I would approach the driver, who was still in the car in an obvious defensive manner and tell them there was some problem with their credentials. This would lead to me asking them if they had any other forms of identification or any other way they could prove they were the person of the name they claimed to be. I would get around to asking them if they have any identifying scars, marks, or tattoos. That always got them to come clean.

They were always a little frightened that they may be mistakenly in some real trouble and a whole lot more anxious to tell me about their tattoos if they had any. If they did possess critical donor criteria credentials, you know the rest. If they didn't, I would go back to my cruiser again and then return, telling them the mistake had been corrected, issue them a verbal warning and send them on their way with no one the wiser.

For most of the others, I had various ways of knowing, many times I saw them exposed enough to know before an induction. Sometimes I heard they had tattoos during conversations with someone who knew them well. However, most of the time, it is pretty obvious. Tattoos are fairly synonymous with gaudy over-excessive men and women's jewelry. Some wear tons of heavy chains and necklaces. I look carefully for tiny tattoos on fingertips, hands, and faces. Body piercing is another giveaway. In general, I have learned over the many years, be it man, woman, or a combo platter of both, if they are ostentatiously ornamented, you can be pretty damn sure they have accented their ensemble with some form of appreciable body-art inking's."

"You're very clever, and while I naturally can't condone what you've done, I sure do admire your creativeness and attention to detail." Said Sharkey, "It's just too bad you didn't use your genius for the good of society. You could be a true hero today!"

"What did you do with the bodies of the abandoned car and missing persons?" asked Sharkey.

"I gave them a fitting service and mass burial amongst other expired contributors." Said Randy, solemnly.

"Did you put their bodies in one of those mine shafts you told me about? Is that why you wanted the secret revolving door between your shop and the mine?" asked Officer Matt Sharkey.

"No, Matt." Said Sheriff Randy Dobbs of Roxi. "Follow me, and I'll show you where they are."

Randy lead Officer Sharkey side by side up a long winding pathway that led past the buildings and along the foot of the mountainside. It intersected a driveway, then through some heavily shrubbed and brushy area, about 100 yards from the nearest building. Hidden deep inside a maze of brush and other plant life, was a large round covered and well-sealed water well-looking structure approximately 35 feet in diameter. There was a ship hold like door and latching mechanism on the top surface of the structures cover platform.

"This is an old water well that my Great Grandfather had dug to have adequate water for the mine mules he sold or leased to the mine operators many years ago. When the mine explosion happened, it changed the course of the underground water, and the well went dry.

My father said that our water went into the now-defunct mine tunnels. I was very young when one-day my Grandmother told my Grandfather that he had better seal the well before someone fell into it. I think she was worried about me falling into it because no one else even knows that it is there, and no one ever is allowed in this area. Things do get a little ripe from time to time when I open the airtight hatch to admit a new contributor, but when it is closed, it seals everything in. I occasionally spread some lime over the contributor's stock to help the natural decaying process and hold down the stench."

"I think I've seen and heard all of this part of the story I want to." Said Sharkey. "Let's go back down!"

"What did you do with the bodies of your other missing persons," asked Sharkey.

"They're all resting quietly in the well too." Said Randy.

Officer Sharkey figured that this is probably as good a chance to unload his big question on Randy, as there was no one else in sight if he had to try to make a break for it.

"Does or did anybody else help you? Are you the only one involved?" asked Sharkey.

"It's just me." Said Randy. "I never needed or wanted to involve anyone else, and I don't think there is another living soul anywhere else in the world that would want to be part of this. I know it's bizarre and gross. Besides, I would never have wanted to share my accomplishments or my acclaim."

Officer Sharkey had been sweating bullets waiting for that reply. He now felt pretty confident that Randy had resigned to the fact that his pursuit of horrifying fame was over and was accepting responsibility for his awful unlawful actions. He figured Randy didn't care so much now as he once did because he had already met at least 80% of his main objective. Further activity would surely provide little more acclaim and recognition.

"Does or did anybody else ever know about your operation?" asked the officer.

"No one still feeling the heat of the sun," replied Sheriff Dobbs. That reply only served to renew some of Matt's fears.

"Are you ready to show me the rest of your enterprise now?" asked Sharkey inquisitively.

Officer Sharkey was hoping the tour might bring him with-in dashing distance of his weapon back at his car if he felt the need to take the opportunity. Even if the Sheriff was under the impression Officer Matt did possess a gun, as Officer Matt suspected he did, he was not holding it and pointing it at Randy.

He knew Randy could have made an attempt to overpower him several times before when they were so close to one another but he did not. They both knew Randy was younger, faster, and had superior strength. Because of the story, Randy told him about Leonard Quisko, the water sports enthusiast and how he showed him around and conversed with him before he killed him, he couldn't shake the feeling that Randy might be showing him around for his gratification and when he was done, he would try to jump him.

"I guess now is as good as good a time as any." Replied Randy. "Let me show you the building I've told you so much about."

As they a returned to the building's area of the property and while approaching the enormous new building Randy was so enthused about, Officer Matt felt the need to question Randy about the other structures.

"What are these other structures used for? Are they for your legitimate businesses?" asked Sharkey.

Randy pointed at specific buildings as he described their uses, "That one, the tall building, is the building I use for my taxidermy business. It is all because I used to have to hang many of my deer and bear hunting client's massive trophies to skin them out. Though I farm most of them out anymore, some seasons I'd have as many as 50 or 60 large game customers and many smaller mounts, like birds, fish, and rabbits. I do a pretty good business providing jackalopes for displays all over the country." Said Randy.

"Except for a new hide tanning and curing room I built into the new building, everything else was done right there in that building. However, of course, as I told you earlier, I do farm out the majority of my current business to another reputable shop. No one knows, not even the other shop's people, and no one complains. Everyone seems very happy with the work my business partners do.

The other shorter building is my upholstery business. Like the taxidermy business, I have one room that I built into the new building for more modern sewing machines. Everything else is in that building. I don't do very much of that work myself either. However, you know," said Randy, "even though I farm almost all the work to others, I still rake in some pretty good coin. There's much to be said for being a middleman. By the way, they are the only buildings, I ever allow my visitors and customers to enter."

Sheriff Randy Dobbs tours Officer Matt Sharkey through his massive new structure describing and explaining things as he goes.

"This building is specifically dedicated to the support and creation of artifacts for my Special Donors Memorial. I want to start by showing you the truck I built and told you so much about. This is something to tell your grandkids about. There's not another like it anywhere in the world." said Randy.

Matt liked the part about telling his grandkids about the truck, hearing that statement gave Officer Sharkey much relief. He now felt reasonably sure Randy was only too happy to have been discovered so he can get to tell his story to everyone. Sick as he was, and as sick as it sounds, Randy was proud of his accomplishments, and Sharkey was sure Randy wanted the world to know it. Randy gets enthusiastic as they approach his particular truck.

"Look at how well built this truck is, said he pridefully, weighs almost six tons itself! Powerful enough to move a small mountain! Here, lets pop the hood. Look at that engine! Full 540 cubic inches, fuel-injected, cranks almost 600 horsepower when the turbo's kick in, yet runs as cool as a cucumber even on the hottest days. Amazing ain't she?"

Randy says, "Watch this," as he reaches inside the cab and pulls out a handheld remote, startling Officer Matt momentarily as he thought he was possibly pulling out a gun.

"I can operate the entire truck and all its functions from outside the cab if I want to."

Randy pushes the start button on the remote, and the engine comes to life and though powerful sounding, it purrs like a kitten.

"Now watch," he commands. "I'll put her through a dry run load sequence. This button will make it all happen. Now, of course, I can also jog the machine through the sequence if I want to, but I want you to experience the speed at which the sequence is performed during an actual load cycle."

Randy pushes the button, and the sequence starts, the entire enclosed box of the truck begins to move upwards, and a vehicle Sharkey didn't even know was inside the enclosed box starts to move to the rear of the load platform. As the entire platform kneels to ground level, the door was already wholly open, the vehicles inside rear tires made contact with the floor of the building. Two long telescopic arms attached to suction cups that were holding fast to the windshield completed the unload cycle very gently and systematically. This was done by pushing the vehicle completely off of the load platform and on to the concrete floor behind the large truck.

Next, leaving the vehicle in place on the floor of the building, the procedure begins to reverse itself. The suction cups on the two long arms release their grip on the windshield. As the arms begin retracting, the load platform and enclosed box portion of the truck are being drawn back into its original position, and the door slowly closes.

Officer Sharkey was astounded at how remarkably fast and smooth the operation was.

"My God," remarked Sharkey emphatically. "This is genius! It's so damned fast I never could have imagined it, and it barely even shook the car!"

However, Officer Sharkey did have questions about what an automobile was doing inside the truck's enclosure. Of course, those questions would have to wait for the time being.

"Can you show me a reload?" asked Sharkey.

"Thought you'd never ask!" joked the Sheriff.

Randy ran the truck through an entire load sequence very much similar to the unload sequence except for the arms and suction cups firmly attached to the windshield assisting the vehicle being retrieved onto its load platform.

"I can see why the patent for this is worth much money to towing companies," Said Officer Matt, "But what if the car is in park and you don't have a key, or the brakes are left on? Solve that one and many car thieves will want your idea." said Sharkey snidely.

"That's never been a problem for me." said Dobbs, "I never leave a vehicle that way. However, if you remember correctly, there were a couple of standard shift transmissions involved. However, it proved not to be a problem as both the arms and the strength of the windshield were both superior in strength than the vehicles high gear resistance. Now, perhaps, if a vehicle was left in low gear, it could be too difficult to turn the tires and potentially cause the cups to lose their grip on the windshield or perhaps the windshield might fail or pull out of its mounting."

"Where's the person who owns the car that is on the truck? Was this vehicle intended to be another abandoned car case?" asked Sharkey.

"Let me answer your last part of your question first." said the

Sheriff. "No, this is not an abandoned car designate. I always turn an abandoned car over as quickly as I feel necessary before anyone has any idea that the driver was unaccounted for. It's less risky that way. You never could tell if the driver had very recently called someone on their cell phone and told them where they were at the time and maybe even told them they would call back soon. Nope, too many things can go sour if you wait too long.

To answer your first question, the driver has recently been admitted to the ranks of special donors. A designate not to be taken lightly. Her contributions are special because she is classified as a [multiples]. Multiples are someone that was unselfish enough to bear the pain and spend the dollars on providing my memorial with a multitude of unprecedented beauty. Most of my donors bring with them designs only adequate to meet donors criteria. I love it when contributors go out of their way to enhance the memorials status."

"In the well?" asked Sharkey.

"In the well." replied the Sheriff.

"What are you going to do with the car?" asked Sharkey.

"I'm glad you asked Matt," said the Sheriff. "I was just about to show you that part of my operation."

Randy Dobbs, leads Officer Matt to the mountain end of his new building and says, "This is where they go!"

Officer Sharkey looks for the secret entrance Randy had told him about earlier and sees no sign of hidden access to the mine.

"Where?" said Sharkey, "I see what looks like it might be the turn style you told me about, but if this is a hidden passageway into the abandoned mine, I'm a monkey's uncle." Said Sharkey.

Sheriff Randy walked over to an inconspicuous tile on a wall of tiles about six feet up and taking his open hand, pushed on the tile. "Won't work if I don't do this first. It's part of my failsafe system so someone at one time or another can't accidentally activate my secret doorway."

Randy then went over to a series of pushbuttons, and levered valves explicitly labeled to accommodate the use of the turn style in a typical fashion and not the passage door and said, "Because I activated my door system by pushing on the tile over there, these controls will now operate the entire revolving door hydraulically.

Once the door is in the open position, if I need or want a wider opening, I simply reposition the entire turn style and door system into the building and out of the way."

Randy is the perfect host and had demonstrated each of the door's functions much to Officer Matt's amazement, and when he was done, asked Matt if he wanted a snack.

Hoping to reduce some of the threat he still felt, Officer Matt Sharkey, tried to reassure Randy that things were going to be alright.

"Randy, we got to get you straightened out boy! The world needs your ingenuity!" stated Officer Sharkey with candor and believable sincerity.

"I'm flattered, of course." Said Sheriff Randy candidly.

Randy led Matt through the passageway and into the first level of the old mine. Randy had installed lighting on both levels, which made it easy to see the structure and contents of the shaft. Officer Sharkey must have expected to see a few cars, but what he saw, I'm sure he could never have fathomed. There were several dozen cars and trucks lining one whole side of the upper tunnel. There was a mini-school type bus quartered and stacked against the wall.

"Now, I know what you did with the other missing person cars that were never found." said Sharkey, "But what about this cut-up bus, did you do that too Randy?" asked the Officer.

"Yeah, let me help refresh your memory." Said Randy. "Do you remember the fax about the mini-bus load of possibly illegal immigrants suspected of selling drugs from Texas to Utah who were last seen in early March of 2009?" asked Randy.

"Yes, I remember that bunch," said Sharkey, "Some spooky people from what I heard. I thought they might be part of the cult bunch that all the rumors were about. Something happened to them. I think the feds were just about to pinch them when they seemed to disappear — last seen in our area if I remember correctly. You don't mean that this cut-up bus is the same bus the Feds were watching... or do you?"

"Yes, that's the very same bus." Said Randy kind of braggadocios.

"Mind telling me what happened to the passengers? Or... whoa... wait let me guess... The well?" asked Matt.

"The well!" answered the Sheriff, and he begins his story. "The stories a little lengthy... There were 21 occupants of the bus...."

As he speaks, Randy reopens his contributor's ledger and brings attention to a slew of names on the list all entered for the same day. March 10th, 2009.

"These are the contributors that once rode that mini-bus piled up against the wall." Stated Randy somberly.

"How in Gods gracious name did you ever subdue so many people on the same day?" asked Officer Matt Sharkey with awe.

"All the same day, all at the same time," said Randy as if it were no extraordinary feat.

"I guess I better start at the beginning and bring you up to speed as things transpired. There's no one I dislike more than drug dealers. Especially those that are thugs too! This group of degenerates had degraded the morale and character of youth all across the lower region. They destroyed lives and disabled families. It always seemed like there was never enough evidence against them to satisfy the law, and they were always allowed to continue their trade.

I didn't need a search and destroy order or judge and jury. When I found out they were selling to kids in my town, I decided I would do something about it. Not only because of their illegal acts, but also because I knew they were an anthill of tattoos and potential contributors. These types of contributors deserved much less than an honorable mention in the Special Donors Memorial, but I did grant that to them anyway because they helped serve as a necessary fabric to the overall design of my conquest.

Using a disguise and garb that I knew they would favorably and readily relate to; I drove up to where I secretly discovered them camping just off the main route into Roxi on a chopper that I had stored in my collection. I got friendly with them and offered them my barn and loft to them to stay in overnight as it did have toilet facilities and heat. It was a chilly day in March, and they were calling for thunderstorms throughout the nighttime hours. They accepted my hospitality as I was sure they would and drove right inside the barn where their bus would not be seen.

They knew the Feds were looking for them and wanted me to stash their drugs for them until the heat lifted. They told me they would reward me well if I did. I of course, pretended to accept their proposal and showed my appreciation by tapping a keg of beer for them that I had previously laced with insect spray. I had success using this approach before, so I used it again this time. It was entirely undetectable for they gorged on the whole keg and were already quite schnockered by the time the slow but potent poison began to take its effect. I joined them, to avoid suspicion, but I only pretended to drink from my pewter cup. No one noticed.

As I noticed some of my guests starting to feel and act

uncomfortable, I slipped away while I could, just in case the chemical didn't disconnect them all at the same time. It could have been very dangerous for me if they suspected I had poisoned them before they became disabled. I locked all the doors on the barn from the outside and waited until all the shuffling and sound of voices stopped. When it was safe for me to do so, I cautiously went back inside.

I was prepared to provide their final step into paradise if it were necessary; however, it was not. It sure was a lot less messy that way. I had a terrific fruitful harvest, almost half of those contributors were full body classified donors... They're the best kind! I had to cut their minibus into four pieces to be able to handle it enough to stack it as I did because even though it was considered a mini, it was too way too big and obstructed my tunnel too much. That immigrant event was my best and largest one-time harvest ever. That's a big reason why I reconsidered and gave that bunch of no good, drug dealing, child-corrupting, crop blighting, degenerate contributors honorable mentions in my memorial."

"I... I don't know what to say after a revelation like that Randy," Said Sharkey as he shook his head from side to side reciting the words, "Unbelievable... merely unbelievable. What do you have on the lower, second level?" asked Sharkey inquisitively.

"Why don't we just go see," said Dobbs.

Following the sloping tunnel, they soon reached the second level. Poor Old Officer Matt Sharkey, if there ever was a day he needed to remember to bring his Tums and Rolaids with him when he left home, this surely was the day. There lining the side walls were some of the most beautiful motorcycles he had ever seen in his life. He immediately recognized the markings on some of the bikes as those of typical low-life, scum bags, and gang members.

"Want to tell me where you got all these?" questioned Matt.

"Lot of different stories there." Said Randy. "Perhaps I can fill you in on all of them at another time, but for right now, why don't I focus on the longer lists I have in my ledger. That'll give you the most bang for your buck.

It was Tuesday, September 18th, 2007... Not too long ago, I'm sure you'll remember it. There was a fire at Brad Wates farmhouse over in Bedloe. You, I, and all available team members helped investigate it." Said Randy.

"I...do...I do remember it...I remember it well... very well." Said

Sharkey, "We investigated it because we thought there might be a link between it and the abandoned car cases. We were heavily into the theory that cult activity may be in some way involved and these bikers seemed to portray the persona typical of some of the cult groups supposedly seen. As I remember it, we never really knew for sure how many people were consumed by that fire because it had burned at such a hot temperature that most of the bodies were virtually disintegrated. Forensics suggested there was evidence supporting the possibility of as many as seven bodies."

Officer Sharkey stopped momentarily as his mind computed what this conversation was leading to, and as he continued, he said, "You...you set...did you set that fire?" Sharkey asked Randy excitedly.

"I'm afraid I did," answered Sheriff Randy Dobbs of Roxi, "They're all right here in the ledger." Randy shows Officer Matt the names on the ledger.

"I see seven names." Said Matt, "I guess that answers the question of the number, doesn't it?... But why? Why, did you do this one? Were they terrible people, or were their motorcycles a motivator? Why?" pleaded Sharkey.

"Why I'm surprised at you Matt, weren't you listening, or did you suddenly forget whom you're dealing with here? You know I don't do these things for money." inserted Sheriff Randy, sounding a little perturbed by Matts questions.

"Sorry, it's just that...I guess I would never have suspected it." returned Sharkey, trying to mend the most recent damage fence between him and Randy.

"It's okay Matt. I surprise myself sometimes." comforted Randy.

"If I remember correctly, we never did identify any of the remains... did we?" asked Sharkey.

"Your right, Matt, we didn't, but I sure did." said Randy. "I've got names and addresses in my keepsakes file and ledger."

"We never could find any evidence about how many bikes might have been removed from the site of the fire, do you keep track or remember how many there were?" inquired Officer Sharkey.

"I requisitioned seven bikes at that time and numerous choice specimens. The last seven bikes in the left row are from those contributors and are intended to be part of the archive. Brad Wate also had a motorcycle. He made seven."

"Want to tell me how you pulled that one off?" asked Sharkey.

"Sure, happy to," said the Sheriff. "I patiently waited as they partied, after the tractor trailer driver left, using my gun, I harvested them all through the window after they were all so high to even care. I knew that the old house of tinder would burn hotter than hell and destroy any potential evidence.

"I don't understand, how did you know these bikers were going to be at that old farmhouse so far away in Bedloe?" questioned Sharkey.

"You might remember Tom Adams, the tractor trailer driver that lives by me in Roxi? I told you about him and how he tailgated and forced my girl Marge Betley off of the road with his rig. I had a vengeance against him and just knew if I followed him when I had the chance, I would sooner or later get something big on him, something big enough that I could hold over his head to keep him off of Marge's and my back. I was following him the late-night when all this happened. Though improper and illegal, nothing big developed. However, I did go way out of my way, and the opportunity was there."

"You told me the bum looked like a freak and was covered with tattoos from head to toe himself, why have you never harvested him? That would have made many of your troubles go away." asked Sharkey.

"That is an excellent question, Matt." Said Randy. "There have been times that I've asked myself that very same question. It took great restraint on my part, but I just kept telling myself that there will be a better time to do it, and he would not escape me forever. Naturally, I could have very effortlessly enrolled him at any time, but it served me well to keep him out there. After all, he was getting the blame from a lot of the townsfolk for things I did. It kept the focus on Tom and not I. I never felt he was a real threat to society," answered Randy.

"I seem to remember that there was another mass fire at a tire store long before the farmhouse fire in Bedloe that we talked about at the time of the Bedloe fire. Got the skinny on that one, have you?" asked Officer Matt.

"Are you referring to the tire store fire in Beaumont, back in 1997?" asked Sheriff Randy.

"I believe that's the one and something tells me you're going to know all there is to know about that fire too... aren't you?" asked Officer Sharkey.

"Why, as a matter of fact, I do just so happen to have that data on my contributors ledger here." said Randy, with a slight chuckle.

"I had been seeing advertisements promoting body-art club

memberships for several years. It had stirred my imagination and interest, but I didn't know a lot about it. Then one day late in 1996, I watched a television commercial about this huge body-art convention to be held in Beaumont sometime in December of '97.

They showed clips of the activities from their previous events, and I became like a kid in a candy shop. Members and would-be members from all over the country were going to be there. It was a crop that promised to produce a desirable yield. I planned to get the most I could get out of that field. I knew if I were unsuccessful, I would probably lose the only chance I would ever get to harvest my share of the bounty. Though the conventions were held yearly, they rotated their crops so to speak, and it would be held in a different field in the future; probably someplace very far away from Roxi.

I knew with the vast number of these body-art club members and future club members coming to town, that the town would be packed, and I knew accommodations would be scarce. So, I had planned to rent a building in advance and sublet it to my potential contributors, whoever they might be when they arrived without reservation hoping to find anything available. I, in disguise, visited Beaumont and found out that everything had already been booked for almost a year ahead of time. The convention was an even much bigger event than I had imagined. I worried about the success of my plan.

Sure, the convention was going to be big, and many residents had signs in their windows offering a room here and there, but that was all there was. Many residents that feared that kind of visitors had already put up [keep out] signs. Others planned to be anywhere but Beaumont when the convention hit the town. I continued to visit Beaumont from time to time, looking for a possibility.

Finally, by the grace of the devil himself I suppose, I heard a story about a vicious murder that happened in an apartment complex that was built above The Beaumont Tire Company store a few years earlier. It had been vacant for about three years and pretty much forgotten because no one would ever stay there.

In disguise, and posing as a convention member, I convinced the owner to rent the complex to myself and other fictitious convention-goers just for the time the convention was to be held. I straightened the place up a little bit, enough to attract my potential contributors, and waited for the big day to arrive.

When I arrived late evening on the day before the convention, I had a van, and it was filled with 12 jugs of illegal moonshine that I again in disguise bought from a bootlegger way up in the mountains. It was some pretty damn good stuff if I do say so myself, and it was plenty potent. However, it was a hell of a lot more potent when I got done lacing it with the same insect spray that I used on the illegal immigrant drug dealers in March of 1999. It worked well for me for this induction that's why I used it for the immigrants I told you about earlier. I always stick with a winner; the results are more anticipated that way. The ridge runner I bought the mash from said you could run a farm tractor on those squeezing's.

It didn't take me very long to engage a group of 13 very unlucky young men and women. They were resigned to the fact that they would be sleeping in their small bus because they could find no accommodations. Their bus driver wasn't at all happy about that because he had a sleeping bag for his use to avoid paying for a room.

The 13 young people however, were now ecstatic to have found an apartment complex, especially because it was within walking distance from the convention center and was located in a part of the town where all the exciting things were happening. The youngsters had big party plans of their own for that evening and well into the morning hours. They brought in a half keg of beer and a box of various kinds of liquor. After they got all settled in and the fun was well underway, I brought in a jug of mountain go-go juice from the van and passed it all around. As that jug was near expended, I sent a couple of young men down to the van to bring up the rest of the jugs and watched them party hearty.

There was only one way in or out of the level the party was on, and that was via a stairway located on an inside wall of the tire store storage room. The joint was perfect for my needs because the only door was at the top of the stairway and it opened in towards the stairway of the tire storage. Besides the 13 bus load people I had targeted to stay in the complex, there were only two other people at the party that were not with the bus people. Afraid to act because I felt others that knew the two strangers might come to the complex looking for them, I waited patiently for them to stagger out. Within minutes, the bus group was either sound asleep or in a stupor. After just seconds, I had initiated my new club members, no one resisted. It required two clips. Fortunately, I was cautious about placing my shots appropriately this time. When I confirmed that all contributors had indeed expired, I took my memorial pictures, then I harvested all the specimens and other human keepsakes, put them on some ice, bagged them in drip-proof body bags, and carefully placed them into the safety of my van. It was a bigger job and took much longer than I thought it would. All of the contributors were of full-body status. Some of them took almost twenty minutes apiece to de-hide without damaging any of the specimens.

When I had acquired all that I wanted, I heavily doused the entire complex wherever any of the donor's leftovers was setting. I also doused the door and the complete stairway with almost all of the remaining alcohol and mash. I firmly forced a 2 x 4 between the doorknob and a stairway wall stud, just in case I might have inadvertently missed someone in the room, and they were still alive inside.

I had already prepared a stick with a rag tied to it to be utilized as a torch and prepped my van for a quick departure. I checked the street and alley, and when I was utterly sure no one was around to see me, I poured some mash on the rag, lit it and threw it into the open bottom stairway door. The alcohol was much more volatile than I had anticipated and when it ignited, it sent me ass over tin cups. When the wall where the van was parked got blown apart, it hurled large pieces of brick against the van, smashing its windshield. Fortunately, though bruised and in pain as I was, I was still able to reasonably quickly get into the van and drive away before anyone saw me. I only had to drive about one-half mile to get to my waiting super truck and load the van for its long trip back to the farm.

I had almost left the truck at the farm thinking I probably wouldn't need it, but at the last minute, I foresaw the possibility of my needing to ditch the van quickly, so I changed my mind and brought the truck with the van inside it. It's a good thing I did, or I would have had some real problems! By the way, that's the van I used over there. I borrowed it from one of my contributors who wasn't using it."

Sheriff Randy pointed to the van in the tunnel.

"I could write a book about you and your escapades Randy! Probably make a pretty damn good movie too," said Officer Sharkey.

"Thank you, Matt! Responded the Sheriff, "But nobody would ever believe it. That's why I had to show you in person." he said.

"No one suspected foul play?" asked Sharkey.

"No," said Randy, "The driver of their bus identified the people because he had a list of the names of the people that rode his bus into town, and he knew that complex was where the group was staying. There was absolutely no kind of incriminating evidence left behind, the alcohol, the rubber tires, an old dry structure. There was nothing left. No one had a cause or any reason to think it was anything other than careless drunken behavior that resulted in a massive loss of life."

"You say your motive is specimens, but you seem to have a thing for motorcycles too, are you sure these bikes don't encourage you?" asked Officer Sharkey.

"They're simply synonymous with each other, that's all." Replied Randy

"There has been a boatload of missing person reports involving motorcycles, other than the ones you were involved with and already told me about. Would you happen to know anything about those missing people too?" asked Officer Matt.

Sheriff Randy Dobbs looks into his ledger and shows Officer Matt one particular name.

"This guy here, Tuggy Thrautle. It was just by pure coincidence, happened as I was bringing the van back to the farm the night of the fire in Beaumont that we just talked about. His bike had broken down. I saw him very obviously decorated and standing by it at the roadside. I stopped. There was no one around.

You know the rest. In all likely hood, he would very well have been sent to Munson's, but I sure liked his bike. That's it, the impressive blue one at the front of this next line of bikes." Said Randy as he pointed to the right-side wall of the tunnel.

Tue.	12/18/1997	Tuggy Thrautle		Full body		Shot	Roxi, Hwy.	Cali.

"Truth be known Matt, as I'm telling it to you now, I'm probably responsible for every last one of them! See the rest of the line of bikes on the right side of the tunnel, I got them all in one operation." Bragged the evil but very resourceful Sheriff.

"Please... Please... tell me about how you pulled that one off!" pleaded Officer Sharkey. "I can tell by the markings on some of those bikes that they must have belonged to some awful treacherous thugs!"

Sheriff Randy Dobbs places his finger at another group of names in the ledger all with the same date by their names and says, "See this list of contributors here Matt, all bikers every damn one."

Thur.	8/13/1998	Bill Finch	Full body	Shot	Roxi, barn	Cali.
Thur.	8/13/1998	Larry Jones	Full body	Shot	Roxi, barn	Cali.
Thur.	8/13/1998	Barb Rycz	Full body	Shot	Roxi, barn	Cali.
Thur.	8/13/1998	Joe Savinchino	Full body	Shot	Roxi, barn	Cali.
Thur.	8/13/1998	Sheb Gansanocho	Full body	Shot	Roxi, barn	Cali.
Thur.	8/13/1998	Miguel Venchenso	Full body	Shot	Roxi, barn	Cali.
Thur.	8/13/1998	Melvin Dorknocker	Full body	Shot	Roxi, barn	Cali.
Thur.	8/13/1998	Marie Garnicko	Full body	Shot	Roxi, barn	Cali.

Thur.	8/13/1998	Many Sanchez	Full body	Shot	Roxi, barn	Cali.
Thur.	8/13/1998	Tony Rodrigues	Full body	Shot	Roxi, barn	Cali.
Thur.	8/13/1998	Julio Hernandez	Full body	Shot	Roxi, barn	Cali.
Thur.	8/13/1998	Jose Feluendez	Full body	Shot	Roxi, barn	Cali.
Thur.	8/13/1998	Gomes Gomes	Full body	Shot	Roxi, barn	Cali.
Thur.	8/13/1998	Jose Salinas	Full body	Shot	Roxi, barn	Cali.
Thur.	8/13/1998	Rita Mendoza	Full body	Shot	Roxi, barn	Cali.
Thur.	8/13/1998	Rhonda Jaimenez	Full body	Shot	Roxi, barn	Cali.

"They're less than a year after the Beaumont fire bunch!" said a surprised Sharkey.

"Almost eight months to the day," said Sheriff Dobbs.

"They were a mob of drug-using, drug dealing, no-gooders' from a California strain of vermin. The grapevine had it that they were spreading out to diversify their territory and planned to terminate the Roxi and Apollotown area. There had been an awful lot of buzz about escalating motorcycle traffic, increased muggings, and violence. It was apparent we were in the early stages of a complete take over or infestation as I like to refer to it. Because the weather was warming up when they slithered into our community, they had initially taken up a residence in a large secluded area of Silver Swan Lake, part of a still existing Indian reservation. Due to that distinction, they were out of the jurisdiction of the law enforcement agencies that protect the towns they were encroaching on.

As you've probably observed by now, I believe in reapplication. When I get something that works well for me and isn't difficult to do, I don't waste my time trying to find alternative ways. I figured there was a reasonably good chance that at least one of the biker members would be able to recognize me if they saw me. I may have already arrested one or two of them for all I knew, or they might have seen my picture on TV or in the paper. With what I was planning to do with this dangerous, bloodthirsty bunch, I surely would be doomed if I were revealed.

I did this by wearing one of my many disguises and engaging the use of one of the bikes from my collection, once owned and driven by another contributor named Calvin Gooch. Gooch is from a gang in Chicago, nicknamed "Gooch God" who about two months earlier had made me the beneficiary.

Little by little, I wormed my way in and became known and accepted by the gang. Like all branches of society, what you drive reflects who you are. I figured there was little chance that gang members from California would recognize a bike from a gang member in Chicago.

I waited patiently, and then one day before the gang had a chance to acquire and take up residence in a building, it was getting very stormy as thunder and lightning moved into the area. Naturally being the sharing host that I am, I did like I did with the illegal immigrants and offered them the use of my warm and cozy barn till the weather cleared. More concerned about their great bikes than themselves, they graciously accepted the accommodations. They were as unruly a bunch of degenerates as I've ever had the misfortune to encounter and I was getting increasingly worried that they might accidentally set my barn on fire. They acted and behaved extremely stupidly, brains burned out from too much exposure to the use of some nasty drugs I presumed.

I had to act quickly. Things were getting explosive. I was second-guessing my decision to use this approach with them. I had never seen or even imagined how an extremely animal like a human being could be, and it was a damn good thing I was well prepared beforehand. A half-hour of my time and a half keg of beer with a vermicide chaser was a small price to pay for getting those vermin off the streets forever and for their fabulous bikes. It was scary for a while, but so easy and so handy too, I wished I could centralize all my recruiting like that. I felt like putting a sign on my barn that said Memorial Donors Recruiting and Induction Center."

"Besides this group of outcasts, that I didn't even know about before," said Officer Sharkey, "I knew approximately two dozen bikers were missing over the last ten years. Seven were accounted for during the September 2007 incident you told me about in Bedloe, the Tuggy Thrautle one in December 1997 on your way home from the Beaumont tire fire makes eight, what happened to the other 15 or so bikers?" asked Sharkey.

"There were another sixteen motorcycle riding contributors that I plucked from random fields during the period you're asking about." explained Randy, "Most were role model contributors and not bad people."

"I've even had a few bikers that no one, at least as far as I know, ever reported as missing. Ain't that a real bouquet of flowers for ya? Nothing particularly interesting to tell you about them, I don't think you want me to go into each one, do you?" asked Randy.

"No, not right now anyway." Said Officer Matt.

Officer Sharkey looked around at all the many sites to see in the tunnel and in the large building itself. It was apparent that both men were feeling somewhat spent. When Sheriff randy suggested, "Well, I guess there's nothing else to show you in here. If you like, let's go back to the house, and I'll go over the memorial items with you, especially the photos. I'm sure that will initiate a lot more questions." Said Randy innocently.

Officer Matt Sharkey agreed, but before he left, he said to Randy, "There must be tens of thousands of dollars worth of bikes in here."

"You're much too conservative, Matt," said Randy, "There are hundreds of thousands of dollars worth of bikes in this tunnel. I estimate the approximate street value of these professionally and specially designed and built bikes at between $350,000.00 and $500,000.00, possibly more. As there are no living owners to claim them, I hope they will always stay with the unique Donors Memorial treasures."

"Ya know Randy," said Officer Sharkey, "You're a tough guy to figure out! Sometimes, as you tell me about your adventures, I can't help but think that you did more good for society than you did bad. If it weren't for the good, clean, innocent people..." Officer Sharkey paused for a second, shook his head, and said, "I don't know... I can't figure you out!"

"Oh, I'm no Robin Hood by any stretch of the imagination, I never pretended to be, I have always had my own selfish agenda and reasons." said Sheriff Dobbs.

"I know a lot of the people you snatched were obvious tattoo wearers, but how did you know who was going to be available for you to snatch, and how did you know the less obvious people had tattoos?" asked Matt.

"If one is patient, everything will have its time. Watch and observe... watch and observe, that's what it's all about." said Randy, "Have a plan and be ready when the time does present itself to you. Be prepared for unexpected opportunities. They come when you least expect them. As far as how did I know who had tattoos that weren't obvious or visible to me, I think it's like being a cop. After a while in the business, you may not be able to prove something, but you know it's so. However, sometimes I was wrong. That's why being a Sheriff made it easy for me to let someone that was a non-contributor go and keep my confidence."

"Did it bother you more to harvest women than it did men contributors?" asked Sharkey saying afterward, "Now just listen to me will ya, you've got me thinking and talking like you!"

"Many of my contributors were women. I firmly believe that many people will think I harvested them because I am misogynistic. This is not true. I am particularly fond of women, young or old, short or tall, heavy or not so heavy. That's part of the reason I took that sleazeball Arthur Owind that I told you about before, to protect them from him." said Randy. "I hope my legacy isn't affected by this perception."

"You've continually used the word [non-contributor], why I'm sure if any of your memorials donors had a choice, they would not have been contributors?" asked Sharkey.

"A non-contributor was a diversion, simply someone that had no obvious inked body-art or tattoos."

"You've done so many different kinds of harvesting of contributors, on the surface at least, it sounds like the abandoned car routine didn't produce near the number of contributors your other methods did," said Sharkey.

"The abandoned car routine was almost more trouble than it was worth as far as acquiring specimens go and netted me a tiny percentage of my specimens. Its whole intent and purpose was entirely to give the authorities something to keep their focus on continually. I wanted to take away the urgency from the other seemingly more insignificant incidents that were happening. This allowed me to be able to interface with the people investigating so I could always stay abreast of and knew what they were doing and planning at all times. It worked pretty well, and the majority of my contributors, which were quite extensive, were just those types of random incidents that few people cared about.

Everyone was focused on the abandoned car and missing persons cases. You were a nobody in law enforcement in this area unless you were trying to help catch the abandoned car abductor(s). I threw in the abandoned car that was at operating temperature because I knew it would interrupt the investigations focus as we knew it before the diversion. I also sacrificed an insignificant contributor, that's one with just a few or lousy tattoos instead of a non-contributor because I figured if I didn't, it would be too obvious and stand out that the real abductors took people with inked body-art and the imposters didn't.

The abandoned car routine served me quite well in other ways also. I was privy to other peoples comings and goings. Being a Sheriff, people are free with what sometimes is quite critical information because they feel trust in me. You remember that Mrs. Silvermann from Beaumonte case, who was thought to have been an authentic abandoned car case and whose car was found in Championsburg. Then was determined to be a hoax because she showed up alive and well, never really was missing."

"Oh, come on now...Damn it! You... you did that too! No... No... you didn't...I refuse to believe it! You... You couldn't have done that. You just got to be shittin' me now, aren't you? How could you have possibly known she left town and when?" asked Officer Matt, surprised to no end.

"As I told you, people tell you things when you're a Sheriff! The shuttle bus driver from the Hilltown Hotel in Championsburg that takes guests to and from their hotel and airport, just so happens to frequent a coffee shop that I always patronize when I'm in the area. We've grown friendly over the years. Of course, I don't wear my actual Roxi Sheriff's uniform when I visit the shop as that would be too telling. The uniform I employ is one of the same ones I use for my abandoned car capers. I have a couple of dozen different uniforms with various fictitious towns names on them, as does my cruiser. I have a complete array of magnetic decals from as many as thirty different fictitiously named towns that I can quickly and easily swap out on my cruiser at will."

"Anyway... getting off track again, ain't I?" said the Sheriff. "So when my friend, the shuttle bus driver, told me during a casual conversation about how he saw Mrs. Silvermann getting out of a cab and taking her luggage into the airport terminal, I became very interested in what he had to say and listened very carefully.

I asked my friend some sporadic questions about Mrs. Silvermann, just enough to learn some things but not enough to get his suspicion. Mrs. Silvermann was known by him always to be chauffeured when she went to the airport and never toted her bags. She unknowingly attracted an awful lot of attention to herself by arriving by taxi, handling her baggage, and being unescorted. It stirred up a lot of rumors and even more when somehow the grapevine revealed that she had gone on a cruise. The granddaddy rumor was that she was having an affair behind her husbands back and was meeting her lover for a secret rendezvous on the sea.

Though I was there with my truck to hopefully recruit a new contributor, I am one to recognize an opportunity when it presents itself to me. I did some quick thinking and came up with a plan. So I displaced the chance to get an actual contributor with the chance to sidetrack or derail the new procedures you and the abandoned cars team were putting in place to catch or deter the abandoned car kidnappers.

My friend, the shuttle bus driver, described her car to me and told me where she usually kept it, but the car was not where it should have been. I started putting two and two together and figured she probably left home with the car to put on a normal appearance when she left and probably left it in a parking lot or garage close to the pier. Getting the license number from the division, knowing the make, model, and color of the car, it didn't take me long to find it parked in a large warehouse and superstore parking lot.

I donned another of my many disguises, and while wearing my mock Sheriffs garb, I drove my cruiser to where the car was parked. Just in case I was being watched by someone that I did not see, I took on the appearance that I was looking the vehicle over officially by pretending to be placing some calls about it from my cruiser. Afterward, I jimmied the locked door reached inside and placed the transmission lever into the neutral position so I would be able to load it on my truck later without resistance. Then I relocked the doors and drove away. I felt confident that the parking area was not monitored for if it had been, I most likely would have been approached and questioned.

Changing the magnetized decals on my cruiser again, I found a concealed place to park it and waited till after dark to retrieve the automobile with my super truck.

I dropped Mrs. Silvermann's car off where it was found and left no personal wear items on the drivers' side front seat as I usually did, because I had none to leave.

It made a difficult trip for me because it was at the furthest point that I recruit away from my. There was also the fact that I had to put as much distance between where I acquired the car and where I deposited it as I could. All while staying still with-in the Championsburg town limits to make it harder for there to be any connections with the found vehicle and my recent inspection of it in the parking lot. I was usually able to dump the acquired car when I had it ready only a short distance away from my cruiser, return to the cruiser, load it quickly and be on my way in no time. However, this time, I had to drive the car much further.

"So that's how you did it!... Damn clever... damn clever!" said Sharkey, "No wonder we couldn't figure it out."

"I do my best Matt," said Randy.

"Still, there's something puzzles me." Said Sharkey, "If you had murdered these people, how come we found fingerprints from some of the abandoned car victims and even other missing persons at crime scenes across our networking area very much after the person(s) had been reported as missing, like at the burning scarecrow scene?"

"Damn!" said Randy, "I wish you wouldn't use words like murder and kill. It sounds so harsh!"

"Anyway, it was all part of my total diversion plan to cloud your investigative process. I removed either the thumb or forefinger from each contributor that would go missing. I would tag and freeze the digits until I needed them. Each time I did need to use one, it immediately removed the missing person status for that particular individual and cast shadows on other cases as well."

"I don't know why forensics wasn't able to find any trace of evidence in any of those abandoned cars." Said Sharkey. "You must have slipped up at one time or another."

"You express such a lack of confidence in me Matt, you hurt my feelings!" said Sheriff Randy, "I always took the proper precautions, hospital-issued shoe coverings, disposable overalls, gloves, and everything. Though I sometimes used blankets in the trunk to hide blood and other evidence, I learned I preferred making the recruitment at the original stop and placing the contributor in a body bag, then driving far away and leaving the original crime scene far behind. Nothing was ever found at the crime scene, because the location the abandoned car was found, never was the site of the crime."

As Officer Sharkey and Sheriff Randy started to walk back to the farmhouse, Officer Sharkey began to have feelings he couldn't shake. For some reason, he felt very uncomfortable about entering the farmhouse again. He had a feeling as if he was going to be entrapped, but he knew if he didn't go, he would miss out on a lot of the information that Sheriff Randy was about to share with him. Keeping his composure, Officer Sharkey resisted his impulse and went into the old farmhouse with Sheriff Randy. Once inside the farmhouse, but before entering the room where the memorial was, Sheriff Randy stopped at the doorway to the room and turned on several light switches.

"I turned on the lighting for the collages in the room." said Sheriff Randy, "It'll light up the individual collages on the walls around the room so you can see each one much better. Look them all over, and we'll sit down again and talk about them."

Officer Matt Sharkey examined every one of them intently. You could tell by the look on his face he was utterly overwhelmed, and his rapidly balding head was bursting with questions. He took notes as he examined the pictures so he wouldn't forget to ask some questions. Officer Sharkey didn't particularly know what to make of the collages. He wasn't quite sure what all this information in front of him was telling him, but it certainly did not look right to him, and now again Sheriff Randy appeared more fearful to him.

Officer Sharkey stopped short of examining all the collages on the walls; he stopped and looked around the room that was slightly better lit than it was when he had been in the room before. He looked to see if there were any other crimes related articles in the memorial. He could see nothing else. The only other things in the large room beside his smashed automobile was the bunch of furniture and lamps that were covered to keep the dust off of them.

Officer Sharkey turned towards Sheriff Dobbs and said, "I'm too overwhelmed. There are just too many questions for me on these walls. Let's take one wall at the time and discuss what we've seen."

"Sounds good to me Matt," said Sheriff Randy, "Let's go sit down where we were before, and I'll fill you in by answering any questions you have at all."

They both made themselves comfortable, and the questioning began.

"I noticed that all of the collages have naked pictures of your victims included, why is that?" asked Officer Matt.

"I have one of those new state-of-the-art cameras now and I've always carried it with me since I bought it," said Sheriff Randy, "It's just kind of a before and after thing to me and it kind of helps to show appreciation for the magnitude of the transition between the contributor and their sacrifice for the memorial. It's much easier to get my pictures now than it used to be when I started. Because I couldn't take my pictures for developing before, for the obvious reasons, I had to use an old cumbersome, but useful Polaroid camera that was capable of producing its images almost instantly. However it was a somewhat slow process and limited my ability to get lots of pictures. My new one is great. I can take all the images I want and only develop the ones I want without anyone but me seeing them."

"How perfectly wonderful for your...your clients," remarked Sharkey sarcastically.

"The newspaper headlines that accompany many of your subjects in the collages seem to speak of people and events that seem dissimilar to those of your normal contributors," said Officer Matt, "For example, the articles about the young men that were eaten by wolves or pigs."

"I can appreciate your perception of that, especially after the tour and stories I told you," said Randy, "But they were my creations too. Quite frankly, there have been few strange happenings anywhere within the abandoned car and missing persons perimeters that weren't of my doing. From abductions at or from bars, dance halls, parks, and even a few at churches. If you can believe it, I could devise and execute to any strange or bizarre accident such as a chainsaw, woodchipper, bush or brush hog farm accidents. Even the incidents the F.B.I. the thought was either mob or drug cartel related, I did them all! I had to find ways... as many ways as I could to get my specimens without people knowing or even suspecting that I or anyone else for that matter were gathering them."

"It seems that it was just so much energy and trouble in most cases for what you got out of it." Said Matt.

"You've got to realize and understand" said Randy. "There never were any "how to do it" handbooks printed for what I do. There was a long learning curve, and learning by one's mistakes is how a person improves." Said Dobbs, "But never once was I discouraged. I just kept plugging along and learning as I went. Mostly I was driven by a desire like the one I experienced the very first time I saw that tattoo in Munson's Morgue when I was a child. Once I saw particular tattoo's, as the men or women had that we're now talking about, my mind went crazy devising ways that I could acquire the potential contributor's specimens without getting caught or drawing attention to myself. My ideas always worked... they may not have been the best way or the only way, who knows... as I said, I had no manual to follow, but they worked... they always worked!"

"But don't you agree that your way was a little too messy?" said Sharkey.

"Well, it wouldn't have been if I knew they would have been taken to Munson's or even Scarlet's. Besides, I'm not the one who had to put them in the body bags was I?"

"Yes, that was quite charitable of you, wasn't it?" said Sharkey sarcastically again.

"What did you think of this other one in 2001, young Joe Klugel who got eaten by the dogs?" asked Randy as he found and pointed to the name on his long list.

| Fri. | 2/02/2001 Joe Klugel | Multiples | B. F. T. | Roxi, Dogs | Roxi |

"Yeah, what happened there?" asked Sharkey.

"Young Joe moved to Roxi from Nebraska where he had a family. He was interning as a veterinarian at Parry's' veterinary clinic. He was to intern there for approximately 8 to 10 months, then he would have the option to either buy and take over the business or move back home to open a clinic of his own near his family. Sort of a like a youth apprenticeship program, I guess.

Joe didn't have a car, so he bought a used motor scooter to get from place to place when he didn't have a reason to use the clinics van. One sweltering day when he first arrived, he drove into the ice cream stand where I was enjoying a sundae with Margie. Joe had on only a pair of shorts exposing several tattoos that I didn't know he had before that event. One was particularly fascinating to me, and I just had to have it! I had to have all of them, but I had a problem. Mr. Parry that owned and ran the clinic was a life-long friend of the family and reminded me of Mr. Russel, the kindly, elderly gentleman that helped me get started in taxidermy many years earlier. Like Mr. Russel, he was kind, elderly and in poor health. He desperately needed the help Young Joey could give him to keep the business functioning as he searched for a buyer. A. buyer which he desperately needed so he could retire as all his wealth was wrapped up in the business. He had no other savings or investments. Joes help was important, especially if young Joe decided he didn't want to take the business over.

I couldn't pluck this plump, ripe contributor, at least for the time being because of the invisible and impenetrable fence that had sprung up around him. As Joes decision date neared, a buyer had been found. Of course, young Joe had preference over the potential new business owner, a man named "Fine" who had stated that if he were successful purchasing the business, would want to take it over at the end of the new month, which was a short month as it was in February. Joe turned the offer down, and I heard about it on February 2nd. Mr. Russel had been admitted to the hospital on Feb. 1st because he was seriously ill with the flu and Joe's surprising decision didn't help Mr. Russel's wicked heart condition any. Joe Klugel would be leaving soon, and along with him, he would take my only opportunity to harvest his terrific specimens. I had to think fast. I was sure he would not be taken to the

Munson's' Funeral Parlor where I could collect them in strict confidence, he would surely be sent back to his family in Nebraska.

After the clinic closed at 4:30 p.m. on Friday, February 2nd, I knew no one would come there again until Monday morning because Mr. Russel never had weekend hours. On weekends, Joe usually would come back two times a day to feed and water the animals in the clinic, which were almost all dogs and a few cats. Joe had an unusual way about him, as he would always open the cage pen doors and invite the critters out of the cage to eat so they could move around freely for a while.

I visited young Joe just as he was preparing to leave for the day. I made Joe an offer he couldn't refuse with a 12" taped up bar of 1" steel I usually kept under the seat of my cruiser. Afterward, I emptied all the food dishes back into the containers they came from and made sure they were out of reach of the dogs. I undressed Joe, took my pictures, harvested my specimens, and smeared some of Joes' blood on a metal hand railing shaped similarly to the bar I used to induct him. I added a few strands of his hair to the blood on the rail. Then I redressed him leaving the areas of harvesting exposed and left a rug corner curled up under his foot. I then opened all the cages doors. I slipped out unseen and let the nature of hungry dogs take its course.

It wasn't until noon on Monday when a supply delivery person that Mr. Russel trusted and had given a key to found him. I felt I lucked out, I didn't know about the key, if I had, it might have scared me off, and I would have had to find a different method to do my harvesting.

When I was notified about the dog attack, I picked up Bill Masten, the County Coroner, and we went to investigate. It was Bill who with very little suggestion from myself, came up with the conclusion that young Joe tripped over the curled-up corner of the rug, bumped his head on the railing and virtually killed himself. The dogs were excellent in the role they had to play. They left not a trace of the specimens' extractions. If only Joe had been from Roxi and I was sure his stock would be sent to Munson's, it would have been a lot easier and a whole lot less messy, but I was sure they would send him back home for the preparations," said Officer Randy sounding kind of beside himself.

33
The Conclusion

Sunday, November 7th, 2010 3:50 pm

"I'm afraid I'm not feeling good about you right now Randy." Said Officer Sharkey. "Killing people is not a virtue! I think it's about time we start to wrap this up, don't you?" he asked.

"Whatever you say, Matt," replied Randy.

"You said you needed lots of tattoos, why did you need so many?" asked Sharkey.

"Its simple." said Randy, "More is always better than less! My creations require unlimited specimens and unique ink designs."

Sheriff Randy Dobbs from the little town of Roxi and State Police Investigative Officer Matthew Ezekiel Sharkey were both very tired of discussing the findings by now. Officer Sharkey did not know how to go about ending the conversation and was seriously thinking about moving on to the next step, which would naturally be to take Sheriff Randy Dobbs into custody when Sheriff Dobbs said to him, "Are you sure you don't have any more questions, I certainly don't want to leave you with any blank spaces."

"All right, just two more questions and then we'll get on with wrapping this mess up," said Officer Sharkey.

"First, you talked about special ink design needs that you had. What did you mean?" asked Sharkey.

"My creations, to meet my visions requirements need to be of hundreds, perhaps thousands of different and various designs, shapes sizes and colors to capture the professionalism and essence of my very being, and the intrinsic nature of the contributors as well."

"You keep talking about your creations. I thought you were talking about the collages and ledgers. However, now your tone is lending itself to something entirely different. Just what did you do with the tattoos after you got the pictures of them that you wanted?" asked Sharkey.

"You should be using the word specimens Matt, haven't you learned anything from this?" said the Sheriff with a tone of disappointment.

"Sorry," said Officer Matt. "Please, just answer my question, what else are you hiding in this... this emporium of death!"

"I'll answer it by showing you, please rise," said Randy as he stood up.

Randy and Officer matt were both standing in the room full of nothing but white sheet-covered furniture.

"Remove the cover from your sofa Matt. instructed Sheriff Randy... Go ahead... it won't hurt anything!"

Officer Matt Sharkey turned slowly, leaned forward and grasped an open end of the bedsheet like covering and slowly pulled it towards him and then to one side. As he gazed upon the revelation, Matt stood there motionless and speechless. His mind and fears were running out of control as during the moments before imminent death. It had to be like seeing the Devil himself. Only inches away from him lay the most horrible, almost incomprehensible and revealing truth — the apparent catalyst for Sheriff Randy Dobbs morbid actions. The sofa was unlike any other sofa ever known to man. It was upholstered with human fabric, a fabric made by combining the various ink decorated portions of different tattooed human contributors skin into clothing large enough to clothe the entire three cushion sofa.

The deranged, but exhibitive Sheriff walked over to and removed a cover from another chair, a love seat. It too similarly served to memorialize the donors. Sheriff Randy removed yet another cover, then another and another until all the low living room furnishings were exposed. They were all the same. Matching furniture, I guess you could say, even the recently reupholstered padded top ottoman.

In the low lighting conditions, gone virtually unnoticed before now, where each shuttered window was, there were grotesquely beautifully designed, and sewn human inked hide draperies that matched the set of furniture that went with them. Officer Matt watched with a dropped jaw, still speechless.

Randy escorted the shocked and astounded State Police Officer to another room in the house, that had its furnishings covered with white sheet-like coverings also. It was a bedroom... apparently the master bedroom. In it naturally, was a bedroom set, with a king-size canopy bed that had a padded headboard.

The beds headboard, canopy, and gigantic spread cover were also made from similar grotesquely beautifully inked human contributions, as were the furniture in the other room they just visited. At the foot of the large bed, there was a matching sort of pirate's treasure chest that went with the bed, and it too had a padded top endowed with some of Randy's' spectacular window dressings. The window draperies in that room also matched the unusual furnishings.

Randy then led Officer Sharkey into the kitchen and breakfast nook area. The six padded chairs and a few rugs were contributors provided pieces also, but the real gut heaver was the unmistakable full-body ink design, contributor donated tablecloth! It was hard to believe that anyone except for perhaps Jeffery Dahmer could down even a portion of their meal off of it without returning it.

Randy took real pride as he showed Officer Sharkey his special, one of a kind matching table and countertops. They had been heavily laden with extraneous contributors personal wear items such as earrings, piercing pins, nipple and other body part rings. The top looked very professionally done, and if one can appreciate the sacrifice and work it took to create them, they might even say they were pretty. Officer Sharkey reluctantly persuaded himself to feel the smoothness of Randy's work as Sheriff Randy suggested he do. He said nothing, just stood there with his back arched back and his head turning from side to side such that he looked like the walking corpse of weekend Bernie.

After the kitchen tour, Randy escorted Officer Matt to a completely remodeled and modern bathroom.

Of course, he didn't take him there because he thought that he needed to use the facility. The first thing that caught Sharkey's eye was the shower curtain, both the inner curtain and the restrained drapery portion were made similar to the other human flesh draperies Randy hung in the houses other rooms. Something different was added there. The toilet tank and top seat cover were the typical human hide scheme. The lower donut seat, as well as the cabinet top, had also been laden with contributors wear items and pieces of human design material. They were suspended and captive with-in a clear acrylic type binder as were seen in the kitchen. The seats and countertop looked very professionally done. Officer Sharkey was at this point little surprised to hear Sheriff Randy mention that he had a top for the living room coffee table cooking and curing in his shop as they spoke.

They left the bathroom area, and as they were returning to the collage decorated, car intruded room, the prideful Sheriff Dobbs unleashed a full 50 caliber barrage of fear on Sharkey when he fully revealed his incessant evil intentions as he continued.

"I've just started my den. It will be wallpapered with specimens. I already am soaking and tanning some fabric for the walls, drapes, and carpeting. I've saved and am treating one particularly unique full body decorated contributors hide and head. One that is decorated from the very tips of his toes to the very top of his head where the multi-colored designs only disappear as they run into his hairline. I will use this to make a human version of a bearskin rug to hang on the wall near the fireplace. The contributor once held the prestigious title of the tattooed man at a sideshow that came through town a year or so ago. This one of a kind creation will be both a tribute to the donor as well as the memorial and show him individual honors for his significant contributions. I am still searching for an equally exquisite female donor for the floor in front of the fireplace. I plan to border her outline with scalping from all the various contributors that have enlisted since I started saving scalps years ago. I believe it may even outshine the wall rug. Moreover, oh yes, he said, I'm cooking and curing a mantelpiece for the fireplace as we talk also!"

There could be no mistaking that revelation. Officer Matt was so frightened that he shook from his head to his toes. His fear weakened him to the point he could barely remain erect. Though terrified to the point of capitulation, Officer Sharkey thought he could be frightened no more; he found out that was just not so when the Sheriff said, "Aren't my rooms magnificent!" the Sheriff said. "Just wait until my memorial is completed! There will never, ever, be anything like it in the entire world! I know it may sound crazy to someone like you that has never entertained such thoughts and desires as I did, but it is important to me that you understand the labor and sacrifices I endured to make all of this possible. The loss of sleep those many, many nights...those full body decorated contributors took me sometimes as much as 20 minutes each to de-hide.

The pain I endured dragging, lifting, and carrying so many contributors such long distances, the awful odors, the bloodstains on my clothes and boots. The pleading looks on their faces, the tremendous headaches from constant planning and devising. It would be hard to find another that would make the sacrifices I have made! It just is not that easy to come up with ways to do the things I was capable of doing, and as often as I did it, without getting caught or becoming suspect. I am the best at what I do!"

"You... you never had any intention to concede and relinquish your memorial or the incorrigible hold you have on society, did you? You... You've just cleverly have been stringing me along, just so you could have some living, breathing person to boast about your evil accomplishments too, weren't you?"

"Tat...Ta..." said Randy, "You did limit yourself to only two more Questions before! I heard you." said Sheriff Randy in a taunting manner.

"I don't know if you're anxious to go to hell... but you won't be allowed to continue the nefarious relationships you have with your so-called contributors. You will never get away with this!" screamed Officer Matt... "People in Roxi...they know I came out here… They'll see where my car smashed into your house and find all your ghoulish treasures when they investigate. I'll bet they're looking for me right now!"

"And just who would be looking for you right now?" Asked the conniving Sheriff.

Matt answers quickly and sharply. "Bill Patton for one. He has been helping me with this case and he knows I was coming here to see you this morning! And… and… don't forget the whole abandoned car investigation committee… or… did you forget we were meeting first thing tomorrow morning? They are counting on me to get the meeting started. How are you going to explain my absence? When someone turns up missing, they always go after the last person to see them alive; you know that! They will all be out here thick as thieves investigating and looking for leads. You can't possibly think you can hide what's been going on right under your very own nose.

The Sheriff just seems to dismiss him as he says, "That's good to know."

Yet again, the Sheriff just disregarded the Officers rantings and continued on casually and as if nothing had changed from before. "Matt, did you see this fabulous diary I have? It's an incessant journal that I kept updated ever since I started my collections and harvestings back in January of 1990."

Randy holds up the Journal for Officer Sharkey to see, as he holds up yet another binder and says, "And look...look at the collection of photos I took off all my harvested contributors specimens, there all inside! I have pictures of the specimens before and after harvest."

The Sheriff handed Officer Sharkey a folder that had the word TATTOO'S printed across its cover diagonally.

"But... what about your wonderful girlfriend Marge Betley... she needs you. She...she liked me; I could tell." Said a desperate Sharkey as he tried to buy time trying to find a way to get himself out of this awful mess.

"What about her?" said Randy.

"Well," said Sharkey, "How do you think she will feel about you if she finds out you did something to me? Besides, she loves you... she will stand by you through all this. Let her help you...Let us help you!" he pleaded.

"Maybe I should show you something that I guess you must have overlooked," said Sheriff Randy. The evil, corrupt minded Sheriff, hands Officer Sharkey the booklet of listed names of his contributors and opens it.

Officer Sharkey quickly leaf's through the pages and says with astonishment, "There must be a couple of hundred names in here!"

"Two hundred seventy-five names to be exact." Said Randy calmly, "but then, who's counting? I averaged 13.75 contributors per year over the last twenty years!" HE said pridefully.

Randy reaches over and runs his finger down the page until he finds a name and instructs Officer Matt to look at it carefully. He quickly recognizes a name he was familiar with. The name of Sheriff Randy's girl Marge Betleys' deceased husband Frank, who died in a barn fire in 2005 was there.

| Fri. | 7/29/2005 | Frank Betley | Face, neck, head | B. F. T. | Roxi, barn fire | Roxi |

"You...You didn't!... You...You...killed Frank Betley!??" Matt said, wishing all this was just a super bad nightmare.

"There's that word I don't like again, but yes... he did join our ranks," admitted Sheriff Randy.

"You killed her husband so you could get Margie asked?" Sharkey.

"Of course not!" replied Randy, you know me better than that! The relationship just happened, she needed a shoulder, and I had two I wasn't using. It's only a loan. You know I could never get married; how could I ever hide my conglomerate of contributor specimens and artifacts from a wife?"

"But don't you love her? Are you incapable of love? Real love!" asked Sharkey, hoping to open a hole to climb out of.

Sheriff Randy did not want to continue the conversation for apparent reasons and shut Officer Sharkey down again as he changed subjects.

"Matt, now that you've seen how I've incorporated my upholstery business into my ventures and how valuable those skills were to the advancement of my Special Donors' Memorial, I've got something else to show you, something elegant. The prize objects of my collection! You'll love them! They're the epitome of my greatness. My skills runneth over!"

Of course, Officer Sharkey couldn't wait to see it! Hell, his heart was still beating.

The undeniably evil Sheriff Randy Dobbs walks up to what appeared to be a tall, pole type of floor lamp that also was covered with white sheeting. Poor Matt Sharkey's heart, just how much fear can one man's heart stand before it can take no more? Randy tugged on the white covering, and it fell to the floor, revealing what just had to be Sheriff Randy's greatest Masterpiece.

There immediately before them was one of the most beautiful looking motorcycles ever built by man and was formerly owned and driven by a character read about much earlier in this story, simply nick-named [Spokes]. If you remember Mr. Spokes was the fellow that ran off with Randy's betrothed Kathy Johns way back in November of 1994, practically leaving Randy standing at the altar and was never seen again.

It certainly was not the motorcycle that made this monument a masterpiece nor was it the fact that this motorcycle was mounted upon a reliable, pedestal stand in a position indicative of doing what is called a wheelie. It gained its masterpiece status because of the life-like human mounts depicted driving and riding on the tremendous vertical, steel steed, they were the mounted and well-preserved hide remnants of some of Randy's most gracious and generous contributors, Mr. Spokes and Kathy Johns. Even the lampshades were decorated with body art inking's from contributors.

Officer Sharkey started choking and looked as if he was going to heave when he saw the appalling presentation.

"You stuffed these innocent human beings...as if... as if they were expendable animals, how...how could you do such a thing?" snarled a thoroughly disgusted Sharkey. "I don't care what you say, or what you want to call it; this was vengeance, undeniable vengeance!" said he angrily.

"O.K.," admitted Randy, "Maybe just a little. I guess that, plus my taxidermy interests are what gave me the idea. Paybacks are hell, aren't they?" he chuckled.

There was a short period of silence as each digested what had just transpired; then Randy broke the silence.

"By the way, Matt, you never did finish telling me why you came out here to see me in the first place, something about cult members, wasn't it?" asked Randy.

"Well... yes...I guess it was," replied Officer Sharkey... "But I'm not sure that matters anymore anyhow, it was more than just about the cult activity we all were so concerned about. It was more about my daughter Sarah. I've been worried sick about her for quite a while now. She met this motorcycle freak named [Slice], and I think he may be a gang banger. I knew you know more about what's going on with these cult groups that anybody else around. I was hoping that you might be able to tell me how to find out where this guy [Slice] can be found. She left with him, and she was talking about marrying the goon, but I haven't heard anything from her since. I've got to know if she's all right!" said Officer Sharkey.

Sheriff Randy again strangely disregarded the Officers current questions and concerns and started to reply to Sharkey's earlier comments about him not being able to get away with what he did and not letting Sharkey take him into captivity.

"I'm surprised that you didn't hear me drive my business truck after you so rudely broke into my house. I parked it directly in front of the grove of pine trees you smashed through on your mad drive to my living room to hide the slight damage to the trees and your car from view; just in case someone did find their way down the driveway to the house. However, before I did, I closed my power gate at the top of the driveway, and it displays a large closed sign and my normal business hours. There's little chance that anyone will walk down here.

Once I am done here, I will deposit your unworthy car in my tunnel, and hide the damage to the side of my house with a few cut spruce trees from my forest until I can make the necessary repairs. Then I will return to my upholstery shop where I was working before you so rudely disturbed me, open my gate and wait until someone contacts me about your strange disappearance. Then I will inform the investigators that the last time I saw you, which was early Sunday morning, you were on your way to Tom Adams house because you had questioned me about him and his possible cult activity connections."

"I'm sure glad I've held off harvesting Tom Adams, he sure has been very beneficial to me by keeping the heat off of my back! Now, it'll look even more like he and cult members are behind all these mysterious disappearances!"

"You're mad!" said Sharkey.

"Don't try to be nice to me now, Matt, especially after you damaged my wonderful memorial. You can be so cruel," said Randy rubbing salt into Sharkey's wounds.

"Sure, things look pretty grim for you right now, but maybe I can ease some of your pain. You asked me before if I could tell you anything about that guy named Slice that ran off with your daughter Sara, well, I do know a Gangbanger named Milt Vargas that had the nickname [Slice], the guy was a real bad dude! His younger brother Claudio was one of the illegal immigrants on the bus I was telling you about. He had sworn an act of vengeance against the persons that made his brother disappear."

"Do you know where he is?" begged Sharkey frantically, "Sara might still be alive and with him!"

Randy just seemed to ignore Sharkey and was somewhat bothered by his interruption; thus, he just continued with what he was saying before he was interrupted.

"I guess someone told Slice where the bus was that his brother was on when he last saw the bus and Slice came looking and throwing his weight around. He started to hurt some people trying to squeeze out some information. I couldn't let others pay for what I did. So, I lured him away from his gang when I sent them all on a wild goose chase to a place they were all to converge about an hour and a half away from here, and in a northerly direction; drawing them far away from this area and away from populated areas.

His gang never knew how, when, or where I did it, but I inconspicuously snatched the low life and the rider with him too, and they didn't even know he was taken until after they arrived at the fictitious location that I sent them to."

"You snatched him!" said Sharkey with great interest. "Is he in your memorial? Did he say where he lived? Did he mention a wife, or a woman named Sara?"

Sheriff Randy paused for a second, took his left hand and rubbed it up and down around and under his chin as if he were deeply thinking about it and said "Let's look at my ledger again and see if it tells us anything, shall we?" suggested the Sheriff.

Sheriff Randy Dobbs again shows Officer Matt Sharkey the entire listing he has.

Officer Matt scanned the list again quickly looking for another Vargas name. He found a Milton Vargas. He was from California. His hopes soared! Then as he looked closer, he saw yet another Vargas Name, it was Sara Vargas. Officer Sharkey was now sure his daughter married Slice, and Sara Vargas was his daughter.

| Thur. | 8/06/2009 | Milton Vargas | Multiples | Shot | Oxford, Hwy. | Cali. |
| Thur. | 8/06/2009 | Sara Vargas | Multiples | Shot | Oxford, Hwy. | Cali. |

"What did you do to her? You maniac!" screamed Officer Matt.

"Matt... Matt," said Randy casually, "She's on the list, do you have to ask?"

"Where is she!" screamed Officer Sharkey at the top of his voice.

"You know Matt, you seemed to have been taken with the first prize object of my collection, that boss motorcycle lamp of my ex-girlfriend Kathy Johns and her friend Spokes over there. They look so carefree and realistic, don't they?" asked Randy.

"Look at the joyous smiles on their faces, griming from ear to ear. They look so happy together. I couldn't see my memorial without a matching lamp."

The obviously deranged, but still Sheriff of the little town of Roxi removed another dust cover from a tall piece of furniture and revealed another life-size reared up on one wheel, motorcycle lamp being driven by none other than Milton Vargas. Immediately behind him and holding on tightly while riding with him in her ensemble resembling that of a freak, was Mrs. Vargas, formerly Sara Jane Sharkey from wherever she called home.

Officer Sharkey, understandably fit with unprecedented rage, turned and attempted an attack against the younger, faster, and stronger Randy Dobbs, but was stopped dead in his tracks as Randy took a step backward pulled a revolver from under his jacket and pointed it at the brave State Police Officer and said, "Does this gun happen to look familiar to you? It, your badge, and cell phone will make great memorabilia. I'm pleased you came so well prepared with artifacts to fill full the obligations of your legacy as your destiny unfolds."

The insane Sheriff Randy, however not yet through providing Officer Sharkey surprises said, "Before your daughter Sara became a five-star member of the Special Donors Memorial, she told me something significant."

"What was that you Bastard?" questioned Sharkey.

Randy replied, "She told me that you also have a few tattoos. You've been holding out on me, haven't you? So, to think... you called me the bastard!"

The Mysterious Abandoned Cars

Special Donors' Memorial Events Listing

Date	Contributor/Donor	Contribution	Method Collected	Donors residence
Tue. 7/23/1991	Charles Stint/Cycle Chuck	Multiples	B.F.T., Orville Dancehall	Utah
Tue. 7/23/1991	Mary Hardau	Multiples	B.F.T., Orville Dancehall	Oreville
Tue. 7/23/1991	Betty Bell	Multiples	B.F.T., Orville Dancehall	Oreville
Wed. 12/18/1991	Mildred Reilly	Multiples	Funeral home	Roxi
Sun. 2/09/1992	William Rapsey	Face, hands/fingers	Shot, Benton highway	Kansas
Thur. 3/12/1992	Brad Lee	Upper/lower right arm	Funeral home	Roxi
Thur. 4/30/1992	Madge Crackest	Breast, neck	Shot	Championsburg
Sat. 6/06/1992	Ted Basinn	Both arms	Shot, Bigelow Alley	Texas
Tue. 7/06/1992	Lisa Durkin	Multiples	Bedloe Market	Wyoming
Wed. 12/02/1992	James Mc'Rackin	Multiples	B.F.T., Oreville Dump	Oreville
Fri. 3/06/1993	Emma Grossen	Both arms, U&L	Shot,Championsburg, Hwy.	N. Dakota
Sun. 7/18/1993	Edward Kasmarinski	Multiples	Shot, Roxi, flood	Championsburg
Sun. 7/18/1993	William Wright	Multiples	Shot, Roxi, flood	Championsburg
Sun. 7/18/1993	Nick Beltraws	Multiples	Shot, Roxi, flood	Championsburg
Sun. 7/18/1993	John Simonsini	Multiples	Shot, Roxi, flood	Championsburg
Sun. 7/18/1993	Marcus Yogaurt	Multiples	Shot, Roxi, flood	Championsburg
Wed. 9/01/1993	Louis Clavis	Full body	B.F.T., Benton, store	New Hampshire
Fri. 9/03/1993	Andrew Klegin	Full body	B.F.T., Benton, church	Indiana
Mon. 11/22/1993	Janet Wentz	Multiples	Shot, Bigelow, Laundry	Bigelow
Sat. 2/10/1994	Jerry Mc Dougal	Full body	B.F.T., Apollotown, bakery	Apollotown
Mon. 4/25/1994	Larry Hilgertt	Multiples	Shot. Roxi, woods	Roxi
Mon. 7/04/1994	Mary Speck	Multiples	Drown, Home, pool	Roxi
Tue. 8/30/1994	Joe Fayette	Full body	B.F.T., Justice, pizza	Justice
Sun. 10/02/1994	Mike Rowhling	Left, upper arm	B.F.T., Ronny Lord	Roxi
Wed. 11/23/1994	Kathy Johns	Full body	B.F.T., Roxi motel	Roxi
Wed. 11/23/1994	Spokes(motorcyclist)	Full body	B.F.T., Roxi motel	Roxi
Thur. 12/08/1994	Wilt Bonning	Both arms, U &L	Shot, Beaumont, club	Beaumont
Fri. 2/17/1995	Milo Zukowsky	Multiples	Shot, Beaumont, ski	Aspin
Mon. 3/27/1995	Tony Rillion	Multiples	B F.T., Porktown, park	Penna.
Wed. 5/17/1995	Bill Dawsonn	Full body	B.F.T.	Championsburg.Hwy.
Wed. 7/26/1995	Alice Dankos	Multiples	Drown	Apollotown
Wed. 7/26/1995	Milly White	Multiples	Drown	Apollotown
Tue. 9/26/1995	Bonnie Gluntt	Multiples	Shot	Justice

Visit www.themysteriousabandonedcars.com
for the entire list of "special donors"!

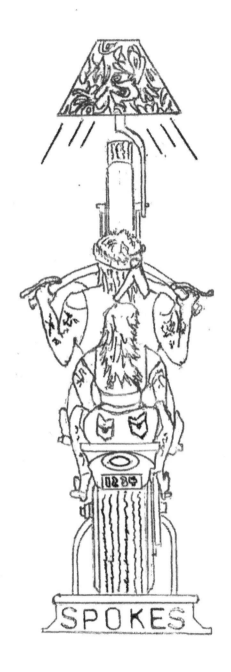